ONLY I CAN SAVE THEM

BOOKS BY IMOGEN MATTHEWS

THE DUTCH GIRLS

The Girl from the Resistance

The Girl with the Red Hair

The Wartime Nurse

WARTIME HOLLAND SERIES

The Girl Across the Wire Fence

The Hidden Village

Hidden in the Shadows

The Boy in the Attic

IMOGEN MATTHEWS

ONLY I CAN SAVE THEM

Bookouture

Published by Bookouture in 2025

An imprint of Storyfire Ltd.
Carmelite House
50 Victoria Embankment
London EC4Y 0DZ

www.bookouture.com

The authorised representative in the EEA is Hachette Ireland
8 Castlecourt Centre
Dublin 15 D15 XTP3
Ireland
(email: info@hbgi.ie)

ISBN: 978-1-80550-204-3
eBook ISBN: 978-1-80550-203-6

*In memory of
Ursula Breslauer, Auschwitz survivor*

PROLOGUE

WESTERBORK TRANSIT CAMP, HOLLAND, 1944

The tiny boy couldn't have been more than three. He stood all alone bawling his eyes out. Close by, a man with a cinecamera was torn between filming this heart-rending scene and going to see if he could help. Just then, a woman came pushing through the jostling crowds and hugged the little boy to her with tears flowing down her face. Their reunion was touching, made all the more poignant because they were just two people amongst hundreds swarming onto the platform – nobody had any idea of what lay ahead.

The man quickly filmed the reunited mother and son. He then turned his attention to filming as much as possible without being spotted by the Nazi officers who were gathering to jostle the crowds onto the cattle train bound for Auschwitz. The most pressing thing on his mind was to get as much footage as possible before they caught wind of what he was doing.

If he could get enough footage showing the truth of what the Nazis were really up to, then he would leave quickly so he could hide the spool of film and hope he was never found out.

He froze as several Nazis in grey-green uniforms and knee-length black leather boots strode along the platform in his direction. They were yelling orders and lashing out with leather straps when people didn't move quickly enough. It was pure chance they showed no sign of noticing what he was up to for he was able to move about surreptitiously. They were there to keep order and ensure that everyone on the deportation list climbed onto the train. Logically, the man knew, he should have nothing to fear – he was, after all, Westerbork's camp photographer – but if he was caught filming this Tuesday deportation he knew he would be in deep trouble.

Taking the opportunity while he could, he was able to melt into the throng of people who were queuing to board the train without being seen. He didn't have long before the cattle train departed, so he began filming again. He recorded everything he saw: men and women of all ages, families with children, babes in arms. They carried suitcases and duffel bags slung over shoulders stuffed with everything they owned. Fear was written on so many faces, both young and old. As if they knew they would never return.

People were now crushed onto the platform with barely any room to move, and tempers were fraying. Many were simply too sick or frail to stand and were being shoved and jostled into the carriages by the Nazi officers. None were spared. These poor souls were the unlucky ones whose names had been called out from a list only moments before. The victims of the Tuesday transport who had been ordered to come here had no idea where they were heading.

It was the first time the man had witnessed these excruciating scenes he knew took place every Tuesday. He hadn't known what to expect when he'd come, but was humbled by the courtesy and dignity of people thinking of others before themselves as they helped the old, the very young and the sick climb aboard and find somewhere to sit on the bare wooden floors of the carriages. Did they have any idea of the fate that awaited them? He couldn't be sure, but he guessed he knew the answer to that.

He swung his camera round to film those who weren't boarding, who were saying their goodbyes and waving as if they'd come to see a relative off on holiday.

Then, moving along the platform, all the time filming and hating himself for it, he felt a compulsion and desperate need to record every detail of this appalling scene as it unfolded. To provide a new urgency that this was actually happening, because, if he didn't, he knew that no one would ever believe the terrible things that had taken place at the hands of the Nazis in this awful transit camp.

A whistle blew and he stood aside, the lens of his camera still following the movement of the enormously long train as it began to pull away, clanking and creaking, white smoke billowing around the engine. He frowned in disgust on seeing several SS officers clinging to the sides of carriages as if hitching a ride, then jumping off before the train cleared the platform.

He looked up and saw frightened eyes peering out from the few carriages with windows – a boy his son's age, his cap pulled over his forehead, his dark desperate eyes just visible beneath it. He moved his camera level with the side of the carriages and saw there were numbers chalked on the side: 74, 88, 113. People, he realised. These numbers represented people.

He filmed it all, when suddenly he was stopped in his tracks by the face of a young girl between the doors of one of the carriages. She looked straight at him, her wide dark eyes uncomprehending and fearful. She had a pale blue scarf covering her head, and he wondered if her mother had tenderly tied the ends beneath her chin before setting out as she tried to reassure her that everything would be all right. Or maybe the girl was all alone, separated from her family, who'd been left behind. In that split second, he saw her lips part as if she wanted to call out to him. But his mind was racing as he realised this was his last chance. He lifted his camera one last time and began to film. The footage he took could only have been five or so seconds before the carriage moved away and she was gone.

Instantly, the man agonised over his actions. He should have called out a few words of comfort, but could he really have done anything to save this poor innocent girl? He knew why he'd taken the liberty of filming her distress, that it was in the desperate hope that someone somewhere would eventually find his film and discover the truth.

Turning away, he shivered violently at the danger he faced if he were discovered filming. It meant he would jeopardise his own family's safety and they would all be condemned to board the next train out of Westerbork. He took a deep breath to steady himself. It was a risk he knew he had to take.

ONE

LEIPZIG, 1936

The day Rudolf Breslauer stood looking up at the sign above his photographic studio was the proudest moment of his life, but it was also tinged with sadness. He'd been waiting so long for this, but now it was finally here he found it hard to believe that the family business, Breslauer Photography, was actually his own.

Ever since he'd been a small boy, Rudolf had been fascinated by everything to do with photography. His father often allowed him to watch quietly as he set up his bulky cameras and tripods and politely asked his customers to stand in a certain way to obtain the best pose. When he was finally ready, he would press the buttons on the camera, which whirred and clicked until he was satisfied he'd got the image he wanted. It wasn't until Rudolf was nine years old that he was allowed into the darkroom tucked away at the back. There he would witness the alchemy of photographic images appearing like magic on wet shiny paper. Even now, the sharp vinegar smell of chemicals made his eyes prick, bringing back sweet memories of those precious times.

Rudolf owed everything he'd learned about photography to his father. Portraits were what Breslauer Photography was famous for, and clients travelled from all over Leipzig and beyond to the small photography shop. Several times a day, the tinkling bell above the door announced the arrival of customers, which included the celebrities of film and stage flocking to have their portraits taken. This was the thriving, bustling Jewish quarter and the small shop was nestled between a high-class jeweller and a bakery whose enticing aroma of golden plaited challahs attracted people from far and wide. And if young Rudolf had been particularly good, his father would buy him a chewy chocolatey babka pastry to eat on the walk back home.

The family were well off and lived in a comfortable apartment on the top floor of a large house in a quiet part of town. The living room had a picture window looking out over a communal courtyard with a flowering magnolia tree in its centre. Rudolf shared a bedroom with his older brother, Wolfgang. At the far end of the hall was a locked cupboard, which their father had turned into a small workshop. Often, he would disappear inside in the evenings to work on the negatives of the photos he'd taken that day.

In retrospect, Rudolf recognised just how idyllic his childhood had been, with its gentle rhythms and a sense that time was never-ending. His parents often took the boys out on day trips and they enjoyed frequent visits to the zoo to see the exotic animals and go on thrilling rides at amusement parks. Neither boy had any inkling of a threat to their safety – their parents made sure of it. As they chased one another, laughing, along the tree-lined paths of the Johannapark, the boys had no idea how hard their parents worked to protect their young sons from the terrifying reality that Jews were being singled out and increasingly ostracised from society.

It wasn't until Rudolf was married to his childhood sweetheart Bella and living in their own apartment with their two young children Ursula and Stefan that the family became targets themselves in the safety of their own home.

It was early one evening and the two of them were in the kitchen clearing away the dishes after supper. Bella was at the sink and Rudolf was bending down to put the plates into a cupboard when there was a deafening crash as an object came hurtling through the window. He straightened up in alarm and saw a large stone crash to the floor. Shards of glass and splinters sprayed the entire kitchen. He heard Bella's moans and saw she had dropped onto her hands and knees. He crouched beside her. 'Bella! Are you hurt?'

'I don't think so,' she said in a wobbly voice.

They both raised their heads as several pebbles came hurtling through the broken window accompanied by the sound of raucous laughter and footsteps running in the street.

Rudolf tried to make light of it. 'Sounds like high-spirited youngsters,' he said. 'You go back into the sitting room while I clear up. I'll board up the window, and get it seen to in the morning.'

Bella struggled to her feet and held on to his arm. 'Rudolf, I think you're wrong. I have a nasty feeling about this. What have we done to deserve it?'

The words were no sooner out of her mouth when a chant went up from the street:

'Jews out! Jews out!'

Shaken to the core, Rudolf quickly led Bella out of the kitchen and shut the door behind them. As much as he wanted to believe it was nothing to worry about, he knew that Bella was right. This was no youthful prank. It was a deliberate and personal attack on them and their property. And then he had a terrible flash of foreboding – that the comfortable life they enjoyed would come to a sudden and brutal end.

TWO
LEIPZIG, 1938

It was after six when Rudolf went to lock up the shop, a lengthy procedure since his recent fitting of sturdy locks throughout the premises. The stories of attacks on Jewish businesses were becoming worryingly common and he didn't want to leave anything to chance. He picked up the small leather suitcase he used to store his Leica camera, the one his father had always used and which took the best photographs. Even before installing the extra security, Rudolf had never gone anywhere without it by his side.

Head down, he hurried back home, taking a shortcut through the narrow streets and alleyways. Bella didn't like it when he went this way. Since the incident with the smashed window, she often warned him about putting himself in danger of an attack. But things had been so much quieter on the streets recently. He was musing to himself that the dangers were not as great as they had once been when he was stopped short by a commotion up ahead. He moved into a doorway where he couldn't be seen and watched a gang of thugs hurling threats at a man who was locking up his barber shop. They were taking it in turns to push the man violently while shouting abuse in his face. Rudolf couldn't stand by and let this happen, so, with his heart in his mouth, he rushed towards them, yelling out to them to stop. Fortunately, several people came out of their houses and joined in and between them they saw off the thugs.

The man had fallen to his knees and was clearly distressed. He was young, no more than twenty. Rudolf went to help him to his feet. 'Would you like me to walk home with you?'

The man sniffed deeply and seemed to regain his composure. 'I can manage. Thank you for offering.'

Rudolf didn't want to force this issue, even though it was obvious the man was still very upset, so he nodded and waited till he had gone on his way. But as Rudolf resumed his walk home, his legs felt shaky, and he realised how easily they might have turned on him. He suspected it was only a matter of time before Nazi thugs came rampaging down his own street.

The photography business ticked over but things could always have been better. Rudolf toyed with placing an advertisement in the local paper but knew it would only draw attention to himself for all the wrong reasons. He started going round the theatres and concert hall to present his calling card, but he didn't hold out much hope of drumming up additional business. These days, having one's portrait done professionally was seen as a luxury and most people had other more pressing things on their minds. Rudolf consoled himself that everyone was finding things difficult these days, but really he knew it was the Jews who were finding it especially hard. In his father's day, Breslauer Photography had a broad customer base. By the mid-1930s business had dwindled; anyone who wasn't Jewish never dared venture inside this once-bustling and prosperous part of Leipzig. No one felt safe any more. Everyone knew it was only a matter of time before the situation rose to a head.

Rudolf's brother, Wolfgang, had been badgering him for

some time to move to Amsterdam, where he was now living with his wife, daughter and their widowed mother. They had taken the decision to move there not long after the Nazis had banned Jewish university lecturers from teaching. Singled out for his religion, Wolfgang, a professor of history, had known the only option was to flee the country. Fortunately, Amsterdam University welcomed Jewish émigrés and Wolfgang was offered a post in the history faculty.

So far, Rudolf had resisted the idea of following his brother, believing that he could still make a go of his photography business in Leipzig. He told himself that if he could just get through the next few weeks then things would settle down and maybe even return to some semblance of normality. But he'd been promising himself this every time there was an escalation of tensions within the Jewish community, and things never did improve. Just one more month, he kept on telling himself.

Rudolf had stayed on late at work one evening when there was a sharp rap at the door of the shop. He'd put the Closed sign up early so he could get on with developing the photographs from an earlier portrait session, so knew it wasn't a customer. He went to see who it was and looked through the peephole to see the distorted but visibly anxious face of his neighbour, the owner of the bakery next door.

'Johann, do come in.' Rudolf opened up and gave him a friendly smile. The two men were the same age and had known each other all their lives; they used to play with other children in the street in front of their fathers' shops. Like Rudolf, Johann had inherited the family business.

'I'm not here for a social visit.' Johann spoke in a rush. 'There's a large pack of young men heading towards the Jewish quarter. They're members of the Hitler Jugend and they mean business. I was just putting up the shutters on the shop and saw your light was on. I thought I'd better come and warn you, but we need to get out now.'

Rudolf's stomach gave a sudden lurch of fear, but he couldn't just leave. 'I'm in the middle of developing some photos. I'll be finished in fifteen minutes.'

'Did you hear what I said?' Johann cried. 'You can't put your customers before your own safety. It's too late for that. I'll help you with the shutters, then I'm off. Are you coming or not?'

'All right. I'm coming but give me one minute.' Rudolf rushed into his darkroom and pulled the dripping sheets out of the chemical bath, roughly pegging them up on the line above the workbench. They hadn't been developing long enough, but he hoped there was a chance he'd be able to salvage the prints. They were for a high-ranking German official, whom he was sure wouldn't take kindly to sitting again for his portrait. Rudolf's thoughts quickly turned to Bella and the children waiting for him to return home. Bella hated it when he was home late and would only worry if she caught wind of the trouble.

He picked up his keys from his workbench and hurried to the front door. Johann was already pulling the shutters down. Rudolf quickly secured the bolts, then double-locked the door behind them.

Up and down the street, people were shouting to each other and securing their properties as best they could before joining a procession of people desperate to get away before the thugs arrived with their missiles and batons. It soon became clear that their area wasn't the only place being targeted and that Nazis were on the rampage against Jews across the whole of Leipzig.

Rudolf and Johann joined the crowds of people surging in one direction to the central Marktplatz. When they eventually got there, they found a mass of people congregating by the imposing town hall in large groups. Tension was building, though things didn't seem nearly so threatening away from the seething streets. Rudolf allowed himself to relax a little and believe that things weren't quite as serious as Johann had suggested. He turned to thank him. 'If it hadn't been for you, I'd probably still be working obliviously in the back of the shop. I dread to think—'

A roar went up from a small group of men who had gathered on the opposite side of the square. 'Nazis – we have to get out!' Johann yelled in Rudolf's ear. He grabbed him by the arm and gripped tightly as they began to run. It was pandemonium as people on all sides bumped into each other in their haste to get away. Along with countless others, they made for a side street. All Rudolf was aware of was the deafening noise of thundering feet as the crowd tried to escape the melee. The two of them kept running until they could be sure that the clamour behind them had receded. Finally, out of breath, they stopped at a busy road intersection.

'This is where I must leave you,' said Johann, gesticulating left.

'Of course. And thank you,' said Rudolf, as he tried to catch his breath, 'for everything.'

'No need. We're not out of danger yet. In fact, we won't be even when we think we're safe in our own houses. Those thugs have got it into their heads they're going to drive all of us out. I only hope I'm wrong.' He gave Rudolf a fearful look and walked away quickly without looking back.

THREE
OXFORD, OCTOBER 2022

Eloise

Eloise turned her head to gaze at the red and gold autumn colours out of the window of the car. Her father had just remarked on how glorious the leaves were this year. Just like he always did every autumn when they drove along the M40. He'd kept up his patter ever since they'd left the house in West London and she was grateful for it. Her stomach had been in knots all morning and she just wanted to get the journey over and done with.

At the top of the hill at Stokenchurch, he said as he usually did, 'Downhill all the way,' though Eloise didn't reply. She was miles away, wondering anxiously if she'd fit in with all the rich confident kids who'd been to private schools, whether she'd be able to keep up in tutorials with students so much cleverer than her, and whether she would manage to produce the standard of essays that would be expected of her. It seemed inconceivable that she would make new friends. These thoughts churned round and round in her head and she was only half listening to her father still talking about how lucky they were to see the autumn colours at their best.

'Dammit, you idiot!' he suddenly burst out and slammed on the brakes. The car came to a violent halt, narrowly avoided ramming into the car in front. Eloise looked up in alarm to see that they had come to a sudden halt in a queue of stationary traffic.

'David! What on earth are you doing – didn't you see that car stopping?' shouted her mother angrily.

'He gave me no warning whatsoever,' her father protested, throwing his hands up in frustration.

'Keep your hands on the wheel,' her mother scolded.

'I'm. Not. Moving.' He spoke slowly, labouring the point.

'Mum... Dad. Can you please stop it?' said Eloise, and put her hands over her ears to block out their bickering. She couldn't bear another hour of this torture. Why was it that as soon as her father got behind the wheel he always lost his temper? But he kept on.

'Look at that car on the right, all loaded up. Is it any surprise they can't see ahead of them? I bet they're all students heading the same way we are.'

Eloise rolled her eyes and sighed. 'Yes, Dad, that's precisely what they are. I did tell you it was going to be busy at this time.'

She sank back in her seat, closed her eyes and thought of Tom. He'd been so shocked and upset by her announcement last night. Only now did she realise what a coward she'd been, leaving it until the last minute. She'd seen the hurt in his eyes and had almost retracted her words, but had stopped herself from doing so. They were going their separate ways – she to Oxford and Tom to Manchester. It would be a fresh start and she was genuinely surprised Tom didn't see things her way. He'd been her first boyfriend and she did love him – really she did – but she was on the cusp of a new adventure and she couldn't imagine how he'd fit in.

'We don't need to be apart for long if you let me come and visit you at weekends. Or you could come up to Manchester. And really, it's not that long till the holidays. Please don't destroy what we have,' he'd said, his eyes red-rimmed as he tried to hold it together.

It had felt like emotional blackmail. She had to stay firm, but still she had a niggling doubt she was acting rashly.

The traffic was moving again and she was relieved to see they had reached the outskirts of Headington. Eloise was still pondering what to do about her ex.

At last they had navigated the queues into Oxford and arrived outside her college. Miraculously, her father found a parking space, and was in a much better mood.

Eloise got out of her side as a young man came forward and introduced himself.

'Hello! I'm James. I'm showing freshers where to go. Do you want a hand bringing your gear up?' He gave her a wide grin, which disappeared when he saw the open boot of the car stacked high with her belongings.

Eloise was about to apologise when her father called out, 'No need. We can manage.' He grunted as he hoisted two heavy bags onto the pavement. 'Eloise, you can bring the suitcase... Clare, can you manage the big cheese plant on the back seat?'

Eloise felt her face heat up with embarrassment as she told James they could manage, thank you.

'No problem. Do you know which room's yours?'

She pulled a piece of paper from her bag and showed it to him.

'Second floor. Two doors down on the right. Good luck and see you around.' He shot her another smile and was gone.

It took several trips up two flights of stairs for Eloise and her parents to cart all her belongings, which now lay in piles on the floor of her room. She looked around at the neat shower cubicle with its toilet and sink, the bed along one wall and the empty shelves above the desk, which stood under the window. It was nicer than she'd been expecting. She then moved to the window to look at the view over the nearby University Parks. The trees dazzled in their crimson and deep gold foliage. A smile lifted the corners of her mouth.

'I don't know about you but I could do with some lunch,' said her father, rubbing his hands together. He looked expectantly at Eloise. 'I thought maybe we could walk into town and find somewhere?'

'Dad, if it's all right with you, I'd rather just get on and unpack.' She gestured at the muddle of bags and cardboard boxes in the middle of the floor.

'We've come all this way – are you sure, darling?' said her mother, looking disappointed. 'You must be starving.'

'You don't need to worry about me, Mum. I'll be fine,' Eloise said, but felt a pang of regret as she moved in for a hug. 'And thanks for the lift, Dad.'

'Not at all... not at all. Come home soon, won't you?' he said. She was surprised to hear the catch in his voice. It wasn't like him.

'Of course, Dad. Oxford's not a million miles away and there's a bus to London several times an hour,' she said with a light laugh.

'Well, bye-bye, darling,' he said and hugged her awkwardly.

After she'd shut the door on them, she stood in the middle of all her belongings, uncertain what to do next. She knew her parents meant well. She'd been so anxious to be rid of them and get on with moving in that she hadn't fully appreciated how they must be feeling about leaving her here. She blew out her cheeks and went over to the window. Down in the street, her father was manoeuvring the car out of a tight spot. She could just make out her mother in the passenger seat saying something to him, and imagined her father starting up again. Smiling, she shook her head and turned back to her new room and began to unpack.

Soon she was down to one last box, which contained her books from home. With the box at her feet she picked them out one by one, examined each title and placed them on the shelf above her bed. It was a tight squeeze and she regretted bringing so many, but these books were like old friends and reminded her of home.

The bookshelf was now full and she was unable to make room for the last one. It was a red leather-bound vintage copy of *Pride and Prejudice* that had been a present for one of her birthdays, but she couldn't remember which one. She'd never got round to reading it, but now that she was embarking on her English Literature course it was high time she did.

As she flicked through the flimsy tissue-like pages, something fluttered down and landed on the carpet. Puzzled, she retrieved it and turned it the right way up. It was a faded black-and-white photograph of a girl with two white bows holding her dark plaits in place; she smiled sweetly for the camera. It was perfectly charming. Eloise vaguely remembered having seen this photograph or something similar once in a photo album of her grandmother's. Was this girl her own grandmother, and who had taken the photo? She wondered if it had been taken professionally, it was that good. She turned it over but couldn't see anything written on the back. So why did she have it? Eloise concluded that she must have been intending to use it as a bookmark but forgotten about it. Sighing, she slipped the photograph back between the pages and laid the book down on the bedside table. She would start reading it later.

There was a knock at the door.

'Come in,' she called out.

It was James, the student who'd welcomed her. 'I saw your parents leave and thought I'd come and see how you're getting on.'

She thought he winked at her but perhaps she'd imagined it. 'Actually, I'm doing just fine,' she said.

He didn't wait to be invited in, and strode over to the window. 'Nice view,' he said, glancing out, then he pulled out the chair from under the desk and sat down.

Eloise tidied the empty box away and turned to him. 'Which room are you in?' she asked casually.

'Me? I don't live here now. I'm in digs this year.' He gazed around her room with an approving look. 'I quite miss these rooms, you know.' He swivelled round to face her. 'Hey, I thought you might want to come for lunch. There's a cheap café that's popular with students. It's not far. And I can show you where things are in town.'

'Thanks. That would be lovely.' Eloise felt inexplicably happy to be asked.

'Good,' he said, getting up and crossing the floor in three strides. 'See you at the front door in five minutes?'

Exactly five minutes later, she tripped down the two flights of stairs, pleased to have made the acquaintance of at least one new person. He seemed nice and they might even become friendly, she thought.

He was waiting at the door with a small group of students around him, and for a millisecond she was disappointed that it wouldn't be just the two of them going off for lunch.

'This is Eloise,' James said easily and smiled at her. 'You'll have to let the others introduce themselves. Everyone turned up at once and I'm afraid I've already lost track of names.'

Pleased he had at least remembered her name, she found herself unable to concentrate on everyone else's, but no one took any notice as they set off in twos and threes. She found herself walking beside Holly, a first-year student, who also came from London and seemed as nervous as Eloise felt. They swapped details, their previous schools, whether they already knew anybody at Oxford – neither did – and what courses they were on – Holly was studying French and German. Eloise was glad to find out that Holly was in the next room to hers.

'Here we are,' said James, who was at the front of the group. He stopped outside a café whose windows were so steamed up it was impossible to see inside. At that moment, the door flew open and a noisy group of students came piling out. A girl with long flowing blond hair caught sight of James and shouted his name, then came over and kissed him noisily on both cheeks. She turned her head to glance at the cluster of people watching them and shrugged at James. 'See you later?' she said airily and ran to catch up with the rest of her group.

'Sure,' said James, watching her go.

And for the second time since she'd met him, Eloise felt a tinge of disappointment.

When everyone dispersed and Eloise returned to her room later that afternoon, she found herself at a loose end. Her eye was caught by her copy of *Pride and Prejudice* that she'd left lying on her bed. She sat down and opened it at the first page, where the photograph lay, and was once more struck by the face of the young girl who stared out at her. She gazed at it for a long time before turning the photo over and noticed that there was something written there after all, but it had become illegible through the mists of time. Frowning, she tried to make out the unfamiliar words, but soon gave up. So she carefully inserted the photo back between the pages of the book. She had a strong desire to find out more, but for now she couldn't think how she would go about it.

FOUR
LEIPZIG, 1938

Rudolf

When Rudolf walked through the door of his apartment, his heart lifted as he heard the joyful sound of his children's voices laughing at something that Bella was saying. Composing himself, he walked into the kitchen, where the three of them were sitting at the table playing their favourite board game. Ursula had just rolled the dice and was frantically banging her red piece from space to space across the board. He slipped into the fourth chair round the table and asked who was winning.

'Me, Papa! I'm winning,' Ursula cried out in delight and threw herself into his arms. He held her and closed his eyes, breathing in the scent of her newly washed still damp hair. *This is all that matters*, he thought with a wave of tenderness mixed with sadness. After all that had happened tonight, would he really be able to protect his wife and children?

'It's not fair. I was winning... Ursula's a cheat.' Stefan slid off his chair so he could stamp his foot.

'Well, let's have another game now that I'm here,' said Rudolf, gently removing Ursula's hands, which were clasped tightly round his neck. 'Come here, Stefan,' he said, stretching out his arms. He pulled Stefan onto his lap next to Ursula and winked at Bella, who was watching the three of them in amusement. They played two more games, Rudolf letting Stefan win one and calling a draw on the second, before Bella stood up and announced it was bedtime. 'Who do you want to read you a story?' she asked, knowing full well that the children would insist that Papa read to them.

'Papa, Papa!' the children chanted, leaping up and tugging him by the hand.

Bella smiled at Rudolf, but there was fear in her eyes. Even though he hadn't had a chance to tell her about the riots he'd been caught up in, he sensed they could no longer carry on pretending that everything would be fine.

'There's a letter for you on the sideboard,' Bella called out from the kitchen after Rudolf had finished reading to the children. 'From the postmark, it looks like it's from Wolfgang.'

Rudolf felt his heart lurch, as it always did when he heard from his brother. Deep down, he knew he should have followed him to Amsterdam. Wolfgang had asked him enough times, but Rudolf always had an answer as to why the time wasn't right. Sighing, he opened it and began to read.

I have an acquaintance who can help you set up in business here. It'll be a fresh start for you all and you'd make Mama very happy. The children are young enough to pick up Dutch and will make new friends at school. Annaliese is virtually bilingual and absolutely loves her school in the centre of town. Do think about it.

Rudolf scanned the rest of the letter and folded it away. His brother was offering Rudolf the perfect way out of their dilemma, but still he prevaricated. He and his family weren't just Jewish, they were German Jews. Why hadn't Wolfgang mentioned that fact? Amsterdam wasn't so very far from Germany, and Rudolf found it hard to believe they would be welcomed with open arms. And yet, Wolfgang's suggestion made perfect sense in the light of the threat they were facing here in Leipzig. But would Bella accept the upheaval of moving away from everything she held dear? He needed to find the right moment to persuade her of what was for the best.

'How's Wolfgang?' Bella asked brightly, coming through with their supper.

Rudolf slipped the letter into his pocket. He wasn't ready to talk about Wolfgang's offer until he was sure what the best course of action was for him and his family. 'It's the usual talk about how we should move to Amsterdam,' he said, taking his place at the table. 'Ah, my favourite – pork schnitzel and sauerkraut.' He sniffed appreciatively.

Bella didn't press him for further information as they ate and talked about the children's day, how Ursula was thriving under a new teacher and that Stefan had been picked to play in the school football team, but there was a thread of tension between them that Rudolf knew only he could address.

He waited until they had cleared away and Bella had brought through a tray with the silver coffeepot, two cups and saucers and a silver sugar bowl.

'Isn't there any cream?' he asked. He never did like drinking his coffee black.

Bella frowned at him. 'How can you ask for cream at a time like this? The grocer has a poster in the window barring Jews from entering and the only place where Jews are allowed to shop is across town. Buying cream for the coffee is the least of my worries right now.'

Rudolf was chastened to hear her talk like this. He had no answer. As much as he tried to ignore what was happening, hardly a day went by when there wasn't another Nazi rule preventing Jews from leading normal lives. Unable to bear Bella's critical gaze, he walked over to the window and looked down on the street. A couple of men on bicycles rode past and only a few pedestrians were out at this time. In fact, it was so quiet that he could almost convince himself that nothing could affect them in this corner of Leipzig.

Stop deluding yourself, said a voice in his head. Wolfgang's voice. He knew he could no longer ignore what was staring him right in the face. There were simply too many signs that the Jews were under attack and he would never forgive himself if he hadn't taken heed of them sooner.

With a heavy heart, he spun round to face Bella. 'I've been waiting for the right time to broach the subject with you, but I didn't want to say anything in front of the children. Things are turning ugly out in the street, and dangerous. Tonight was no exception.' He told her about the Hitler Jugend thugs who came to storm the Jewish quarter, how Johann had helped him escape and that they had ended up running for their lives.

'Rudolf... why didn't you say anything earlier?' She got up and went to hold him tight.

'Oh, Bella,' he whispered. 'I'm so worried about our situation.' He held her face and looked deep into her eyes. 'Whenever I've received letters from Wolfgang in the past, I always thought he was exaggerating about how bad things are here and that he can't possibly know what it's like. And then I witnessed it first-hand tonight. I don't think we can stay in Leipzig any longer.'

Bella held his gaze. 'I agree... but Amsterdam? It'll be such a big move for us.'

Rudolf had just opened his mouth to speak, when there came the sickening sound of splintering glass from down below. They both hurried to the window and saw an angry mob of men prowling along the length of the street, whooping and shouting and brandishing heavy clubs above their heads. Close behind came a black van with the windows blanked out; it stopped in front of a neighbour's house opposite and several uniformed men jumped out. Without knocking, one of them began kicking violently at the door. When it didn't open immediately, the man ran at it with his shoulder several times, until it flew open with a resounding crack that could be heard two storeys up.

'Oh my God,' said Rudolf, unable to tear his eyes away. Bella stood at his side, clutching his arm so tightly he gasped out loud. Or perhaps the gasp was because of what he'd just seen. Manfred Friedmann, his neighbour and friend, who had lived across the road for as long as Rudolf could remember, was being dragged out of the broken door of his house. He held his head high in defiance but the pained expression on his face spoke volumes. Why would they come for Manfred, well-respected doctor and pillar of the Jewish community? But of course Rudolf knew – that was precisely why he was being targeted. If even doctors were under attack, this meant that no Jewish person was safe. The Nazis were trying their utmost to deprive Jews of their livelihoods, homes, their society – their whole lives.

'It's Manfred,' Rudolf said, his voice shaking with the shock.

'Why? What's he done?' Bella clung to him, staring down at the scene unfolding before their eyes. Manfred, normally so neatly turned out in suit and tie, was completely dishevelled. His shirt was torn and his hair was falling over his face. He was being restrained by two uniformed men, who hauled him stumbling towards the back of the waiting van. The doors had been flung open to reveal that it was packed with men. It was impossible to guess how many, but they all looked so young, some mere teenagers. Two of them leaned out of the van to give a helping hand to Manfred, who was trying to resist his captors. Suddenly, he received a blow to the back of the head and fell forward. Two men inside the van reached out to catch him and managed to drag him on board. He looked so utterly helpless that it made Rudolf's heart constrict with pain.

The doors were immediately slammed shut, the perpetrators jumped into the front and the van drove off.

Bella stood weeping beside her husband. 'After all Manfred's done to serve his patients – I can't believe anyone can be so cruel,' she managed to say.

'Nor can I,' Rudolf said, still unable to believe his eyes. Down below, a gang of thirty or more men were charging down the middle of the street, lashing out at whoever crossed their path. Many smashed batons against windows. The noise of splintering glass was deafening, along with ear-splitting screams and the constant screech of tyres as vehicles sped through the streets.

'Come away from the window. We've seen enough. And we need to make sure the noise hasn't woken the children and upset them,' said Rudolf, trying hard not to show his terror at what this meant for his beloved family.

They tiptoed down the hallway together. Rudolf pushed open the children's bedroom door and they peered into the darkness. Ursula and Stefan lay side by side in their beds, fast asleep. Thanks goodness they were oblivious to the raucous noise, thought Rudolf. 'Let's leave them to sleep in peace. I'll go and lock up,' he said, even though he'd secured the door tightly after he'd come in. But would it be enough? Would the Nazis come for them next?

When he was satisfied that the locks were secure, he walked back to the living room and found that Bella had drawn the curtains. She was sitting on the settee in the dark. Rudolf sat down beside her and took her hand in his, while they listened fearfully to the crashing and crunching sound of shattering glass accompanied by triumphant whoops from the thugs who had caused it. It seemed to be never-ending, but eventually things quietened down.

'I think they've moved on,' said Rudolf in a whisper and squeezed Bella's hand.

Neither spoke until they could be sure that the fracas wasn't about to start up again, then they slowly went off to bed.

The next morning Rudolf was up early to go and see what damage had been done to his shop. He found Johann already there, along with many of their neighbours who were picking their way through broken glass and rubble. It was worse than Rudolf could possibly have imagined. As if a bomb had hit the place. None of the businesses had been spared.

Together, Rudolf and Johann crunched over shards of glass and arrived in front of the baker's shop, which stood window-less, hollowed out and desolate. There were no lovingly arranged displays of freshly baked goods, nor any customers queuing halfway down the street as they normally did on a Sunday morning. Johann stood staring in disbelief, white-faced and speechless.

'I'll help you clear up and get things back to normal,' said Rudolf softly, knowing his words were meaningless. How could any of them recover after this? Even if they did manage to start again, what was the point when the Nazis were determined to drive them away?

After Rudolf had helped those less able to help themselves, he went to his own studio. Like all the other shops and busi-nesses, the window had been shattered and a brick lay on the pavement, evidence of what had caused the damage. His care-fully conceived window display had been knocked about and the framed portraits that he'd positioned on easels lay strewn across the floor. The plum-coloured velvet settee he used for sittings had several long gashes across its fabric and the pale stuffing billowed out onto the floor. Where there had been light fittings were only loose wires. But the worst of it was that someone had daubed 'Jews out' in black paint on one of the white walls. The only positive sign was that the vandals seemed to have missed the darkroom, which was still locked. Rudolf went inside and saw that all the bottles were lined up neatly on the shelves and the trays still contained chemicals waiting to be emptied. Even the photos he'd hastily pegged up on the clothes-line had by some miracle been spared. But it was small consolation in the light of knowing those vandals had trodden through his studio with their heavy boots and left that hateful slur daubed across the wall.

Bella was waiting anxiously for him when he arrived back home, exhausted and dejected. 'Rudolf, I can't take any more of this,' she announced after he'd recounted what he'd seen. 'For the sake of the children, we have to get out of Leipzig.'

It was a relief to hear that she had reached the same conclusion as he had. He smiled weakly. 'I'll make the arrangements with Wolfgang in the morning. We must leave for Amsterdam while we still can.'

FIVE
OCTOBER 2022

Eloise

Eloise was finding it difficult to settle into student life and the heavy demands of her course. Two weeks had passed since her first day and she was struggling to keep up with her growing reading list. Dickens was on the syllabus this week and she'd only managed to read two of his novels. There was still a stack of books to get through and just four days till her tutorial. Feeling panicky, she reached for her phone.

Her mother picked up straight away. 'It's lovely to hear from you, darling. How are you getting on with Dickens?' It wasn't the first time her mother had asked, but Eloise knew she could no longer pretend everything was fine.

She gave a shuddery sigh. 'I gave up after *Bleak House*. Don't get me wrong, it's brilliant, but it's so long. I simply haven't time to read it, let alone *Martin Chuzzlewit* and *A Tale of Two Cities*. There's a pile right here on my desk and I've made hardly any headway. I don't know how the others on my course manage it, but they do. Mum, I'm not sure coming to

Oxford was such a good idea.' She took in a sharp breath, waiting for her mother to offer words of support.

'Now come on, you know you're just saying that. You passed all your exams and the interview with flying colours, so you've already proved yourself.'

Eloise sighed. How could she expect her mother to know what it was really like being a student when everyone was so much cleverer than her?

'Have you spoken to anyone else about your workload?' her mother went on.

'Of course not! I barely know anyone... besides, the people in my tutorial group are so much more confident than me. I just know they're breezing through the books.'

'If you barely know them, then how can you say that? Listen, darling, I have an idea that might help.'

Eloise didn't respond. She took several deep breaths to steady herself.

'I think you need a bit of a break—' her mother said.

'How can you say that?' Eloise butted in. 'I've only been here two weeks.'

'I understand that, but it sounds as if you need to get away from your desk and clear your head. Why don't you pay Grandma a visit? She's only a short bus ride away from the centre of Oxford.'

Eloise paused as a thought occurred to her about the photograph that she was sure was of her grandmother. She had been there for Eloise's entire life and Eloise loved her dearly. She was her father's mother, now in her nineties and still as bright as a button. She'd always been so kind and loving towards Eloise, as she was towards all her family, which was extensive. At the last count, she'd told Eloise, she had twelve grandchildren including her.

'It might be more. I'm afraid I've lost count,' Grandma had

said the last time Eloise had asked. She'd looked genuinely upset about the matter. Eloise had helped her remember by offering to write down everyone's names in bold black ink on a large piece of paper, but when she'd asked the names of her grandma's parents she'd waved a hand dismissively in the air. 'Don't complicate things.' And she refused to say any more.

'Are you still there, darling?' Eloise's mother was saying.

'Yes, I am. I was just thinking about a photo I found in one of my books I brought with me. It's of a girl with ribbons in her dark hair. It's quite old and I'm sure it's of Grandma. I was just wondering if you knew anything about it?'

'I'm sorry. I can't say I remember it. But you should take it along and ask her. By the way, I took the liberty of ringing her and asking if she'd like you to visit and she gave a little whoop of delight. You know how much she loves your visits.'

It was a sunny day and Eloise decided to walk up the Banbury Road, which led to Summertown. Her grandmother lived in sheltered accommodation, a short walk from a parade of well-appointed shops that supplied her with all of her needs. Eloise turned into the tree-lined street of large townhouses to the block of retirement flats and glanced up to see her grandmother framed in one of the windows. She stopped to wave and kept on waving until the old lady noticed her and began waving back. How sweet of her to look out for me, Eloise thought, her heart lifting. She ran to the main entrance, rang the bell and was buzzed in by the warden, a middle-aged woman whom she recognised from the last time she'd been.

'Mrs Moses has been talking non-stop about you coming to visit her. You know where to go. Do go on up.'

The door to the flat was open. 'It's me – Eloise,' she called and stepped inside the narrow hallway that led to the living room. Grandma was slowly making her way towards her with a look of great concentration on her creased face as she cruised from one piece of furniture to another for balance. When she reached the living room door she clung on to the handle, her face erupting into the biggest smile, her dark brown eyes shining with pleasure. 'My dear Eloise,' she cried. 'What a delight to see you.' Her voice was strong and firm and she spoke with that familiar faint accent that Eloise knew was Dutch mixed in with something else, but that was every bit a part of her as her infectious smile. Eloise couldn't help but feel comforted whenever she was in her presence.

'It's lovely to see you too, Grandma.' Eloise kissed her warmly on her pillowy soft cheek, but didn't hug her. Grandma never went in for hugs and the times that Eloise forgot she'd be given short shrift.

'Push the door shut, will you? Come inside. I'll make us a cup of tea.'

Eloise did as she was told and walked behind the old lady as she traced her passage handhold by handhold towards the small kitchenette. Eloise knew better than to offer to make the tea for her. She'd offered only the once and been given such a look that she'd never done it again, though she noticed how much slower her grandma was than she remembered. Yet she still took pride in doing things for herself. In fact, it was a condition of the sheltered accommodation that its residents must be able to lead an independent life. But she'd recently celebrated her ninety-first birthday and Eloise worried what would happen when she was no longer able to fend for herself.

Eventually the tea was made, and Eloise was allowed to carry it through on a tray. She put it down on the low coffee table, pushing some magazines and today's paper aside, and sat down in one of two big armchairs.

'I'll pour,' insisted her grandma, who was moving steadily towards her chair. When she got there, she held on to the chair wing to steady herself before sinking down into the cushions with a sigh. Eloise thought how frail, how birdlike she seemed amongst the cushions, but she perked up immediately as she leaned forward to pour out their tea. She pushed a cup and saucer and the milk jug towards Eloise.

'Now, dear Eloise. I was so pleased to hear that you were coming to study at such a prestigious university, and just down the road from me. When your mother called to say you'd be coming today it made me very happy.' She beamed at Eloise as she sipped her tea.

'You know I always love to see you, Grandma. Oh, I've got something to show you.' Eloise dug into her canvas bag and brought out her copy of *Pride and Prejudice*. She opened it at the page where the photograph lay. 'I've had this photo for some time and recently found it. I've been wondering – is it of you as a young girl?'

Her grandmother's smile dropped as she concentrated on examining the photograph, which she held close to her face. She took so long over it that Eloise wondered if something about it upset her. Perhaps it wasn't of Grandma at all, but of someone close to her she'd loved and lost. She had begun to wish she hadn't shown her it when her grandmother suddenly handed it back to her. 'It happened such a long time ago,' she said vaguely.

Eloise frowned a little as she wondered what she could mean. 'Would you like to tell me about it?'

Her grandmother slowly shook her head and drew in a deep breath. 'No, not now. But perhaps one day.'

Eloise didn't think she could press her for more information, but decided on a different tack. 'What was it like for you when you were my age? Dad told me you wished you'd gone to university but never had the chance.'

'Things were very different for young people back then. I never had the opportunity to go to university, though my papa always hoped I would one day.' The old lady paused, gazing straight ahead as she remembered. 'When I was eighteen, I was living in another country, newly married and with my first child on the way.' A wistful smile crossed her face as she went on, 'With your father, as it happens. Now, there's a thought.' She continued to tell Eloise about young married life on a kibbutz looking after four young children, while her husband worked as a librarian.

Eloise listened in wonderment, unable to imagine what it must be like to have a baby at such a young age. 'It must have been hard looking after four little children,' she said.

'No, it was never hard. There were always people around me to share childcare and household chores. In fact, we shared everything. We all felt extremely blessed after all we had been through. And after the children were grown up and had moved away, Chaim was offered a job at the Bodleian Library, which is how we ended up in Oxford.'

It was comfortable sitting here and listening to her grandmother's reminiscences. Eloise only wished she could stay all day, but she began to have a nagging feeling that she should get back to her studies. She leaned forward and took her grandma's gnarled bony hands in both of hers. 'I should go now, but it's been so lovely seeing you.'

'Must you leave so soon?' said her grandma, a look of worry briefly crossing her face.

Eloise felt a pang of pity for her, knowing that she didn't receive many visitors, but she did need to get back to work. 'I'm reading Dickens this week and I've a lot to get through before my next tutorial.' She suddenly felt better about the task ahead having taken this break.

Grandma nodded understandingly. 'Come again soon, my dear, and I'll show you the family album with photos of when I was young. There's so much you don't know about the family.' She briefly had a faraway look in her eyes, then she turned to Eloise and chuckled. 'I'm sure it must be hard to believe that I was ever young.'

'Not at all, Grandma.' Eloise kissed her warm cheek, breathing in the faint powder scent. 'I'd love to see your photos. You must definitely show me them next time.'

She left with a lighter heart and an intention to raise the question of the girl in the photo again the next time she visited.

SIX

Eloise kept mulling over the significance of the black-and-white photo in her possession. Her grandmother had seemed reluctant to acknowledge it was of her, but why did she refuse to talk about it? Straight after, she'd been quite happy to chat about her life when she was a young woman living in Israel, so maybe Eloise was simply overreacting. She told herself it was probably nothing and that there would be a perfectly simple explanation.

The following weekend, she walked over to Summertown and popped into the deli on her way to buy cinnamon buns for tea. But when her grandmother took the bag, opened it and saw the buns, tears filled her eyes.

'I'm so sorry,' she said and handed them back.

Eloise was appalled that she'd made some terrible faux pas and made to put them away in her bag. 'Is there something wrong, Grandma?'

'No. You misunderstand. These are tears of happiness. They suddenly brought back a memory of when I first came to Amsterdam with my family. Our aunt Gertrude took us into a cake shop on our first day and bought us cinnamon buns just like these ones. I insist we eat them.' She gave a little laugh, and Eloise smiled, relieved she hadn't done something to upset her.

After tea, her grandmother picked up her treasured photo album that lay on the table between them. She took her time explaining who was who in each of the photographs, which were taken in the late 1940s.

'It was a bitter-sweet time for me coming so soon after the war,' she said after they'd been poring over pictures of herself as a young wife and mother living close to Tel Aviv. 'I had four beautiful children, a wonderful husband, but neither of us had any other family to enjoy it with. It was the same for all of us living on the kibbutz. We were all far from where we'd grown up as children and that created a special bond between us. We had all lost family. It never got any easier.'

Eloise could see the pain etched in her grandma's dark brown eyes as she tried but failed to put herself in her shoes. From the small amount she'd been told by her father, Eloise had been able to piece together that Grandma's family had suffered terribly at the hands of the Nazis. They had fled Leipzig before the war, leaving all their possessions to settle in Amsterdam, where they were happy for a while until Germany occupied the Netherlands and drove out the Jews. That was when the details of their story became hazy. Her grandmother never talked about it and her father had given up trying to discover what happened to the rest of the family during the war and after it had ended.

Eloise had never understood her grandma's reluctance to speak of the past but, now that she was beginning to open up, she sensed it was as good a time as any to bring up the subject of the photograph.

'Grandma,' she began, as she extracted the photograph from the bag at her feet. 'Do you remember I showed you this when I came last week?'

Her grandmother reached out a bony hand that shook slightly as she took hold of it. She gazed at it for several moments. 'Of course I remember. This was taken when I was thirteen.' She nodded her head and smiled at the memory.

Eloise was relieved, if not somewhat surprised her grandmother was reacting to it differently now. 'Did you have it taken professionally? It's very good.'

'Oh, no. We never needed to. My father always took our photographs.' Suddenly, her smile dropped as if something had caused her great pain. She handed back the photograph, saying, 'It was the last photo he took of me by myself. But I am pleased you still have it.'

'It's a lovely photo,' Eloise said, wanting to hear more.

Her grandmother smiled and seemed to have forgotten the painful memory, whatever it was. 'I remember being so happy that day and Mama telling me I looked quite grown up.'

She glanced down at the album that still lay open in her lap. When she closed it with a sigh, Eloise was certain that that would be the end of the matter, but the old lady took up her theme again.

'You've reminded me – I have another album that pre-dates this one by some years. I haven't looked at it for a long time. It makes me too sad, because all the people in those photos are long dead. I've kept it locked away all these years, but as you are close family I think you have a right to see.'

Eloise's heart beat faster as she waited for her grandmother to elaborate, but she felt disappointed when the old lady sat back with a long sigh. 'Not now. I'm far too tired. Remind me to show you the next time you come.'

SEVEN

AMSTERDAM, 1938

Rudolf hadn't seen Uncle Thomas since his father's funeral, so it was with great anticipation that he craned his neck out of the window to catch a sight of him as the train pulled into Amsterdam Central station. The platform was crowded with people waiting to welcome the arrivals. Uncle Thomas was tall, distinguished-looking, with silver hair and black-rimmed glasses. He would be easy to spot.

'There he is!' cried Rudolf, waving frenetically, as the train drew to a halt alongside the teeming platform with a prolonged screeching of brakes.

'Uncle Thomas, Uncle Thomas!' chanted Ursula and Stefan, egging each other on and jumping up and down. 'Can we get off now?' cried Ursula, who reached up to open the door of their compartment. Their mood had alternated between excitement and boredom throughout the ten-hour journey and they were visibly relieved that it was at an end.

'Calm down, children, and gather your things together,' said Bella, reminding them not to forget their small knapsacks. 'It's very busy on the platform. You must stick close to Mama and Papa.'

Rudolf heaved their heavy suitcases down from the luggage rack. 'Hold their hands, Bella. I can manage these.'

They shuffled along the narrow corridor behind a long line of weary-looking passengers weighed down with enormous pieces of luggage. Soon, the children were squabbling over who had the better knapsack, and didn't believe it when their mother pointed out that they both had exactly the same.

'Over here!' boomed a voice, and Rudolf caught sight of Uncle Thomas, weaving through the crowd towards them. Close behind him was a porter wheeling a luggage barrow, ready to receive their baggage.

Bella was the first to disembark, lifting each child out into Uncle Thomas's outstretched arms. 'My goodness! How you two have grown,' he said, raising each child up high until they squealed.

They were suddenly hemmed in on all sides by crowds of people and Bella put her arms protectively round her children. 'Hold hands and stand next to your great-uncle Thomas.' She then offered her cheek to him for a kiss.

Rudolf was left to manhandle the two heavy cases onto the platform. Uncle Thomas instructed the porter to take them, then went to give Rudolf an enormous bear hug. 'I'm so glad you finally came,' he said gruffly.

With a lump in his throat, Rudolf replied, 'We didn't have any choice. But thanks for all you've done to make it happen.'

Uncle Thomas had worked tirelessly to make sure they received their visas and train tickets out of Leipzig. He was now a Dutch citizen after leaving Leipzig with his wife a few years before the Nazis came into power. He counted himself lucky to have escaped before people realised that Hitler wanted to rid Germany of its Jews. Ever since, he'd dedicated himself to helping other family members and close Jewish friends achieve a safe passage to freedom.

'It's the least I could do. You and Wolfgang are my closest family now.' Uncle Thomas's voice was deep and he gave a small cough and covered his mouth with his handkerchief. Rudolf's heart went out to his dear uncle, who had always been so kind to him and his family; he had never had children of his own.

'You must be starving after your long journey,' said his uncle, who now seemed in better control of his emotions. 'Gertrude is preparing supper and you'll be staying with us tonight. Then tomorrow, we'll show you your house, which is right on one of the canals. I think you will all love it. It's close to the flower market and even has a back garden where the children can play.' He smiled indulgently down at Ursula and Stefan and Rudolf wondered if he'd forgotten their names.

'Come on, Ursula, Stefan. Follow Great-Uncle Thomas,' said Rudolf and the children obediently clasped hands. Rudolf slipped his own hand into Bella's and, when she turned to him, they exchanged a smile. It came to him that it was the first time they'd smiled at one another in weeks. She nodded and he understood what she meant by it – that the decision to move to Amsterdam had been the right one.

Early next morning, Uncle Thomas and Aunt Gertrude took them the short distance to the tall, thin black-and-white canal house that was to be the Breslauer family home. The children raced inside and up the steep staircases that led to a tiny attic room with views over the canal where a few boats were moving along at a lazy pace. To avoid arguments, it was agreed that this would be their bedroom, as it had just enough space for two single beds below the eaves. The sitting room was on the first floor and had large windows that let in the light from both ends of the house. On the ground floor was a neat kitchen with a door leading onto a small patio and garden.

After they'd viewed the house, Rudolf shook Uncle Thomas's hand. 'You've done us proud here. This is like a palace after our apartment in Leipzig.'

'I was lucky to hear it was available. I thought it would be perfect for the four of you. Until your furniture arrives, we can lend you anything you need. Now.' He turned to speak to Ursula and Stefan, who were growing restless at all this grown-up talk. 'Who would like to go down to the canal and see the boats?'

'Me! Me!' they shouted, both trying to outdo the other.

They stepped out into the bright sunshine and onto the narrow cobbled pavement. Rudolf held the keys to the house in his hand and lifted his gaze to see how tall it was. He could hardly believe this house was theirs after all the worry and tension they'd suffered these past months. To have escaped Nazi Germany was a miracle in itself, but to move into such a beautiful house in a city where Jews weren't being threatened was even harder to comprehend.

Bella came to stand next to him and touched his elbow. 'Is everything all right, *Liebchen*?'

He turned to look into her eyes and felt a sudden rush of love for her. 'Yes,' he said, kissing her on the lips. 'It's marvellous. In fact, it couldn't be better.'

Thomas and Gertrude gave the Breslauer family a tour of Amsterdam, showing them the nearby Vondelpark, where they would be able to take the children to play, but more importantly, the best Jewish shops in their neighbourhood. When they stopped at a baker to buy bread and pastries, Bella wiped away a tear at the sight of such an abundance of familiar food in the shop window.

After the children had gone into the shop with Aunt Gertrude, Bella said to Uncle Thomas, 'It's been so hard recently. The Nazis have forced all Jewish shops in Germany to close and anyone who defies them has their property smashed up. And if that wasn't bad enough, we've been banned from shopping anywhere else. Seeing shops like this one so full of the food we love is quite unbelievable.'

Uncle Thomas put an arm round her shoulders. 'It may take some getting used to, but you'll soon see just how safe things are for Jews here,' he said quietly.

The children came bounding out of the shop, already hungrily chewing their sweet cinnamon pastries. Smiling, Gertrude came out, holding several loaves of bread in her arms. 'I've bought enough for all of us, but if not you can always pop back. It's only a few minutes' walk from your house.'

Rudolf had been listening attentively to Uncle Thomas's conversation. He wanted to believe that Amsterdam was so much safer than Leipzig, but he was left with a queasy feeling. He'd witnessed first-hand the brutal treatment of Jews in Leipzig and had heard that similar horrific scenes were unfolding throughout Germany and Austria. It was impossible to believe that Amsterdam could be any different.

EIGHT

Bella met Rachel on the first day of school, when she became aware of the young woman beside her waving her children goodbye.

'It's never easy, is it?' said Bella, noticing the tears in the woman's eyes. 'I'm Bella, by the way,' she went on, smiling.

'I'm Rachel.' The woman sniffed. 'I don't believe I've seen you here before. Do you have a child starting today?'

'Two, actually. Ursula's the oldest, she's eight, so I'm hoping she'll take care of her little brother Stefan. He's just turned six.'

Rachel's face brightened. 'Same age as my two, Max and Klara. That means they'll be in the same classes. You'd think I'd be used to it by now.'

Bella nodded sympathetically, then said quietly, 'I'm not sure how my two will cope with speaking Dutch. We've only been living in Amsterdam a few weeks.'

'The German children always pick it up soon enough. I wouldn't worry too much. And you speak Dutch well.' Rachel glanced at her approvingly.

'Do you think so?' said Bella, feeling herself redden, for she hated her German accent. 'I don't expect I'll ever be taken for Dutch.'

'Maybe not, but no one round here will judge you. We're all friends. Where are you from?'

'Leipzig,' said Bella wistfully.

'I bet you miss it.'

Bella nodded. 'I didn't want to move, but my husband's uncle persuaded us that Amsterdam is a safer place than Leipzig.' She raised an eyebrow. 'What do you think?'

'At the moment it is. Listen, I've invited a few of the mothers over for coffee on Thursday morning. Why don't you come along?'

'I'd love to,' said Bella, glad to have the opportunity of meeting other women in a similar position to her own. With her children at school and Rudolf out all day, she often felt lonely without her Leipzig friends and with only a handful of relatives nearby.

Bella began to settle and looked forward to Thursday mornings, when the women gathered at each other's houses for coffee and cake. Sometimes as many as fourteen women came together and it was always a convivial affair. They enjoyed relaxing in each other's company and there seemed to be an unspoken rule that no one talked about the rumours circulating of imminent war started by the Germans and what that might mean for the Jews. Instead, they chatted about normal things, like swapping recipes, clothing patterns and gossip. Several of the women were German, like herself, and had also moved to Amsterdam when the threat of persecution became too great. Bella relished being able to speak in her mother tongue in this safe haven where it didn't matter that they were German. And it was easier than trying to converse in Dutch.

Rachel became a good friend. She'd lived in Amsterdam her whole life and had a big network of friends and acquaintances who all looked out for each other. She kept Bella informed of everything she should know, and promised to let her know if she heard the slightest whisper of any threats against their tight-knit community.

One morning, as they waved their children off at school, Rachel asked Bella if she knew that their husbands were acquaintances.

'Really?' said Bella, surprised. 'How come?'

Rachel's face softened as she talked about Jozef, her husband of ten years, who ran Cohen's, a high-quality draper's shop that had belonged to his father and his father before him. 'When the photographic gallery opened its doors, Jozef went in to introduce himself. He tells me your husband has a real talent for photography.'

Bella had been relieved and delighted when Uncle Thomas had found Rudolf the premises for his new studio-cum-gallery. Rudolf had been worried about whether he would be able to afford the rent, but Thomas had persuaded him it would be a good investment. He promised to spread the word and was sure Rudolf would pick up business from Leipzig customers who had moved to Amsterdam. Bella hadn't seen Rudolf so excited in years as he was by the studio with its white walls – perfect for displaying prints – and the room at the back, which he'd straight away turned into a darkroom. Around this time, Rudolf had begun to dream of developing a sideline in framed prints of Amsterdam's tall houses on the canals and people milling round the pretty floating flower market, to show a side to the city that he was already growing to love.

Bella basked in the glow of Jozef's compliment. She'd always known how good Rudolf was behind the camera, but hearing it from someone who'd only just met him was indeed sweet. 'As long as I've known Rudolf he's been tinkering with his camera or disappearing into his darkroom. He's passionate about his work and is always striving for the perfect picture that reflects more than what you see on first viewing. He's following in the footsteps of the father he revered.'

'Sounds just like Jozef. Cohen's has been in the family for generations and Jozef takes the business very seriously. I hope they can be friends, just like we are.' Rachel reached over and touched Bella's hand. 'We're so lucky both having a family business. It's something to be cherished.'

'Yes,' said Bella, remembering how everything had changed for Rudolf after they'd been forced to flee their family home. Without thinking, she laid a hand on her belly.

Rachel broke into a smile. 'Are you...?' She left the question hanging.

Bella found herself blushing. 'Expecting? Yes, I am. It's not great timing though with all the talk about war these days. The news from Germany is pretty grim. I'm so grateful we made it out in time, but it makes me nervous about bringing another baby into the world when things are so uncertain. But when is it ever a good time?' She sighed.

Rachel beamed her delight. 'The arrival of a baby is always something to be celebrated. I'm sure Ursula and Stefan will be thrilled to have a baby brother or sister.'

'It's still early days and we haven't told them yet. But I'm sure they will be.' Bella stroked her belly pensively. Rachel's kind words had cheered her up and briefly she was able to forget about the troubling thoughts that had begun to plague her.

NINE

JULY 1942

Rudolf

Rudolf was lost in concentration as he moved prints around the gallery when the bell above the door tinkled. He turned to see a man dressed in the distinctive grey-green uniform of the German SS step through the door. He removed his cap and greeted Rudolf in German.

Rudolf stiffened. 'Good afternoon,' he replied and put down the framed print he was holding and leaned it against the wall. 'How may I help?'

It wasn't the first time he'd had a visit from an SS officer, but each time it happened he was careful not to say anything that might antagonise them. Although these SS officers were always polite, they never appeared particularly interested in his work, but Rudolf wasn't fooled. He'd seen and heard too much from when he'd been living in Leipzig, a view that hadn't changed since moving to the Netherlands. And his suspicions about their motives were proving correct. History was repeating itself all over again with the slow creep of anti-Jewish laws. Only last week, the Germans had introduced a curfew forbidding Jews to be out on the streets after 8 p.m. or before six in the morning. It was another nuisance and didn't affect him overly, but it came not long before a law came in forcing Jews to hand in their bicycles and the keys to their cars. Seeing this Nazi taking up space in his gallery felt like an insult. He had to restrain himself from venting his anger at this stranger and all he represented. Instead, he took a deep breath and reminded himself that he was still able to carry on with his business. But why had this German come now and what were his intentions? Rudolf had an inkling that things were about to take a turn for the worse.

'I was passing and noticed the photographs you have displayed in the window. They are very good,' the man said with a disarming smile.

'Thank you. Do take a look round,' said Rudolf. The man seemed different to other Germans who'd come to his shop and snooped around and left without saying much. And a compliment was a compliment. He would simply have to humour him, he thought, and went on, 'In addition to the framed prints on the walls I have other unframed ones in portfolios. Let me know if you'd like to see them.'

The man nodded but didn't answer. With his hands clasped behind his back, he began examining the prints on display. He took his time moving from one to the next, sometimes leaning forward to examine one more closely.

Rudolf had just that morning been rearranging the framed prints on the walls of the small gallery to his satisfaction and had been keen to make space for a selection of framed photos he'd taken when wandering through the streets of Amsterdam. One, in particular, he was proud of. He'd taken it when he'd first moved to the city and had been spellbound by the sight of the man who ran a flower stall handing over an armful of tulips to a customer. He'd been particularly pleased with how this picture had turned out, and displayed it on the wall of his gallery as a poignant reminder of how life once was in Amsterdam before the war. After three years of Nazi occupation, it seemed inconceivable that life had ever been that carefree. Rudolf hadn't expected the street scene to attract so much interest, but several customers had admired the print and asked if he had any others. It gave him the idea of experimenting with different kinds of photography, which brought in new customers who might not necessarily be interested in sitting for a portrait. He duly obliged and was able to build up a sizeable portfolio of prints, until it was no longer safe for him to wander through the streets with his camera without being stopped by the Germans.

From his desk, where he pretended to busy himself with some paperwork, he kept glancing surreptitiously at the SS officer and tried to ascertain his motives. He seemed to take a genuine interest in what he was viewing. They must be about the same age, Rudolf thought, and he wondered briefly if he was married and had children back home. Did he miss them? He shuffled the papers in front of him.

Suddenly, the man cleared his throat loudly. Rudolf looked up in surprise to find him standing right next to his desk and towering over him.

'May I take a look in your portfolios?' the man said.

'Of course.' Rudolf quickly stood up, knocking over a pile of papers, which scattered across the polished floor. Feeling foolish, he cursed himself. What must the man be thinking?

'Here. Let me,' said the man, bending down to help him gather them up.

Rudolf hadn't realised how nervous he was, but he quickly regained his composure and went over to a wide chest of drawers in which he kept the portfolios. He didn't want the man fingering them, so stood by ready to show him each one.

Most were scenes around Amsterdam, such as trams passing well-known landmarks, people on bicycles – no longer Jews, he thought bitterly – riding over humpbacked bridges.

'You certainly capture the spirit of Amsterdam,' said the man, with an approving smile. 'I would like to buy a selection. Four or five will do. Unframed. How much do you charge for prints?' He pulled a leather wallet from his inside pocket, which Rudolf saw was bulging with banknotes.

Rudolf named a price and, feeling rash, offered a discount if he was interested in taking half a dozen.

'And if you were to do my portrait? Will you give me a better price for the whole lot?' This time the man's smile was less pleasant. Rudolf knew he could hardly refuse.

'It would be my pleasure,' he heard himself say. 'Let me book you in for a sitting.'

'I'll come back tomorrow. Ten a.m. sharp,' the man said before Rudolf had a chance to consult his diary. The man put his wallet away, then took his time selecting the prints.

Rudolf realised he wouldn't be paid now after all, but he maintained a professional facade. 'I'll have everything set up ready for you at ten. And the prints will be wrapped to take with you.'

Rudolf walked him to the door, then remembered he didn't have his name. Before he could ask, the man said, 'Kurt Schlesinger. Chief Service Officer, Westerbork. Pleased to meet you, Herr Breslauer.' The genial smile was back as he carefully replaced his cap and stepped out of the door, which Rudolf closed behind him.

Had he heard him right? Rudolf racked his brains, trying to remember something that someone had told him about Westerbork, but he couldn't remember what. He was left with a feeling of deep disquiet, wishing he'd had the nerve to ask this Kurt Schlesinger why he wanted his portrait done. After all, it was a conversation he always had with his clients when they booked a sitting as it helped him when setting up.

He hurried back home, barely noticing the army vehicles and groups of soldiers massing outside the station. They were a common sight these days and he knew that as long as he kept his head down and walked quickly no one would bother him.

It was a relief to turn onto the canal street. He was looking forward to getting back home and putting the day behind him.

He put his key in the lock and heard quick footsteps approaching in the hallway. He broke into a smile at the prospect of seeing his family, but when he saw Bella standing there, holding their toddler by the hand, he knew instantly that something was wrong.

'Thank goodness you're home... have you heard the news?' she said in a rush.

Frowning, Rudolf shook his head as he shut the door and dragged the bolt across as normal. He turned to kiss her on the cheek, which felt reassuringly soft and familiar, then chucked Mischa under his chin, making him giggle. At that moment, Ursula and Stefan came bursting into the hall and threw themselves at him.

'Papa, Papa, have you brought us anything nice?' pleaded Ursula, tugging on his hand. These days, she spoke exclusively in Dutch, after her teacher had suggested all the German pupils do so in order to learn the language more quickly. In private, the parents were told it was to protect the children from the taunting some of them had been subjected to in the streets.

'Not today, my darlings,' said Rudolf, bending down to kiss each of them on the top of their heads. He caught Bella's eye and frowned. How could he tell his children how hard it was to buy them treats when their favourite places where they'd always shopped were being forced to close down?

At least they could still enjoy the games they'd always played together as a family. 'Who wants to play our favourite board game?' He clapped his hands and Stefan jumped up and down.

But Ursula scoffed and almost spat out her words. 'That game is stupid. It's German. I hate the Germans,' she said with a vehemence that took him by surprise. Where had she learned to say this – surely not at school? He glanced over at Bella and they exchanged a worried look. Things had gone too far, he thought. They would have to speak to her teacher about this.

'Then let's play ball,' he said, turning back to the children and letting them drag him downstairs and out into the small back garden.

It wasn't until the three children were tucked up in bed that Rudolf had a chance to speak to Bella. She was in the kitchen, stirring a saucepan on the stove.

'What news did you want to talk to me about?' he said from the doorway. 'I didn't want to ask in front of the children.'

She turned off the flame beneath the saucepan and wiped her hands on a tea towel. 'I'm not sure how much longer we can protect them from what's going on. They see the soldiers out on the streets, hear the name-calling, even if they don't fully understand what it means. But Ursula's old enough to grasp it – she knows a lot more than she lets on.'

'This outburst from her... this hatred. Against her own people?' Rudolf was having difficulty comprehending what had happened to his sweet innocent daughter to make her behave in such a way.

'That's not how she sees it. She's a child who lives in Amsterdam and goes to a Dutch school. Every time she goes outside the door she sees German soldiers. What do you expect her to think?'

'She's being brainwashed—'

'Stop this, Rudolf. This is the reality of the world we live in. Wouldn't you rather our children were brought up as Dutch citizens than German Jews?'

They stared at one another, as Rudolf let the awful truth sink in. Bella was always so clear thinking and unafraid to speak her mind. It was what had attracted him to her when they first met as students in Leipzig twelve years ago, when war seemed impossible.

She seemed to sense his inner turmoil and softened a little. 'This war won't last forever, but we have to stay strong for the children's sake. In the meantime, things are going to get a lot worse before they get better.'

'Yes, you're right,' said Rudolf, but he hoped she was wrong. 'What about this news you were about to tell me?'

Bella huffed out a long breath. 'I'm surprised you haven't heard. Everyone round here is talking about it. We're now only allowed to go into non-Jewish shops between three and five each day. I thought it was bad enough when they banned us from buying fruit and vegetables from non-Jewish shops. What will they think of next? Stopping us from going into shops altogether?'

'I don't think they can do that. There are too many of us. They can't let us starve,' said Rudolf, though he wasn't so sure. He thought of Kurt Schlesinger, who must have known about this latest announcement, and the thought disgusted him.

'Rudolf, I don't know how we'll manage. And what really worries me is that, when we are all queuing up for food, we'll be targets. Who's to say it's not a ploy to round Jews up and shoot us?'

He took her in his arms, held her to him and stroked her hair. 'Don't think like that. You don't know how it'll be.' His mind kept going back to Schlesinger, whom he'd agreed to see the following morning. If only he could think of a way of getting out of it.

Bella pulled back and looked at him critically. 'What's the matter with you? You don't seem particularly concerned. This is serious.'

He considered not telling her about Schlesinger, but he knew from the look she gave him she would drag it out of him anyway. He sucked in a breath and began to tell her about the surprise visit of the SS official, about how uncomfortable he'd made him feel, and that instead of just selling him a few prints he'd agreed to take his portrait the following morning. He waited for her to reproach him, but she didn't.

'What do you think he wants from you?' she said, her brow wrinkling with concern.

'I wish I knew. Perhaps I'll get the chance to ask when he comes tomorrow. People often open up when I get them to relax in front of the camera. They let down their guard.'

She made a scoffing sound. 'From what you've described, I can't believe he will. It sounds to me as if he's planning something and is waiting till you've let down your guard before springing it on you. He already knows who you are and where you work. He probably knows where you live, then we'll all be in danger. I have a terrible feeling about it.'

And then he remembered where he'd heard the name Westerbork. It was a Jewish refugee camp on the German border, set up by the Dutch government to help Jews fleeing from Germany and Austria. But was it much more than that now? He thought back to Schlesinger, dressed in an SS officer's uniform. What was going on?

He quickly composed his features, unwilling to cause Bella any further worry. 'Let's not jump to any conclusions,' he said evenly. 'He came to the studio and didn't ask any searching questions. In fact, he was perfectly civil.' He so wanted to believe his own words; he didn't want to give Bella any more reason to be worried. 'Why don't we have a drink before supper,' he said, eager to change the subject. He went over to the cupboard where he kept the spirits and took out a bottle of jenever and two small glasses. 'Will you join me?' He tilted his head and gave her a long look, wondering why he hadn't noticed before how tired she looked these days. But when she smiled, he was relieved to see all traces of tiredness disappear from her beautiful face.

He took her drink over to her and kissed her gently on the lips. 'We'll get through this together, *Liebchen*,' he murmured. 'I promise.'

TEN

Rudolf had set up portraits hundreds of times before, but never once had he experienced such nerves. He'd even come in early to arrange the equipment, but on this occasion nothing seemed to be going right – the props he'd always used looked awkward and the tripod jammed when he tried to put it in position. He hurriedly removed it and found the tripod he'd long discarded and stored at the back of the darkroom. By the time everything was set up, he was unable to quieten his trembling hands.

At ten o'clock sharp, the door opened, activating the tinkling bell. Kurt Schlesinger walked in, resplendent in a jacket covered in Nazi insignia. His metal buttons glinted in the sunlight that shone in from a window high up on the wall.

'*Guten Morgen*, Herr Breslauer. I was just thinking what a wonderful morning it is to have my portrait taken.'

'*Guten Morgen*, Herr Schlesinger, if I may call you by your name.'

The German officer smiled indulgently. 'Of course. No need for either of us to stand on ceremony. Let's get down to business. The reason for my visit is to have my portrait taken for my new position at Westerbork camp.' He pulled himself up a little straighter, then went on, 'The photographer we normally use is no longer available, but you come highly recommended for your excellent photography, which is why I'm here. You do know of the camp, don't you?' He tilted his head, enquiringly.

Rudolf chose his words carefully. 'I know it was set up by the Dutch government as a safe place for Jewish refugees. A stepping stone for those who have been displaced.'

Schlesinger let out a harsh brittle laugh. 'No longer, my friend. I'm surprised you haven't heard that it is now under German control.'

'Have you worked there long?' Rudolf asked, trying hard to disguise his dismay at not knowing about this development that had somehow passed him by.

'No. Not long. Enough of the small talk.' Schlesinger moved over to the small velvet settee Rudolf had positioned beside an occasional table with a pot plant placed strategically in its centre. He sat down and flung his arm across the back. 'We'll come on to the formal photograph, but first I rather fancy the idea of you shooting me in a more casual pose. Like this. What do you think?' He stared up at Rudolf, then added, 'I'm keen to see what photographic skills you have. And as everything is already set up, why don't we start with a few informal ones?'

'That's an excellent idea. Stay just as you are and I'll get started.' Rudolf went over to the camera, which was attached to the tripod, made a few adjustments and peered through the viewfinder. Schlesinger was smoothing a few strands of lank hair across his bald head, then he tugged at his small dark moustache before pulling himself upright. He looked straight at the camera – his expression was tense, his dark stare unnerving.

Click.

'Would you please put your arm on the back of the settee again?' asked Rudolf, with his head bowed over the camera.

Click.

'Perfect. Now please look to the left?'

Click.

'Very good. The other way, please.'

This time Schlesinger didn't move.

Rudolf sensed his approach wasn't working but wasn't too concerned. It often happened when people were ill at ease in front of the camera. But these poses were too staged for his liking and he was sure Schlesinger wouldn't approve the results. He was searching his mind to say something to break the ice and make him relax, when Schlesinger spoke in a quiet voice. 'I'd rather not move my head that way. It isn't my good side.' He glanced over at Rudolf with a look of embarrassment, then went on, 'It's for my wife, you see. I thought I'd surprise her.' There was a brief moment when his face softened into a natural smile. Rudolf quickly pressed the shutter button once, twice, hoping to capture the image before Schlesinger became aware that he was no longer posing. Then, while he was adjusting his settings, he asked Schlesinger if his wife liked Amsterdam. Anything to get him to open up and talk about himself, he thought.

But the moment was lost. Schlesinger frowned as he stiffened. 'I really don't know. She's never been, as far as I know.' He spoke abruptly, then cleared his throat. 'I'm just passing through on business. There is no time for socialising.' His lips parted as if he were about to elaborate, but he seemed to think better of it. 'Are we finished with the informal poses?' he said impatiently. He rose to his feet.

'Yes, I have everything I need. Please come and stand here and rest your hands on the back of the upright chair. You won't see them in the photo, of course, but I find it makes for a better pose. I can do a head and shoulders shot, making sure your er... badges are visible.' He was gabbling and he knew it, but Schlesinger seemed unaware of Rudolf's nervousness and did as he was asked.

The rest of the session passed off without incident. Schlesinger appeared more comfortable posing for the formal portrait and Rudolf mused on how often he'd done this. Perhaps every time he was promoted to a new rank, he thought, as he went through the motions of taking more shots. There was no time to dwell on what the man's new role within Westerbork camp would involve. By the time Rudolf had used up an entire roll of film, he was sure that he had everything he needed, though he would need to edit the best ones and spend time fine-tuning them to make sure they were absolutely perfect.

'Will tomorrow at ten be convenient for you to come back and view the photos? It shouldn't take long,' said Rudolf.

'No,' Schlesinger said bluntly. 'I need to have everything concluded by the end of today. I'll come back at five p.m. It's not necessary to view the photos in advance. I will leave it to your good judgement to pick out the ones that are most suitable. Remember, I want one formal and one informal one.'

Rudolf did a quick calculation in his head and knew the timing would be tight. There was the processing time and the editing, which he usually allowed more than a few hours to complete. 'If you're absolutely sure you don't want to choose for yourself...'

'That's what I said. Is there a problem with that?' The SS officer's dark eyes glinted threateningly.

'No, of course not. I'll make sure everything is ready for you,' Rudolf found himself saying.

'Good. On my return, I will settle up with you for the prints I chose yesterday and the studio portraits. Good day.'

ELEVEN

It was a big responsibility choosing something so personal as a photograph on behalf of a client, especially one as powerful as this one. Alone with his thoughts as he worked on the images, Rudolf convinced himself that, whatever the outcome, there would be unforeseen consequences. What if Schlesinger disliked the photos? Would he, Rudolf, be made to suffer for it? Although Schlesinger said he'd come highly recommended, Rudolf felt nervous about taking his portrait. How come the Breslauer name was already known in Nazi circles?

These unsettling thoughts bothered him, but, once the images began to emerge on the wet photographic paper, Rudolf was able to relax a little. The formal shots showed a man in authority, severe and self-assured. There was little to differentiate the photos, so Rudolf had no trouble choosing – any would have done. But as he went on to the others, he found the task more difficult. His favourite was of Schlesinger sitting back and looking beyond the lens of the camera, his lips parted in a smile – but he guessed that Schlesinger would find this one too revealing, maybe a little too intimate? So he chose another, of him gazing forward with only the ghost of a smile. It was relaxed, but not too much so, and, to Rudolf's mind, showed a softer, more human side to the upright German officer presented in the formal portraits. In the end, he decided to make only minimal changes to the two photos he'd chosen. He hoped that Schlesinger would approve of them.

He was ready at 5 p.m. when Schlesinger walked through the door promptly. He wasn't wearing his cap but he had on a long leather coat, which Rudolf took as a good sign. Perhaps he was feeling more at ease than on his previous visits.

'I've been looking forward to this all day,' Schlesinger said, rubbing his hands together. 'What have you got for me?'

'Come and see for yourself.' Rudolf moved to the trestle table, where he'd displayed the two photographs.

Schlesinger was silent as he picked up each of the photos; he frowned and began examining them minutely. Rudolf left him to it and went to fetch the prints Schlesinger had selected the day before.

'These really are very good,' Schlesinger said over his shoulder. 'I commend you on your skill. I especially like the one where I am seated. I can tell you now that I found the whole experience uncomfortable, but you wouldn't guess that from looking at these photos. Yes, indeed. They will do.'

Rudolf silently let out a breath, relieved he'd passed the test, though puzzled at this last remark. 'That's very kind of you. I only take what I see and the camera never lies.' It was a line he used that always seemed to please clients. He never let on about the small adjustments he made to the prints behind the scenes.

Schlesinger beamed. 'Pack them up for me then, while I take another look at your splendid gallery.'

Rudolf waited for him to come to the desk, where he'd written out a receipt for the goods.

'I have a proposition for you,' said Schlesinger, as he counted the banknotes into Rudolf's hand.

Taken aback, Rudolf held his breath in anticipation of something unpleasant about to come his way.

Schlesinger went on, 'I can put a lot more business your way if you would be prepared to come to Westerbork and meet the kommandant. He needs a good reliable photographer and I think you are just the person for the job. What do you think?'

Rudolf was too shocked to reply at first. Schlesinger must know he was Jewish... but to go and work inside the camp? Trying hard not to display his fear, he looked at him, his gaze steady. 'I'm afraid I am the only one running this studio and gallery. I can't possibly leave it unattended.'

Schlesinger frowned, which Rudolf interpreted as displeasure. Then, almost as suddenly, he smiled. 'I'm sure the kommandant would make it worth your while.' He lowered his voice, even though he was standing quite close to Rudolf and there was no one else to hear them. 'Your business here in Amsterdam may be doing well. It's not for me to say. But I can tell you that things are going to get a lot worse for Jews like yourself. I'm offering you a way out. Come to the camp and meet the kommandant. I'm certain he will be very impressed with your work.'

Still Rudolf refused to relent, and regarded Schlesinger as calmly as he could. 'Everything I have worked for is here in Amsterdam. My family too. Westerbork is a long way from Amsterdam.'

Schlesinger seemed unperturbed by this reply and tapped the items he'd just purchased. 'Give it proper consideration, Rudolf. And don't leave it till it's too late.'

TWELVE

OCTOBER 2022

Eloise

Eloise couldn't stop thinking about the photo album her grandmother had kept locked away all these years. Why had she never thought to share it with her before? She wondered if it was linked to the black-and-white photograph in her possession and somehow served as a painful reminder of all her grandmother had suffered during the war. Maybe that was why she'd been so reluctant to bring those memories to the surface. The more Eloise thought about it, the more she wanted to understand what had happened in the past to cause her so much pain.

The next time she visited, she tentatively broached the subject, as there was no sign of the second album her grandmother had mentioned.

'I was hoping you would ask, dear Eloise. I haven't looked at those photos in years and it's high time I did.'

'Can I fetch the album for you?' asked Eloise. She was eager to find out more before her grandmother changed her mind.

'Would you?' Her grandmother leaned back in her armchair with a sigh. 'It's in the bureau. You'll find a little key on a red ribbon in one of the pigeonholes at the back. The key will open the bottom drawer.'

Eloise went over to the corner where the handsome polished bureau stood. She held her excitement in check as she admired the delicate mother-of-pearl inlay on the drop-down flap. When she opened it the ancient hinges creaked. It was full of papers, many crumpled and yellowing with age, that threatened to spill out onto the floor. She quickly pushed the flap to, then gingerly opened it wide enough to insert her fingers so she could feel around for the key. It took several attempts until she found the ribbon and pulled it free. Then, crouching down, she inserted the small rusty key into the tiny lock of the bottom drawer and jiggled it until it sprang free. Pulling on the small brass handle, she carefully wriggled the drawer open, and saw the weathered photo album lying on top of some old yellowing newspapers that had become brittle with age. The album was faded black, leather-bound and slightly bigger than a paperback book.

'Here it is!' Eloise exclaimed, getting to her feet and holding it aloft. She brought it over and placed it on her grandma's lap.

The old lady stared at the worn black leather cover for several moments as if trying to gather her thoughts, then slowly opened it at the first page with her knobbly fingers. Passing a shaking hand over the black-and-white photograph, which was accompanied by some writing, she said, 'I would like to read this to you, but first I need my glasses. Now, where did I put them?'

Eloise patiently searched and eventually located the glasses under that day's newspaper on the low table between them. She handed them over and crouched beside the armchair so she could see the photograph more clearly. It showed a girl with short dark hair secured with a hairgrip, leaning over the crib of a tiny baby whose eyes were screwed tightly shut. On the opposite page was an announcement of some kind written in German. She saw the name *STEFAN* written in large capital letters and guessed the photo must be of Grandma and her newborn brother.

With her glasses perched on the end of her nose, Grandma read out the words in fluent German, then smiled at Eloise. 'This card was sent out by my parents thanking well-wishers on the birth of Stefan. I was very excited to have a baby brother and have always treasured this first photo of him.'

'He looks very sweet. How old were you when he was born?'

She shook her head. 'I can't honestly remember but I know I was very small. We lived in Leipzig at the time. Stefan and I had such a happy childhood. I remember how my parents took us out on trips to the park and the zoo. My father always liked to take photographs of us. You see, photography was what he did for a living. Let me show you the others.'

She turned the pages, proudly explaining who each of the people was in the photographs. There were mainly family snap-shots of the children as they grew older, laughing and playing in the garden, and of their mother holding on to their hands as she swung them around. Eloise's grandmother explained that the family were living in Amsterdam then. Another of their mother gazing into the camera with the sweetest of smiles. Eloise thought it seemed such an idyllic family life, all the more poignant because of what she was beginning to discover about them. She felt a strange but powerful connection to these people she'd never known existed before now. With a shiver of recognition, she considered the fact that she was related to every single one of them.

'Who is this?' Eloise said, leaning over a photograph that looked much older than the rest. It was sepia coloured and badly faded at one corner. It showed an elderly man with a full white beard and round wire-rimmed glasses smiling down at a little boy with curly blond hair on his lap. 'That was my grand-father – Opa as we called him – and that is Stefan again. Opa was so proud of his grandchildren. You can see that on his face, can't you?' The old lady's face crinkled up as she touched the photo.

Eloise felt tears prick in her eyes. 'And this photo was also taken by your father, the photographer?'

'It was special, because his father, the old man you can see here, owned the family business – Breslauer Photography. I think he believed that eventually his grandson, Stefan, would follow him into the family business.' She nodded her head, as if remembering a long-forgotten conversation.

'But he didn't,' said Eloise softly, wary that her grandma might suddenly clam up and refuse to reveal any more about her family.

'No. He didn't. That poor boy never had the chance,' the old lady replied sadly. 'But that's enough for one day.' She shut the album with a soft thump and a finality that brooked no further discussion.

THIRTEEN

JULY 1942

Rudolf

Rudolf's mind was in turmoil. He knew he couldn't avoid telling Bella about Schlesinger's proposal, though he knew full well that wasn't what it was. More like an ultimatum, he thought grimly. But what if he refused to meet the kommandant? What would the consequences be if he didn't go? If he turned him down, Schlesinger was bound to return to his studio and leave him no choice but to comply. And if he did go all the way to Westerbork, would he even be allowed to leave? He trembled as he imagined what terrible schemes Schlesinger was plotting for him.

It was past six by the time he left the gallery, making sure the shutters were secure and double-locking the door. After Leipzig, he never took any chances.

Turning to leave, he heard his name called from across the street. Glancing up, he saw it was Jozef Cohen, the owner of the draper's shop opposite. He waved, then looked right and left for any vehicles before crossing over to Rudolf's side.

Rudolf smiled, feeling himself relax a little. He liked Jozef and appreciated the effort he'd made in getting to know him when he first opened his gallery as well as introducing him to the other shop owners in the street. It was small comfort to learn that they were experiencing the same concerns as himself – the singling out of Jewish districts by the Germans and being forced by law to display a sign in the window advertising that they were Jewish. It was bad for business and they all knew it could only get worse. Jozef's family had traded here since the turn of the century and had contributed hugely to the local Jewish community. Rudolf thought how terrible it was that such a long-established business as Jozef's should be threatened in this way. And yet, Jozef always looked on the bright side and did his utmost to keep people's spirits up.

As Rudolf watched Jozef approach, he debated whether he should mention Schlesinger's visit and wondered what he'd make of it. Not here, he decided, as he spotted two Germans in uniform patrolling the end of the street. German soldiers were a common sight out in public and mostly didn't interfere with him, but still Rudolf was careful to avoid any kind of confrontation.

Jozef gave Rudolf a hearty handshake. 'I thought we could walk home together. We don't often get the chance, do we?'

'Why not?' said Rudolf, trying to match his cheerfulness. 'There's still time before curfew.'

They fell into step, striding down the street past the two Germans, who were more interested in watching the traffic passing on the busy road that skirted the Nieuwe Herengracht. After they'd crossed the bridge that spanned the canal leading to the quiet Plantage Middenlaan street, Rudolf asked Jozef how business was.

'Busy as ever, though I've had to adapt to the times. There's not much demand for dress shirts and cufflinks these days, which is a shame because it's what Cohen's is known for.' Jozef gave him a rueful smile, then added, 'People don't want to buy new items of clothing but are making do with what they've got. These days, we've become more of a haberdashery. Our customers come in for needles, thread, wool for knitting, that kind of thing. Fortunately, we've managed to hang on to most of our clientele.'

They reached the park and caught a glimpse of the majestic tall trees with people strolling along the avenue between them. Only a year ago, Rudolf and Jozef would routinely cut across the park, for it was always a pleasant walk home, but now the gates were heavily guarded by grim-faced German soldiers whose eyes followed them suspiciously as they walked past. It was yet another Nazi restriction to Jewish freedom, and, in Rudolf's opinion, one of the more irrational measures.

Once they were out of earshot, Jozef suggested stopping by a nearby Jewish bar. Like so many other public places, it was off-limits to the non-Jewish population, but at least it was a place they could talk and have a drink without having to look over their shoulders the whole time.

'I can't stay long. I promised Bella I wouldn't be late home tonight,' said Rudolf with a tight smile.

'So did I. Rachel will be waiting with supper on the table. We'll have just the one beer and be on our way,' said Jozef, with a pat to his arm.

They entered the wood-panelled bar, where a few men stood drinking at the counter. The bartender greeted Jozef by name and they exchanged a few pleasantries. While Rudolf waited for them to finish, his thoughts returned to the conversation he needed to have with Bella. He was pondering how much to tell her about Schlesinger when Jozef presented him with his drink and indicated to a table at the back where they could sit.

After they'd both taken a mouthful of the cool beer, Jozef looked Rudolf in the eye. 'Do you want to tell me about the man who visited you today?'

Rudolf was so shaken by his remark that he almost knocked

over his drink. He had no idea that Jozef had been watching his premises. 'You saw him?' he said.

Jozef shrugged. 'I was sorting out stock yesterday when a customer came in. She was worried for you because she'd just seen a uniformed German enter your gallery. I didn't think it was any of my business. To be honest I forgot about it. This morning, I happened to glance out of the window and saw him going in again – at least I assumed it was the same man. I hope he wasn't causing you any trouble.' Jozef frowned a little and looked concerned.

'He was no trouble. At least not yet. He turned up out of the blue yesterday and behaved like any other normal customer wanting to take a look at my prints. He was keen to buy, which was fair enough. I hoped that would be all but then he asked to have his portrait taken. He wanted to come back this morning for a sitting. I tried to put him off, but he was insistent. He was a paying customer, so how could I refuse?'

Jozef didn't reply and looked as if he was waiting for Rudolf to say more.

'Then he told me what he wanted. Apparently, he has a new job at the refugee camp over at Westerbork.'

Jozef took in a sharp breath. 'He came all the way from Westerbork to Amsterdam to have his photo taken? He must have had his reasons. Did he say why?'

'That's the worrying thing. He told me that their usual photographer wasn't available and that I'd come recommended. They could have chosen any number of photographers, but why me? He knows I'm Jewish – and Westerbork is a camp for Jewish refugees, at least it was until the Germans took it over. I'm not sure what its function is now.'

'Rudolf, do try to get some perspective. You know the Breslauer name is well known, and not only in Jewish circles. That's probably why you were recommended.' Jozef sat back and took another mouthful of beer.

Rudolf wished he could be as relaxed as Jozef, but then Jozef wasn't the one being asked to go and work for the Germans. 'I'm afraid there's a lot more to it than simply taking his photo. When he came back and saw the photos, he was quite effusive in his praise and wanted to recommend me to the kommandant. To take over as the official photographer at Westerbork. Did you know the place is now run by Germans?'

'From what you said I guessed as much,' said Jozef.

Rudolf held his gaze and said, 'I have this terrible premonition that they've done something to their photographer and expect me to step into his shoes. I told him I couldn't just leave my studio to go to Westerbork, but he didn't leave me any option. He didn't threaten me, but the way he presented it I didn't really have a choice. I have to go.' He wanted Jozef to disagree, to offer an alternative optimistic point of view, but Jozef remained silent as he drained the remains of his beer.

The bartender rang a bell and called out that he'd be closing up in ten minutes.

Rudolf stood up without finishing his drink. 'Come on, Jozef. I want to get back home.'

'I'm so sorry, Rudolf.' Jozef got up and put an arm round Rudolf's shoulder, his eyes reflecting the fear that Rudolf himself had been trying to suppress.

FOURTEEN

Despite his reluctance to discuss this latest turn of events with Bella, Rudolf felt an overwhelming sense of relief when he walked through the door. Before they'd left the bar, Jozef had been sympathetic and promised him that he would keep an eye on his studio if Rudolf was forced to work at Westerbork. Jozef agreed that he should keep the studio running at all costs, even if it meant closing on days he was out of town. That way, his family could stay put in Amsterdam and he'd always have a safe haven to return to.

Rudolf went into the sitting room, where Ursula was sitting with her head in a book. Stefan was playing with the wooden train set that used to belong to Rudolf. Bella raised her head from her sewing, her smile lighting up the room. 'Ursula, Stefan. Say hello to Papa.'

'Hallo, Papa,' said Ursula, deliberately using the Dutch form of greeting, and without lifting her head from her book.

Rudolf exchanged a shrug with Bella, who came over for a kiss. He held her in his arms, squeezing her against him, and breathed in the faint aroma of her familiar scent – roses and something that was always indefinably linked to her. 'Sorry I'm late. I stopped off with Jozef for a quick drink,' he murmured. She looked up at him, her dark eyes questioning, but he couldn't elaborate now in front of the children.

'Am I too late to say goodnight to Mischa?' Rudolf thought of his dear little boy, the apple of his parents' eye. They'd never expected to have another child but he'd brought such joy to them. Rudolf couldn't bear the idea of anything bad happening to him or indeed any of his family.

'He'll be asleep by now. Leave it till Ursula and Stefan have gone to bed and then go on up.'

Stefan was now tugging at Rudolf's hand, pulling him on to the floor and begging him to play trains with him.

'Remember what I said, Stefan,' said Bella. 'Ten minutes playing with Papa, then it's time for bed. Ursula, you can read for a few more minutes, but you must go to bed when Stefan does.'

'Can't I finish my book? I've only got a few more pages,' said Ursula, shooting her a sullen look.

'It's a school day tomorrow. You know what the rules are,' Bella replied.

'It's not fair!' Ursula slammed shut her book and stomped out of the room.

Rudolf stood up to go after her, but Bella stopped him. 'Leave her be. She's upset that Bekkah didn't come into school today. We're hoping it's because she's unwell. I'll check on her when Stefan goes to bed.'

'Papa, can you make a station?' said Stefan, looking up from busily fixing carriages onto his engine. 'Papa?'

Rudolf was miles away, thinking of Ursula's schoolfriend and the very real possibility that her sudden absence meant she wouldn't be coming back. Absent pupils, and teachers too, were becoming a more frequent occurrence, although parents were careful not to discuss the reasons with their children. But Rudolf knew there was no fooling his perceptive daughter.

He ruffled his son's thick fair hair, dropped to his knees and started gathering the colourful wooden blocks into a pile. Soon, the two of them were laughing and lost in their game of make-believe.

By the time the two older children were tucked up in bed and Rudolf was sitting down to a supper of meat loaf and potatoes, he felt the tension of the day melt away. At last he was able to think more rationally. Schlesinger's visit and threatening demeanour no longer held the same terror he'd been feeling all day. Maybe he'd been reading too much into it and Schlesinger genuinely meant to help him. But he still needed to persuade Bella of the fact.

'Today went pretty well, all things considering,' he began.

'Oh, did it?' Bella looked at him sceptically.

'Schlesinger asked to pose for two photographs and because he was short of time he came back for them at the end of the day. So, with the prints he bought yesterday it amounted to a pretty good day's work.'

'Good. So that's that, then?' Bella's expression softened and she looked reassured.

But Rudolf knew he must now choose his words carefully and try not to worry her. 'Schlesinger likes my work. He wants me to take some portraits... of his work colleagues.'

'Go on.' Bella stiffened slightly, her stare giving him no choice but to elaborate.

'It's going to be tricky, but I'm sure I can handle it. Unfortunately, it means travelling to Westerbork.'

She regarded him in stunned amazement. 'Why Westerbork? You do know it's a camp run by Nazis?'

Rudolf didn't show he was surprised by her knowing and

just nodded briefly. 'Schlesinger works there and it's the reason he wanted his photograph taken.'

'I can't believe you're telling me this so calmly. It sounds to me like they're trying to trap you and once you're there they won't let you leave. Oh Rudolf, please tell me you said no.' She reached for his hand, gripping it so tightly it hurt him.

'I said I'd talk it over with you first,' he replied, gradually extricating his hand.

'I'm not sure I believe you.' She stood up and threw her napkin down on the table. 'When are you going?' Her voice wobbled.

'Listen to me, Bella. I haven't committed to anything, but you have to understand I've been put in an impossible situation. If I don't go and at least listen to what they want from me, I'm sure the consequences will be far worse than if I did.'

She sat back down on her seat. She seemed slightly calmer now, which was something, but Rudolf couldn't bear seeing her so upset. He moved over to her side of the table to hug her, but she brushed him aside, shaking her head. 'Westerbork's in the middle of nowhere and there's no direct train. It's a camp for Jewish people who have nowhere else to go. We live here, in Amsterdam. Don't you see? Before you know it, they'll expect you to move your whole family there.'

He hadn't even considered such a terrifying thought. Schlesinger hadn't mentioned it. But he knew that Bella was right to speculate. 'Not if I can help it, but I do think I have to show willing and at least go and meet the kommandant.'

'The kommandant?' she said, fearfully. 'You mean the Nazi who's in control of the whole camp?'

Rudolf felt increasingly uncomfortable. He felt as if he was losing the argument, but then she said, 'I suppose you must go, but I wish I could come with you.'

'I wish you could too, *Liebchen*, but I'm not sure it would make any difference. I got the distinct impression Schlesinger's mind was made up.'

It was late when Rudolf crept upstairs and into their bedroom, where Mischa lay in his bed. He looked so peaceful deep in sleep. Rudolf bent over and kissed his cheek, breathing in his warm familiar smell. Then he went next door and carefully sat down on Stefan's bed and gazed down at his precious boy. He lay so peacefully, clutching his beloved toy rabbit to his chest. Rudolf lightly planted a kiss on his soft warm cheek and Stefan stirred, drawing in a contented breath.

Smiling, he moved over to Ursula's side of the room. She had a bookshelf above her bed, full of her favourite things, her books and the collection of miniature porcelain animals she'd brought from Leipzig. In the middle of the shelf stood a framed photograph that Rudolf had taken on her birthday, the last cele-bration they'd had before leaving. He peered closely at the family members crowded round the dining room table, their faces filled with such joy. In the picture, Ursula was wearing her pretty party dress with the satin sash and had ribbons holding her hair up in bunches. She was puffing out her cheeks as she was about to blow out the candles on her birthday cake. Bella stood behind her, watching her daughter with pride. Seated round the table were Ursula and Stefan's cousins, ranging in age from three to thirteen, the aunts and uncles, Bella, Stefan and his own mother, the proud matriarch of the family. It seemed so long ago, but at the same time it could have been yesterday that they were all gathered together as one big happy family. With a sigh, he put the photo back where he'd found it. That was all in the past now and there was no point dwelling on it.

His gaze moved to his daughter and lingered there. She was no longer the little girl in the photograph – she was growing up fast – but she was still a child. He wondered what the future would hold for her and it frightened him. Bending down, he brushed his lips against her soft wavy hair so as not to disturb her sleep. Then he tiptoed out of the room, silently vowing that he would do anything in his power to protect the people he loved most.

FIFTEEN

Bella

Bella was buttoning up Stefan's coat and smoothing down his springy hair when she caught sight of Ursula looking at herself in the hall mirror. She seemed to be admiring herself, Bella thought, and then she noticed it. Or rather she noticed what was missing. Her dark blue coat was as unadorned as the day Bella had been given it by a Christian friend whose own daughter had outgrown it.

'Ursula! What have you done with your yellow star?' she said in a quiet but firm voice.

'What, Mama?' Ursula glanced over her shoulder with a guilty look on her face.

'Turn out your pockets,' said her mother, anger swelling in her chest.

Ursula took her time, putting one hand into one of her pockets and pulling it out empty.

'Quickly. You're holding us up.'

Sheepishly, Ursula fished out the crumpled yellow badge with 'Jew' stitched in thick black letters in the centre. It was slightly frayed along one edge, the cut thread still hanging loose from where it had been torn from her coat.

'What's the meaning of this? I've explained to you the importance of wearing your star whenever you go out. What do you think will happen if you're stopped in the street and asked where it is?' As Bella admonished her, Ursula's face turned progressively redder, but she remained silent.

Bella held out her hand. 'Take off your coat and give it to me. You can't go to school without the star.'

After the initial shock of being confronted, Ursula found her tongue. 'I hate this stupid star and I hate that people stare at me like I'm worthless, like I'm not as good as them. None of my friends wear the star. Why should I?' Her eyes flashed defiantly as she stood firm.

Bella held her own emotions in check. It never did to argue with Ursula when she was upset but knew she must make her see sense over this life-or-death situation. 'It's not a question of what your friends do. To be honest, I find it hard to believe they'd even consider not wearing it – but never mind that. In this house, we wear our star, not because any of us want to, but because we don't want to draw attention to ourselves. I've explained why to you enough times. Now give me your coat and give me the star. It'll only take a minute to sew it back on.'

Ursula's mouth was set as she reluctantly peeled off her coat and dumped it on her mother's outstretched hands.

'And the star, please.'

Ursula handed over the star she'd been holding with an extravagant sigh. Ignoring her, Bella hurried to fetch her sewing basket and quickly tacked the offending star back in place using big stitches.

From the hallway, she heard Stefan pipe up, 'I don't want to wear my stupid star either.'

'You heard what Mama said. We have to,' came Ursula's voice.

Bella smiled to herself, grateful that her daughter was being sensible around Stefan. But it saddened her that a child so young felt the need to. She quickly finished sewing the star back on and cut the thread.

Ursula and Stefan were waiting patiently by the front door. They were such good children, Bella thought to herself; they didn't deserve to be put through such an ordeal. As she helped Ursula on with her coat, she felt a pang of remorse for having to be so strict with her daughter. 'It'll have to do for now, but please don't do it again.' She felt Ursula flinch under her touch.

It pained Bella how much the two of them seemed to argue these days. She wished they didn't, for she liked it that Ursula was growing up and starting to voice her own opinions. Of course she didn't always expect to agree with her. But this time, she wondered if her best friend Bekka's absence from school was at the root of her outburst. Maybe Ursula knew more than she was letting on. Bella understood that children as young as eight were disappearing from school, but no one really knew what had happened to them. The only certainty was that the Nazis were behind it. It was a full week since Ursula first mentioned that Bekkah hadn't turned up at school and she must be hurting. Apart from acknowledging Bekkah's absence from class on that first day, the teacher hadn't spoken of it since. Bella didn't agree with the school's policy of shielding pupils from the truth. She decided she must have a conversation with Ursula about her best friend; but now was not the time.

Ursula looked close to tears. Bella put an arm round her. 'Come on, we need to go. We can talk about things later.'

Ursula pursed her lips, defiant again. 'There's no point. I've got nothing to say.'

Bella blamed herself for having snapped at her daughter. If she was honest with herself, the real reason for her short temper was that she was scared. Rudolf had gone ahead with his decision to go to Westerbork to meet the kommandant and she'd been powerless to stop him.

Rudolf had left early that day. Everything was arranged by that Schlesinger man. Bella instinctively distrusted him, even though she'd never met him. Nothing good would come of it, she'd told Rudolf, but his mind was made up. His efforts to placate her did nothing to allay her suspicions.

There was no direct route to Westerbork, so Schlesinger had arranged for a car to pick him up from the nearest station to the camp to take him the remainder of the journey there. Bella knew she wouldn't rest until her husband was home again; she was unable to shake off her fear that he wouldn't come back. Of course she didn't tell him that, but, from the sorrowful way he gazed into her eyes before he left, she knew he must be thinking it too.

After the drama over the yellow star and the rush to get the children to school on time, Bella dropped Mischa off at the kindergarten for the morning. She'd hoped to see Rachel at the school gates, but she'd already gone by the time Bella arrived. She had a few errands to run and afterwards decided to walk the long way home. When she wanted time alone to think she often went this way. She knew all the shortcuts along the canals that avoided the streets where German soldiers were most likely to be patrolling, either in armoured vehicles or standing on street corners looking for trouble, and always took care over where she went.

She was walking quickly, head down, when she became aware of something unusual happening up ahead. Instinctively, she stopped and searched for a spot to hide behind a tall plane tree where she couldn't be seen. Peering out, she saw a long queue of people – men, women, children and babies in pushchairs, snaking down the street and round the corner. Many of them had bags and suitcases. Each one was wearing the yellow star. Horrified, Bella knew at once what this meant. She'd heard the stories but found it hard to believe them to be true, until now. These Jewish people weren't there under their own free will but would have been forced at gunpoint from their homes with no idea what terrible fate awaited them. It was a game the Germans often liked to play with the Jews, instilling fear by deliberately not giving the slightest hint about what they had in store for them.

As she waited, Bella calculated that these people were a short distance from the street on which the SS headquarters were located. It surely had to be some kind of routine check to make sure their papers were in order before allowing them to return home. But the queue didn't move.

Bella stood frozen behind the tree, not knowing what to do. If she came out now and walked back the way she'd come, she risked being caught and ending up in that queue with the rest of them. In a flash of panic, she realised she'd come out without her papers. She fumbled through her bag, praying she was mistaken, but her fears were confirmed. How could she have been so foolish after all the fuss she'd made over Ursula's yellow star? She felt desperate, but knew she was safe, at least for now. She just needed to stay hidden.

Her heart leapt at the sight of a group of German soldiers marching round the corner of the street and heading for the sorry-looking queue of people. They began yelling and many visibly cowered in their presence. No one dared catch their eye. Bella was trying to make out what they were shouting when they began pointing at people and ordering them out of the queue and into a separate one. When one man objected, crying out that he wasn't prepared to leave his wife and baby, they ignored him and roughly held his arms back behind him. His wife cried for them to stop and clung onto his arm while still managing to hold tight to her baby. Startled by the commotion, the baby gave a high-pitched scream. Immediately, one of the

Germans aggressively put his face close to the woman and screamed at her to shut her baby up. But the baby kept crying inconsolably. Several others around her went to help, but they were all put firmly in their place.

Bella was unable to tear her eyes away. What was this all for? she thought in anguish.

Suddenly, she was distracted by two young men whispering at the back of the queue. They kept looking furtively around them, then they made a break for it and sprinted down the street in her direction. Several deafening shots rang out close to where Bella was concealed. The two men, no more than teenagers, crashed screaming to the ground no more than a few feet from where she stood. Trembling violently, she watched the backs of their shirts bloom bright red. She hesitated, torn between rushing to help and staying put. Then more shots rang out. The queue was descending into chaos. Others were trying to escape but were beaten back by Germans wielding batons.

'Bella! You can't stay here – run!'

Startled to hear her name, Bella looked up to see a wild-looking man she didn't recognise come racing towards her. Bewildered by this turn of events, she tried to fend him off, but he grabbed her roughly by the wrist.

'Come with me. Quickly!' he ordered and wrenched her from her hiding place.

'No! Please stop!' she cried out, trying to wriggle free, but he was stronger than her and she couldn't pull her arm free. Half crying, half begging him to stop, Bella found herself powerless to resist as he dragged her away.

Only when they came to an alleyway between two tall houses and were halfway down did he stop and turn to her. 'I'm so sorry I had to do that, Bella. I hope I didn't hurt you.' He passed a handkerchief over his face, which was shiny with sweat.

She shook her head, rubbing her wrist. Still not recognising him, she blinked, and then realised she was looking at Jozef, Rachel's husband. Relief flooded through her as she gasped, 'Jozef! What are you doing here?'

'My best friend is in that queue. His neighbour came to tell me he'd been arrested early this morning and will be sent to Westerbork. I came as quickly as I could. I thought I might save him, but as soon as I saw the Germans I knew I'd made a mistake in coming. I'm glad I did, because if I hadn't seen you I might have been gunned down. And you might have been too.'

Bella nodded absently as she tried to process what he'd said. These people were about to be sent to Westerbork against their will – it was the very place Rudolf was travelling to right now. Then it dawned on her that, had Jozef not appeared by chance, she could easily have lost her life. 'I don't know what I would have done if you hadn't turned up,' she said shakily.

He glanced quickly over his shoulder. 'I have a feeling nowhere is safe today. Let's keep walking. I'd see you home, but I'm needed at the shop. I'm sure you'll want to see Rudolf after all this.'

She quickly looked sideways at him. 'Didn't Rudolf tell you? He's gone to Westerbork today to meet the kommandant.'

'Oh Bella.' Jozef sighed and she saw the same resigned expression in his eyes she'd seen in Rudolf's that morning.

SIXTEEN

Rudolf

Drenthe, where Westerbork was located, was an area of the Netherlands that was unfamiliar to Rudolf. In fact, he'd never heard of it before this train journey. When he looked it up on the map, he remembered how close it was to the German border, a fact that made him tremble with fear. Schlesinger had made the arrangements for Rudolf's visit and booked his ticket – Rudolf had made sure it was a return one.

The journey was long, involving several changes of train and many stops along the way. The train was full leaving Amsterdam, but as it drew nearer to its destination it emptied out, giving Rudolf the impression that no one willingly made the journey as far as Westerbork. Each time the train pulled away from a station, a ticket inspector passed through the carriage. After he'd shown his ticket the first time, he kept his head down and tried to concentrate on the book he'd brought to pass the time. Unable to concentrate, he became distracted by his troubling thoughts, so he stared out of the window at the endlessly changing landscape, which alternated between

uniformly vast flat green fields, rural villages, swathes of heathland and dense pine forest. He tried to imagine what he'd find
when he got there and hoped that the view outside the camp
provided some solace to those locked up there. He knew only
the basic facts, that it had until recently been a prison camp run
by the Dutch, but nothing about any changes the German SS
had made since they'd taken it over. He suspected that there
was now a stricter, more brutal regime and life for the prisoners
had deteriorated. More demanding work, longer hours, more
punishments... it was hard to know exactly what they were
forced to endure, because the Germans never revealed their
practices. Few prisoners had been released from German camps
to give their side of the story.

At Beilen, he was the only passenger to get off the train. He
stepped on to a deserted platform and watched the guard blow
the whistle and the train slowly pull away from the station. He
looked for the exit, which was at the far end of the long platform. It felt like he'd reached the end of civilisation. He began
to walk, every step leaden with apprehension.

Outside the station was a shiny black car, which Rudolf
knew at once was for him. A uniformed chauffeur in a peaked
cap was standing beside the car, and moved forward to enquire
if he was Herr Breslauer. He then opened the passenger door
wide and invited Rudolf to step inside and make himself
comfortable. Everything about the car was opulent, from the
leather seats that squeaked when he sat down, to the click of the
passenger door when the chauffeur closed it and the smooth
purr of the engine as it pulled away. Rudolf allowed himself a
small smile, pleased he would at least have something positive to
relate to Bella on his return.

'I have been given instructions for you to meet Herr
Kommandant at his residence,' said the chauffeur after they'd
been travelling for several minutes.

Rudolf nodded, although this was news to him. He'd

assumed he'd be taken inside the camp, but was relieved to hear this wasn't to be the case. 'Does he live nearby?' he asked.

The chauffeur glanced quickly at Rudolf with a surprised expression, then turned his attention back to the road. 'Of course. His villa is close enough to see over the top of the perimeter fence from the first-floor windows.' He sniggered to himself. Rudolf felt slightly sick at the idea of the kommandant keeping an eye on the prisoners at all times.

Rudolf's first inkling that they had arrived was when the car rounded a bend and they were faced with an imposing black wooden watchtower overlooking a long perimeter fence topped with barbed wire stretching far into the distance. He took in a long silent breath. The camp was significantly larger than he'd imagined.

'Seeing as you're not going inside, I thought I'd show you how big the camp is,' said the chauffeur, as if reading his thoughts. He spoke with pride in his voice.

Please don't bother, thought Rudolf, distinctly unnerved at the unfolding spectacle. He turned his head to look up at the razor wire stretched along the top of the fence as if seeing it through the lens of his camera. He knew what an arresting image this would make, and couldn't help wishing he'd brought it with him. The urge to record what he saw was never far from his mind and he was sure he'd never get the chance again to see the camp from the outside. But even if he had his camera, it was absurd to think he could simply snap away with the kommandant's own chauffeur at his side. Rudolf shifted uneasily in his seat, which no longer felt as comfortable as when he first stepped inside the car.

Just beyond the end of the fence, the chauffeur turned off the road onto a long gravel driveway bordered by mature trees. Moments later, they pulled up in front of a large house with green wooden panelling and a first-floor balcony facing the camp. He must have had it built here deliberately, Rudolf thought, feeling nauseous, but he had no time to dwell on the matter.

The chauffeur came round to open Rudolf's door. As he got out, another uniformed German greeted him.

'Welcome, Herr Breslauer. I take it you had a pleasant journey,' he enquired.

'Yes, thank you.' Rudolf was finding it hard to believe that this charade had been put on for his benefit.

He was led into the spacious entrance hall. The walls were adorned with framed paintings that must have cost a small fortune. A polished oak table with an enormous vase of lilies stood in the middle. Their sickly-sweet scent hung thickly in the air.

'This way,' said the German with his hand on the polished wooden banister.

At the first-floor landing, a window gave Rudolf his first glimpse inside the camp, but he didn't have time to stop. The German was already striding along a carpeted corridor to a door at the end, which he opened. He waited for Rudolf to catch up before standing aside to let him go through.

The room was magnificent. Antique furniture, oil paintings hanging on the walls and a large picture window overlooking a lush green lawn edged with beautiful flowering bushes. A fence was half hidden in creeper – the dividing line between the grounds of the villa and the camp. Rudolf glanced across at rows upon rows of wooden barracks with a path that cut through the middle. He was surprised to see that the people – prisoners – weren't wearing prison uniform. In fact, the scene wasn't at all how he'd imagined it.

'It's quite something, isn't it, Herr Breslauer,' said the kommandant, a portly man with short fair hair, who had stood up from behind his wide desk. He shook Rudolf's hand enthusiastically and gave him an appraising look. 'My name is Herr Gemmeker. I wanted you to come here and see for yourself that this is no ordinary prison camp.' He turned his gaze to where Rudolf had been looking and smiled indulgently. 'The people are happy here,' he said, in a sing-song tone of voice.

Rudolf wasn't taken in by the kommandant's smiling pink-cheeked countenance, nor his genial manner, and knew it was a ploy to put him at his ease before getting round to the real purpose of his visit. 'So it seems,' he said, non-committally.

'Please, do take a seat.' The kommandant gestured to one of two dark green leather armchairs and sat down on the other. 'Herr Schlesinger speaks most highly of you. And I admit, I am very impressed by your work.' He opened a folder that lay on the low table between them. Rudolf recognised the top photograph he'd taken, the one of Schlesinger standing and staring at the camera. His expression was serious, formal. The kommandant held it up. 'It's very good.' Putting it aside, he turned to one of the prints Schlesinger had selected, of two young children sitting on a bench eating ice creams, which dripped onto their hands. As he fingered each one, Rudolf felt a wave of revulsion. It was such a simple subject but represented Rudolf's desire to use photographic techniques and skill to tell a compelling story and portray the truth. This was his work that he'd spent so much time crafting, and now he feared it would in some way be used against him.

Smiling, the kommandant said, 'I can see you're very versatile in your handling of the camera. That will come in very useful. But tell me about Breslauer Photography. You used to live in Leipzig, I believe.' He settled back in his armchair, ready to listen.

Rudolf nodded. 'The business was started by my grandfather in 1910. My father took it over when he died, and he taught me everything I know about photography: we had an excellent reputation for high-class portraiture in Leipzig. The business passed to me after he died.'

'But you didn't stay in Leipzig and moved to Amsterdam. You're Jewish. Is that why you left?'

Rudolf felt backed into a corner. There was no point pretending he wasn't Jewish, but neither did he feel inclined to admit to it. 'I wanted to be closer to where members of my family were living. So we could all be together.'

'I see. Well, let's get down to business. Did Herr Schlesinger tell you what I had in mind for you here?'

Rudolf swallowed down the feeling of panic rising in his throat. He racked his brains, trying to recall exactly what Schlesinger had said, but it was hard remembering anything under the kommandant's penetrating gaze. Had Schlesinger actually said anything to him about what the job would entail? The only thing he could remember from that conversation was that the kommandant would make it worth his while coming here.

When Rudolf shook his head, the kommandant carried on, 'Herr Schlesinger may have told you that our photographer is no longer with us.' He tilted his head in a remorseful gesture. 'This means that a vacancy has arisen, and one, in my opinion, that you are well placed to fulfil.'

He stood up, and paced the short distance to the window, stared out, then paced back again. 'It's an important position. You will be in charge of photographing each new arrival, making portraits of key functionaries, recording official dinners and luncheons, which take place in our spacious reception centre. Just last week, I threw a garden party here at the villa for our new dignitaries. It was a great success, but such a shame we had no one to provide photographic evidence of the occasion. But now you are here, I won't need to worry about that any more. You will be my official photographer.' He beamed at Rudolf and rubbed his hands together. Clearly, he thought everything had already been settled between them.

Rudolf plucked up the courage to speak. 'With respect, Herr Kommandant, I have a thriving photography studio and gallery in Amsterdam. I have many clients who have been coming to me for years. It simply isn't possible to leave Amsterdam to take up a position here.' Rudolf felt his palms grow clammy and his mouth go dry. He was desperate for a drink of water, but didn't dare ask.

The kommandant nodded sympathetically. 'Herr Breslauer, this job I am offering you is important. I will personally make the arrangements for you and your family to move here with the minimum of inconvenience to yourself. We have everything here that you could possibly need or want – an excellent school, a doctor's surgery, dentist, even top-class entertainment, which our... er residents appreciate.' His voice drifted off as he smiled to himself. 'And all your photographic materials will be paid for by the SS. Naturally, we will provide you with space for you to develop the photos, a nice accommodation for your family and schooling for your children. I understand you have a girl and two boys.'

'Yes, that's right,' said Rudolf, suddenly wary on hearing how much the kommandant knew about him. He wondered what else he knew, and resolved not to give away anything else about himself. He must remain on his guard. Then he considered the kommandant's proposal, which did not include payment for his work. In any other situation he would flatly refuse, but instead he found himself asking, 'What am I to do about my studio and my clients?'

'Herr Schlesinger will take care of it.' The kommandant spoke dismissively, and stretched out his arm so he could look at the expensive-looking watch on his wrist. He took to his feet and so did Rudolf.

'I have an appointment now. Manfred will take you into the camp and show you round. It has been a pleasure meeting you and I look forward to seeing more of your work.' He shook Rudolf's hand, but Rudolf was convinced he did so with considerably less enthusiasm than when he'd arrived.

SEVENTEEN

The journey back to Amsterdam seemed to take forever. Rudolf kept turning over the implications of the kommandant's demands but was unable to come up with a satisfactory reason as to why his whole family should all go to Westerbork. The kommandant had made the position of camp photographer seem like a privilege, but with no pay or contract this definitely was a job without prospects. Instead, it was a one-way ticket into a potential nightmare from which he could see no escape. Rudolf wished fervently that he'd had the resolve to refuse the job outright. It was what Bella would want too, but how could he convince her he had no choice without sounding weak?

By the time he arrived home and put his key in the lock, he felt weighed down by the enormity of what he was about to impart. The moment he opened the door Bella came running out of the kitchen towards him, her face wet with tears.

'You're home! I thought I'd never see you again,' she wept.

'Oh Bella! Of course I'm home.' Rudolf held her trembling body tight and struggled to stop his own tears from flowing. But the relief at being safely back with his beloved wife and children quickly vanished.

Bella turned her anguished face up to his, 'Surely it's good news that they let you come home? Please say it is.'

He felt an almost physical pain grip his chest. 'Let's not stand out in the hallway. I don't want the children to hear us. Are they in bed? Is Mischa settled?'

Bella gave him a weak smile. 'Yes, they're all tucked up in bed asleep. Let me get you a drink – you look as if you need it.'

He sorely needed a stiff one, but didn't want to prolong the agony any longer. He needed her to know. 'Later,' he said and planted a kiss on the top of her head.

Closing the door of the living room behind them, Rudolf moved over to the settee and patted the place beside him. Bella sat down warily and met his gaze.

'You accepted the job, didn't you?' she said.

Rudolf pursed his lips before nodding his assent. 'But that's not how it went. The kommandant gave me no opportunity to turn it down.'

Bella's face fell. 'When do you start?'

'I'm afraid it's not just about me and the job. It will affect all of us. He wants us all to move to Westerbork straight away. I'm to start next week.'

'No! Please tell me it's not true. What about the children? We can't just take them away from school. They're so happy and settled there. And little Mischa... how can I properly care for a young child in a place like that?'

'Bella, the situation is out of my hands. Believe me, if I refused to go, the Nazis would have come for us anyway and we would still end up there, but as prisoners. At least this way there's a chance we will get through this and come home. I promise I will do everything in my power to keep you and the children safe.'

Bella shook her head vehemently. 'You say that, but what can you possibly do?'

'By showing willing and doing the job to the best of my ability. The kommandant wants me to photograph all the new arrivals and to take photographs of official functions and dignitaries. It won't be a lot different to what I do now. If I keep my head down and work hard I don't believe they'll bother me.'

Bella nodded half-heartedly. 'I only wish it were true, but I have a really bad feeling about it all. It feels like a monstrous trap and I don't want our children to be caught up in it.'

'They won't... not if I have anything to do with it. I promise to do all I can to keep them out of harm's way.'

Bella's face softened slightly, but still her eyes carried so much worry. 'I know you will, Rudolf. You're a good man. We can only pray that it's enough.'

EIGHTEEN

Bella

Bella fought back tears as she walked the short distance to Rachel's house. She was clutching the battered leather suitcase that had belonged to her mother and which banged against her leg with every step she took. It was the same one her mother had asked her to look after when she herself had been forced to leave Leipzig. The irony wasn't lost on Bella, knowing she must soon part with it herself, but she pressed on, knowing that this was no time for sentimentality.

Rachel was waiting at the window and came running out to help Bella bring the heavy suitcase into the house. Once inside, and with the front door firmly closed, the two friends hugged each other hard.

'I don't have long,' said Bella, tearfully. 'We're leaving tonight. We've been told we can only take two suitcases between the four of us. I just don't know how we'll manage.' She wiped the back of her hand against her eyes. 'I wish we didn't have to leave so soon. In fact, I wish we didn't have to go at all,' she said through her tears.

Rachel looked shocked. 'Why so soon? I thought it was only a few days since Rudolf went to find out about the job.'

'They want him to start straight away. There's no time to get our affairs in order. I tried to persuade him to ask for longer to prepare, but he said they wouldn't listen to him. I've tried so hard to support him in this, but I'm afraid we rowed. I accused him of being weak and I immediately regretted it, but I was so angry – not with Rudolf, but with those Nazis who are hell-bent on making our lives a misery. The worst of it is that Rudolf didn't disagree with me – he just seems to accept it without resisting. I saw then that our situation is much worse than I could ever have imagined.'

Rachel listened, her large dark eyes round with fear for her friend. Bella's words hung heavy between them, for she knew that whatever she said could so easily happen to Rachel and her family.

'What will happen to Rudolf's studio?' Rachel asked.

Bella sighed and gave a half-hearted shrug. 'He's there now, putting the framed photographs into crates and locking them in the back room. He's worried about looters.'

'Jozef will watch out for anything suspicious. You do know that.'

Bella nodded but seemed distracted. 'We're also worried about what will happen to the house once we're gone. Wolfgang has promised to keep a close eye on it and make sure all the windows and doors are secure. But even that won't be enough if the Germans get it into their heads to break down the door and take it over.' She took in a long shuddery breath.

'Come into the kitchen and I'll make us some coffee,' said Rachel. She held out her hand to take the suitcase, but Bella shook her head and only gripped it more tightly against her chest. She followed Rachel and took a seat at the kitchen table, keeping the suitcase close to her side. She'd been on edge ever since she'd packed, unpacked and repacked it that morning.

Now, as she watched Rachel boil the kettle and spoon ersatz coffee into the jug, she felt slightly calmer as she reflected on the many times the two of them had sat companionably at this table. When Rachel placed a cup in front of her and put a warm hand on her shoulder, she gazed up at her and smiled. It was impossible to imagine this visit might be the last time they ever saw one another.

Bella blew on her coffee to cool it and took several sips before she was ready to discuss the contents of the suitcase. It had been a painful business deciding which items to take and which to leave out.

'Let me show you what I've brought,' she said at last, and heaved the case onto the table. She snapped open the clasps, lifted the lid, then removed the delicate white lace tablecloth that had belonged to her mother and which Bella always brought out for special occasions. Beneath it lay the beautiful family seven-branched menorah, two silver candlesticks and several silver engraved plates, a bowl and a jug. Next came a black leather photo album, which she ran a hand over; she hesitated a moment, unsure whether to take it out. With a small shake of her head, she left it inside the suitcase and moved it aside to reveal her mother's precious jewellery. Finally, her own jewellery, including the fine gold chain with its tiny Star of David that Rudolf had given her on their first wedding anniversary. Lastly, and reluctantly, she eased the engraved gold ring from her finger and stared at it for a long moment. Rachel's eyes widened as Bella deposited her ring beside the necklace. 'You can't do that. You simply mustn't leave your wedding ring behind.'

'My mind is made up. I'd rather know it was in safe hands than the Germans steal it from me. Please don't try and dissuade me.' Bella could barely utter the words.

'All right. But there's something I must say,' said Rachel, looking solemn. 'I know I said I'd look after your valuables, but when I told Jozef he was adamant that it's too risky for us to accept them. It's not that he doesn't want to help, but there have been too many raids on Jews and we could so easily be next.'

'But what am I to do?' Bella stared despairingly at her possessions. She began to pack them away when Rachel laid a hand over hers.

'Stop and listen to me,' said Rachel. 'I have another plan. We know a Christian couple who live in a townhouse on the Herengracht. The husband has created a safe hiding place under the floorboards of their living room that runs the entire width of the house. They've helped several families already by agreeing to look after their valuables until they come back. I'm sure they'd be willing to look after yours.'

'Do I know these people?' asked Bella anxiously. The idea of her precious possessions being passed on to strangers filled her with horror. Just because Rachel and Jozef knew people they believed could help didn't fill her with confidence.

'Their names are Hendrik and Annemarie Bos. They live at number forty-two. Remember, in case I'm not here when you come back.'

Bella bit her lip so hard she could taste blood. How could she have forgotten that Rachel, Jozef and their children might find themselves in a similar predicament to her own? What would they do if all their friends had gone? She understood that Rachel was only being sensible and realistic. But still, Bella couldn't quite bring herself to agree to giving away her most treasured items to perfect strangers.

Rachel said, 'I'm so sorry, Bella. I promise to be so very careful with everything you leave with me. I'll take your suitcase to the Bossen myself and see where it's stored. It'll be for the best.'

Bella gazed at her for a long moment. She knew she could trust her friend to look after her family heirlooms as if they were her own. There was no other alternative, she realised, for she simply wasn't prepared to leave them at home for the Germans to pilfer for themselves.

'Thank you for everything, dearest Rachel. You know I'd do the same for you.' Bella dropped her gaze to the items laid out on the table and continued to place them one by one back in the case. Reluctantly, she snapped the clasps shut and slid it over to Rachel's side of the table. 'I must go now.' She stood up and the two women embraced.

'Keep safe,' Rachel whispered.

'And you too,' Bella replied, her voice breaking. 'We have to believe we can survive this.'

NINETEEN
WESTERBORK, JANUARY 1943

Rudolf

It was a bright sunny winter's morning when Rudolf and his family arrived at Westerbork camp. But there was nothing cheerful about the place or the demeanour of the prisoners milling around aimlessly, miserable and lost. Rudolf held Bella's hand, but her pale, stricken face told him all he needed to know about what she thought of this place. In fact, no sooner had the gates clanged shut with a resounding finality behind them than it was obvious they had waved goodbye to their old life.

The first shock had come earlier that day when they arrived at Amsterdam Central station and were intercepted by an SS officer.

'Herr Breslauer,' the man called out. He was out of breath from running along the platform.

'That's me,' said Rudolf in surprise, then grew tense when he saw two other uniformed Germans come up behind him. 'Wait here a minute with the children,' he said to Bella. He suspected this was going to be unpleasant and he didn't want them to hear.

'What is it?' he said sharply, turning to the first man.

'The keys to your house, Herr Breslauer. I am ordering you to hand them over.'

The idea was preposterous. Surely there must have been a mistake? 'Whatever for? I can't possibly let you have my keys.'

'I have orders to remove your keys from you,' the man said, as if rearranging the words would make a difference to their meaning. The two other Germans moved menacingly closer and encircled him.

Rudolf heard Mischa let out a cry and looked over at Bella's worried face. Slowly, he reached into the inside pocket of his coat and reluctantly withdrew his bunch of keys. Not only were there keys for the house, but his studio keys – they represented everything he owned. His fingers trembled as he began to twist the house keys free.

'No need for that, Herr Breslauer. Hand them all over.'

The other men shifted position in a threatening manner, leaving Rudolf no choice but to relinquish his keys, but not before he spoke his mind. 'I want you to know that I do not do this willingly. The kommandant made no mention of it to me. I will have words with him when I see him.'

All three of the men burst into laughter. 'Say all you want to the kommandant, but I doubt he will listen to you. This is standard procedure,' said their spokesman.

Rudolf was lost for words and felt his whole world collapse around him. Silently, he handed over his keys. Only then did the three Germans move aside. There was nothing more for Rudolf to do than return to his family and prepare to leave Amsterdam for the very last time.

On their arrival at Beilen station, a car was waiting for them like the time Rudolf had come for his interview. It was a surprise, though not an unwelcome one, for the alternative would have been to walk the eight kilometres to the camp.

The car took them to the entrance; they were met by a couple of guards, who were all smiles and offered to take their bags and show them to their accommodation. Rudolf found this special treatment unnerving. He was still in shock, as was Bella, so soon after the blow of being forced to give up their home.

The walk down the broad main street of the camp was purgatory. Rudolf felt that all eyes were upon them as they passed row upon row of wooden barracks without stopping until they reached the small number of single-storey houses at the far end. This was the accommodation for the fortunate few who had actual jobs inside the camp. Rudolf couldn't help wondering what the prisoners who stared at them must make of this family group being given preferential treatment. It was an inauspicious start.

But Rudolf and Bella managed to put on a brave face for the children, who couldn't fully comprehend the abrupt change to their circumstances. At first it was relatively easy to deflect their questions about returning home by making out that they were going on a big adventure. The idea appealed to Stefan, who perked up once he'd seen the small two-roomed house and the bed he'd be sharing with his sister. Ursula, however, was appalled by having to share and for the first time in years threw a tantrum. At least Mischa was far too young to notice, and was happy as long as he was close to his mama and papa.

As the small family prepared to hunker down miserably behind their closed door that first night, Rudolf reflected on the terrible situation he'd got them all into. He saw with blinding clarity that the empty promises he'd been made were nothing but a trap from which there was no escape.

TWENTY
DECEMBER 2022

Eloise

Whenever she could, Eloise paid her grandmother a visit, but the demands of student life meant she couldn't go as frequently as she might have wanted. Even just a couple of hours in her grandma's company provided a welcome break from her busy schedule. She made sure she always brought cinnamon buns, which no longer brought tears to the old lady's eyes, but made her smile with pleasure. It was their little ritual, which they both looked forward to.

These shared moments were special. The more Eloise learned about her grandmother, the more intrigued she was to discover what had happened to her and her family in Wester-bork, but she knew not to probe too far as it remained a sensitive subject.

One afternoon, when they'd finished their tea and buns and the photo album was brought out, Eloise wondered if it was time to broach a subject that she'd been contemplating for some time. They had reached the last page of the album, which her grandmother called 'our Amsterdam years', and finished with a sweet portrait shot of Ursula's mother sitting with a child on either side of her. Joy and love emanated from her mother's smile as she stared up into the camera.

'I think this is my favourite photo of the three of you,' said Eloise. 'Did your father take any more after this one?'

Her grandmother looked up sharply and seemed on the verge of speaking, then quickly pursed her lips. She nodded as if remembering something. 'I think so, but these are all that are left. As far as I know, any others are lost.'

It was a perfectly reasonable explanation, but Eloise suspected that something more lay behind her words. 'What a shame,' she said. 'I do love looking at old photos and it would be lovely to see more of the family as you and Stefan grew older.' Eloise then noticed a pained expression cross her grandmother's face and quickly said, 'Don't get me wrong – I love looking at these ones.' She quickly went on to change the subject as she hated seeing her grandmother upset. When the older woman finally relaxed Eloise knew there was no point keeping on with her questions and she would have to wait until another time.

Before Eloise knew it, it was the end of term. Handing in her final essay was a definite cause for celebration and it coincided with a party at a student house in Jericho. All day, Eloise had a delicious feeling of nerves and anticipation as she planned what to wear. She went shopping in town but found that everything she liked was way beyond her small budget. She'd almost given up when she noticed the Oxfam charity shop and decided to go in on a whim. There, hanging on a rail right in front of her, was the perfect going-out dress – it was an off-the-shoulder black velvet number with sequins sewn across the bodice. And it was in her size. She couldn't wait to get back to her room to try it on.

With trepidation, in case it didn't fit, she eased the side zip into position and smoothed down the full skirt before taking in her reflection in the mirror of her wardrobe. 'Hmm,' she murmured and twisted her thick fair hair back from her face into a knot at the nape of her neck. Then she decided she needed some make-up to complete the look. Not wanting to overdo it, she emphasised her grey eyes with a lick of black eyeliner at the base of her lashes, a few dots of blusher on her cheeks and a sweep of rose-coloured lipstick to her lips. As she stood back to assess how she looked, there was a knock at the door.

'Come in!' she called and turned her head to see who it was.

Holly, the friend she'd made on arriving at Oxford, came in and her eyes widened as she saw Eloise in all her finery. 'Wow, you look amazing. Where did you get that dress?' She walked over to Eloise and fingered the soft nap of the fabric.

Eloise laughed. 'I picked it up this afternoon in Oxfam. Five quid,' she said proudly.

'Typical!' said Holly, flinging herself onto Eloise's bed. She had on a floaty cream blouse over black trousers, which she wore with her usual Doc Martens. Her curly hair hung loosely round her face and Eloise saw she'd accentuated her blue eyes with a cat-flick of eyeliner.

'You look great yourself. You always do. You don't think it's too much, then?' Eloise said, smoothing her dress as she worried about it.

'Come off it. You've seen what people wear round here.' Holly sprang up. 'Don't you think we should go?'

'Hang on a minute, I've got nothing to wear over the top. It's freezing out there. I can't wear my parka.'

'Haven't you got anything else?' Holly strode over to the wardrobe and began flicking through Eloise's clothes. 'God, I've never seen you in this.' She pulled out a blue tweed jacket and laughed.

'Stop it! My mum bought me that. Thought I should look smart around college. Hey, why don't you have it?'

'No way.' Holly immediately replaced it where she'd found it. 'Here you go,' she said and produced a plain black cardigan from the back of the wardrobe.

'Where did you find that?' Eloise snatched it from her. 'Another of Mum's bright ideas…' She held it against herself. 'And for once, I think she's right.'

The two girls stopped off at the college bar, where they met up with friends. After a couple of drinks they set off through the middle of town, stopping at an off-licence for wine to take to the party. They were walking down Little Clarendon Street, which was strung with twinkling Christmas lights, when Eloise turned to Holly and asked, 'Is this Jericho?' She had never walked this far, to the other side of town, and her feet were hurting from the cheap high heels she'd thought would look good with her dress.

'Are you telling me you've never been to Jericho?' came an aghast voice from behind.

'No, I haven't. Should I?' Eloise glanced over her shoulder and saw it was her friend Simon walking just behind them; he was swaying ever so slightly and already seemed worse for wear.

'Of course, because it's where all the best parties are,' he said with an exaggerated wink. He guffawed as they carried on until they came to a road lined on each side with terraced houses.

'Here we are,' said Holly, coming to a halt outside one of the houses with the front door standing open to the street. The thud of music could be heard from somewhere deep within, along with the babble of voices. Simon plunged straight in and was immediately swallowed up by the melee of people crammed inside the small corridor.

Eloise exchanged a look with Holly. 'Are we late or something?'

'Course not. Come on. I'm going in,' said Holly, her eyes bright with anticipation. Moments later, she had disappeared along with all the others from their group.

It was hot and stuffy inside, so Eloise slipped off her cardigan, took a deep breath and eased her way through the mass of people congregating in the corridor, who were having to shout to make themselves heard above the music. She came to a room on her left, the source of the booming music, and glanced through the door, just about making out the shapes of bodies gyrating to the thumping beat. She carried on past and came to the kitchen. There were fewer people here, and still she recognised no one. Everyone seemed to know someone else and they stood around in twos and threes, chatting and laughing uproariously and tipping back their drinks.

The countertops were entirely covered with half-empty bottles of wine, stacks of beer cans and open vodka and gin bottles. She still had no idea whose party this was and who to give her bottle to, so she put it down with the rest, then looked around for a clean glass.

'Eloise... is it really you?' said a man's voice close behind her.

She swung round and came face-to-face with James, who was smiling so sweetly that she felt her stomach give a sudden lurch. Could it really have been two months since she'd met him on her first day? He looked incredibly attractive in a midnight-blue velvet jacket, white shirt with the top two buttons undone, and black denim jeans.

'James,' she said, genuinely surprised to see him. 'I didn't know you'd be here.'

'Simon told me you were coming. News travels fast,' he said, with a steady gaze. 'By the way, you look gorgeous. That dress really suits you,' he murmured.

Eloise felt herself blush and her mouth go dry. 'Thank you,' she managed to say.

'You don't have a drink. What do you fancy?' he said, picking up an empty wine glass from the countertop. 'I assume you like wine. Red or white?'

'I'll have white, please.' She watched his face as he poured, and found it hard to tear her eyes away from him.

He handed her the glass and his fingers lightly brushed against hers. 'It's far too noisy in here to have a conversation. Shall we go into the garden?' He grabbed a beer for himself and led the way outside. The cold night air was a welcome relief from the oppressive heat inside. They sat together on a low brick wall facing away from the house, sipped their drinks and chatted.

'I can't believe we haven't run into each other sooner. Where have you been hiding all this time?' said James.

'I live on the other side of town, if you remember,' she retorted, matching his teasing tone with her own. 'This is actually the first time I've been to Jericho,' she admitted.

'Seriously?'

'Don't tell me – it's where all the action is.'

James scoffed. 'It's true there are a lot of students who live here, and the pubs are pretty good.' He paused, then said, 'Actually I'm not that keen on parties. It's just an excuse for people to get drunk and behave badly.' He glanced quickly at her.

'I agree,' she said, relieved to hear him say it. 'I came with a bunch of friends, but they all disappeared as soon as we got here. It's horrible when you don't know anyone.' She shuddered.

'Well, you know me.' He gazed at her for a long moment, then, moving a little closer, said, 'Are you cold?'

'I'm fine,' she said a little too hastily, before realising it was more chilly than she realised.

'Here, give me that,' he said, gesturing at the cardigan she'd forgotten she was holding. She handed it to him and he slowly draped it round her shoulders, keeping his arm round her.

'Do you mind?' he said, gently pulling her closer.

She shook her head and gave in to the blissful feeling of being close to him. It felt so right to be sitting snuggled up to him that, when he turned to kiss her on the mouth, it didn't seem strange at all.

Two days later, Eloise was waiting to board the Oxford Tube at Gloucester Green bus station. James had come to see her off, and wrapped her in his arms against the December cold.

'Promise you'll call me as soon as you're home,' he said, lifting her chin and kissing the tip of her nose.

'Of course,' she said, tilting her face so she could gaze into his eyes. Giddy with love, she seriously considered staying longer, but James had a train to catch up north where he was spending Christmas with his large family – he had two brothers, one older and one younger, who were both at college. His grandparents always came two days before Christmas 'to avoid the traffic'. James had rolled his eyes in mock weariness when he'd told her this, but Eloise could tell it was a tradition he always enjoyed. When she'd told him that her Christmas would be quiet, with just her parents and her aunt on her mother's side, he'd said he was sorry, but she said he shouldn't be.

Then, with a pang of regret, Eloise thought of her grandmother all on her own this year. Her father hadn't been able to persuade her to come to London, even when he had offered to drive to Oxford to fetch her. Grandma had brushed off his offer, saying Christmas wasn't important to her and she was perfectly happy on her own. But it bothered Eloise to think of her all alone with her sad memories, and she vowed to make a special effort to visit her in the new year.

'The bus is ready to leave,' she said, as the queue began to inch forward towards the bus. James pulled her against him again and kissed her deeply before letting her go. 'I'm so pleased I found you again,' he said, but she didn't have time to reply because she'd reached the front of the queue.

TWENTY-ONE
JANUARY 1943

Rudolf

The kommandant had allowed Rudolf to have his own photographic studio, a room located above the Grote Zaal, the large reception centre that doubled up for SS parties and functions. It was a reasonable size, but still a fraction of the studio-cum-gallery he'd left behind in Amsterdam. The only furniture was an adjustable stool positioned in front of a whitewashed wall, a wooden chair and a small table in one corner. A door led to an even smaller boxroom where he kept his photographic equipment and materials. At first, he'd railed against the injustice of losing his thriving business, loyal customers and livelihood that enabled him to provide for his family. But gradually he came to realise that this small space was at least a place he could call his own; it also came with a key, so he could work undisturbed here. He grudgingly accepted that it was a privilege of sorts.

Every Tuesday, hordes of new prisoners arrived by train inside the camp. They poured onto the platform wearing thick coats and blankets round their shoulders, each with as much baggage as they could carry. The remnants of a life they'd been forced to leave behind. The majority of arrivals were Jews, but Rudolf learned there were Roma and Sinti people too. He stood watching on the sidelines, never ceasing to be shocked at the vast numbers of dazed people crowding out of the dirty old wagons, which had never been intended to transport human beings.

Rudolf's job was to take each person's photograph for their identity cards. He found it hard work processing so many people at any one time and was forced to cut corners, which went against everything he'd learned as a professional photographer. The inmates queued in their groups outside his makeshift studio and filed in one by one to give their details to David, his young assistant. He was assigned to write each person's details on a card, which he then slotted into a folder. It wasn't a perfect system, but it was the best that anyone had come up with. More importantly, it seemed to satisfy Schlesinger, who was in charge of the day-to-day running of the camp. Rudolf had been surprised to hear that Schlesinger had arrived in Westerbork in 1940 as a Jewish refugee and had never left – he had never considered that this German who managed to instil such fear in him was Jewish too. But when he made enquiries no one was able to confirm this fact. He found it hard to believe that Schlesinger enjoyed being around so much misery and wondered what had prevented him from leaving the camp when he'd had the chance.

One cold dark Tuesday morning, Rudolf went to open up his workroom. He regretted not bringing warmer clothes. When they were preparing to leave Amsterdam, he'd been more concerned about packing his Leica camera, the one precious thing that linked him to his father and grandfather and which enabled him to carry on his job. It took the place of sufficient warm clothes in his suitcase, so he had to make do with his one and only suit, a waistcoat knitted by Bella and his gaberdine coat, and still he felt the biting cold. He was more concerned about keeping his camera inside his coat for warmth. Condensation was the enemy of photography and he had to take extra care that the camera lens remained free of moisture.

Even at this early hour, many people were out and about walking along the aptly named 'boulevard of misery'. It was bleak, but Rudolf knew things could have been a lot worse. He remembered looking down from the first-floor window of the kommandant's mansion and being surprised at how normal everyone looked. But things were different close up. The people here might not be wearing prison uniform, but this was no ordinary stroll. There were Germans everywhere, patrolling up and down and keeping a watchful eye. Rudolf had yet to witness any brutality since his arrival; nevertheless, it was obvious that no one took anything for granted and everyone was naturally wary of what the Germans were capable of.

As the camp photographer, Rudolf came into contact with every new person. It was a strange feeling being known to everyone, and not something he particularly relished. He hadn't chosen this role for himself, but no one knew that. He had every sympathy for the suffering of those around him, but did they think the same way about him? How could they possibly know that he too was in total fear for his family and felt the need to constantly prove himself so as to avoid harsh treatment? He realised that his position was what set him apart. He would always be an outsider in their eyes.

Inside his studio, he shut the door behind him to keep out the cold, not that it made much difference, because there was no stove to heat the place. He went into the back where he kept his tripod, and set it up ready for the first of the new arrivals. As soon as he heard the first rumblings of the train approaching and the shrill screech of brakes as it pulled up outside, he locked up and walked over to the assembly point. Schlesinger was already in position with several **SS** officers, who were herding the arrivals into their ethnic groups.

'They've come from Amsterdam,' Schlesinger said when he saw Rudolf. Rudolf let his gaze roam over the crowd and was relieved he didn't recognise anyone. The chances of any of his family or friends being amongst these people were small, but he feared that soon enough someone he knew would arrive on the transport from Amsterdam. The place was being emptied out of Jews and two thousand alone had come to Westerbork on the last transport.

Rudolf turned his attention to the crowds of people standing around in a bewildered state. 'Everyone must have their photograph taken.' He addressed them in Dutch. 'Please follow me. When we get to the building over there, please line up outside. There's not much room inside, so wait until it's your turn. I'll take your photograph as quickly as I can,' he added kindly.

Several hours later, Rudolf had all the photographic evidence he needed, and was packing the used film in canisters and into boxes ready to be developed when he heard a young girl speak his name.

'Mr Breslauer. It's me – Bekkah.'

He turned in surprise and shock to see Ursula's friend, Bekkah, who had gone missing from class, standing before him. He would never have recognised her, for it was months since she'd last visited Ursula at their home. Her long dark hair had been cut short in a ragged style; she seemed thinner, but maybe it was the worry etched on her young face that made her appear so.

'You do remember me?' she asked anxiously.

'Yes, of course I do. Ursula will be so pleased to see you. Have you come on the train from Amsterdam? If so, I apologise I didn't recognise you when I took your photo.'

She stared at him, shaking her head. 'I was at the back of the queue with Mama and Papa, so you haven't taken our photos.'

'Are they waiting outside? Please bring them in.'

A dowdy-looking couple shuffled inside holding hands. The woman held a handkerchief to her mouth.

'Mama's not well,' explained Bekkah.

Rudolf felt a wave of sympathy and wished there was something he could do to alleviate their misery. 'I'm so sorry you had to wait so long. Let me remedy that.' Flustered, he realised he'd forgotten their names. Fortunately, David was still working on the identity cards, and came forward to ask them for their details.

Rudolf busied himself putting the tripod back in position and fine-tuning the settings on the camera. David sat Bekkah's mother on the stool and adjusted it till she was staring straight into the lens. Rudolf lowered his head and looked through the viewfinder, seeing a frightened, desperate woman who wanted to be anywhere else except here. 'This won't take a moment,' he said and tried to give her a reassuring smile. The expression on her face relaxed, all too briefly, but it was enough for him to capture it on camera.

When he'd finished, he walked them to the door. 'What happened to bring you here?' Rudolf said quietly.

Bekkah's father spoke. 'We thought we were safe. A friend we thought we could trust offered us a hiding place in his cellar. We were there for some weeks. It was one o'clock in the morning when Nazi bullies came and dragged us out into the street. I'm afraid it's been a terrible shock to us all.' He glanced at his wife.

'How did they know you were in hiding?' asked Rudolf.

'There have been rumours of people turning Jews over to the Nazis in exchange for money. That's all I can think of.' His direct gaze caused Rudolf to drop his eyes in embarrassment. These were his own people, whose daughter was Ursula's best friend, and who now found themselves in such desperately straitened circumstances.

Rudolf tried hard to think of something that might console the man. 'It may not seem like it right now, but things aren't as bad here as they might look. It's actually well organised and there's a doctor, a dentist, and the school is run by proper teachers. And we get enough food, even if it's not what we would normally choose to eat.' He volunteered a smile, but instantly knew his words must sound hollow to these newcomers. They must have guessed he'd deliberately missed out details of this place. How could a prison camp be anything but bad? Then, to his great shame, he realised he was telling the same lies he'd been told when he'd first come to Westerbork. Did that make him a collaborator who was complicit in Nazi lies? The very thought of it shook him to the core.

TWENTY-TWO

Bella

For the sake of the children, Bella put a brave face on their significantly changed circumstances. However much Rudolf had tried to sugar-coat things, the contrast between their comfortable three-bedroom Amsterdam townhouse – their entire life, in fact – and the unheated, uncarpeted wooden hut with no facilities was stark. Of course, other people had it so much worse than they did, crammed into smelly airless dormitories where they were expected to provide their own blanket and forced to share bunks with complete strangers. But Bella was finding it hard to look upon their basic accommodation as a privilege after losing so much.

It was clear to her now that everything Rudolf had been promised was a lie. Apart from being given their own private quarters, they were treated no differently to anyone else. They still had to share basic wash facilities and toilets with other prisoners, as well as go to the communal dining area for their meagre meals, which often consisted of no more than a couple of ladles of turnip or cabbage soup and a piece of stale bread.

Bella was too shocked to discuss with Rudolf what was staring them in the face: they were prisoners and the chances of them emerging from this terrible place and regaining their freedom were virtually none.

Despite everything, Bella was determined to make the best of it and create as normal a home life for them as possible. There wasn't a lot she could do about their spartan surroundings, but she'd managed to lay her hands on some plain fabric, which she made into curtains and tacked above the windows facing out onto the street. Just being able to shut the curtains at night made the world of difference to how she felt. It was the only time they had their own privacy. And in the evenings before bed, they played card games together, just as they always had, first in Leipzig and then in Amsterdam.

Ursula was now thirteen and Stefan eleven, and it worried Bella that both children were developing an awareness beyond their years. Stefan was nearly as tall as his sister and came up to Bella's shoulder, making him appear older than he was. Increasingly, she was finding it impossible to shield them from the reality of their situation, so she resolved to answer their questions as honestly as she could. Thankfully, Mischa, aged three, was still too young to notice what was happening around him. His innocent and cheerful demeanour was the one ray of positivity amongst so much misery.

It was early morning, and Bella was getting the older children ready to walk the short distance to the classroom block. Mischa was playing with his toy car at her feet.

'When are we going home?' Stefan asked her out of the blue. Since they'd come here, he'd been quieter and there was a guarded look about him, which made her sad. Already he'd seen too much.

'Didn't you know? We're not going home,' said Ursula matter-of-factly as she bent down to fasten her shoes. She'd always been the more outspoken of the two and today seemed unaware of the effect her comments had on her brother.

Bella frowned at her. 'There's no need to say that. None of us know how things will turn out. We only got here a few weeks ago and Papa is very busy with his new job.'

'What I don't understand,' said Ursula, standing up straight, 'is why we had to come here in the first place.' She gave her mother a challenging look.

'You know perfectly well, Ursula. Westerbork is too far from Amsterdam for Papa to travel every day. We all want to be together, so coming here is for the best.'

Ursula stared sceptically at her mother. 'Bekkah told me that no one ever goes home.'

'Oh yes?' said Bella with a sigh. 'Bekkah's only been here a few days, so how does she know that?'

'Because her papa told her.' Ursula's cheeks started to redden.

Bella glanced at Stefan and saw he'd begun to cry silent tears that splashed down his cheeks. She took a step towards him to give him a hug, but he shrugged her off. 'Not now,' she mouthed at Ursula, who was gazing at Stefan with concern.

'Stop saying these things,' he sobbed, then looked beseechingly at his mother. 'I hate it here. There's so many people crammed in here. It's just awful. Mama, is it really true we're not going home?'

Bella felt a stab of desperation for her poor innocent boy. How could she tell him that coming here hadn't been their decision and that she feared for all their futures? She hated herself for it, but she knew she must avoid telling him the truth.

She forced herself to smile. 'Not if I have anything to do with it, sweetheart. Now dry your tears. Would you like me to walk you to school?'

He looked at her askance and shook his head vehemently. 'I'm not a baby anymore,' he said with a loud sniff and stomped off to the door. 'Are you coming?' he said, tossing his comment over his shoulder to Ursula. He went ahead and it pained Bella to see how his back stiffened with the emotion he was trying to hold in.

As the two children walked off together, Bella watched from the door with Mischa by her side, hoping they would soon forget their spat with her. The children joined the throng of people on the boulevard of misery; she thought how small and defenceless they looked. Then, pulling herself together, she reminded herself that their family was still intact. They had each other and she was determined they would stick together through thick and thin. As the children disappeared off into the distance she consoled herself that, however much they bickered, Ursula would always look out for her younger brother.

TWENTY-THREE

Rudolf

Rudolf was sorting through long strips of negatives from photographs he'd taken that day. It was a laborious process, but he had always been meticulous about keeping records, and didn't want to give Schlesinger any reason to criticise him. Fortunately, he'd had little to do with him since he'd been appointed head of registering and segregating new arrivals. Schlesinger had his hands full processing the thousands of new prisoners who were still being brought in each week, despite the lack of space.

Inside the camp, conditions were deteriorating. Due to over-crowding and a shortage of beds inside the barracks, some had taken to sleeping outside on the ground under the night sky. Piles of rubbish, including old stinking mattresses, began to accumulate behind the barracks, but this didn't stop people from strolling beneath the oak trees to gaze beyond the wire fence at the wide-open heathland. It was a brief reprieve of sorts from the unending misery. Then a new rule was introduced in order to reduce prisoner numbers. Those in mixed marriages were summoned to Schlesinger's office and offered a choice – if they agreed to be sterilised, they would have their **J** removed from their identity card and could leave the camp immediately and return home to Amsterdam. If they refused, they were sent on the next transport out of Westerbork to a Polish work camp for hard labour.

As he worked, Rudolf mulled over the callousness and impossibility of being faced with such a choice, when there was a sharp rap at the door. He carefully laid down the strip of negatives and went to open up.

Schlesinger stood there with a sour expression on his face. Next to him was a balding man dressed in a suit that was clearly several sizes too big for him.

'I want you to take this man's photograph. He missed registration because he was in the camp hospital. They say he's better.' Schlesinger shot the man a disbelieving look. The man dropped his eyes to his shoes. Even these seemed too large for his slender feet.

Rudolf had to stop himself from staring. 'Yes, of course, Herr Schlesinger. You can leave him with me.'

'Good.' Schlesinger pursed his lips and turned on his heel; he seemed to be in a hurry to get away.

Rudolf laid a hand on the man's bony shoulder and led him into his studio. 'Why don't you take a seat while I set things up?' He went into the back to fetch his camera and tripod.

When he came through, the man was still standing, his hands in his pockets. 'I suppose you'll want to know why I was in hospital,' he said quietly.

'Only if you want to tell me.'

'Why not? Nothing here is a secret. I was brought here from Kamp Amersfoort. They broke my hands by stamping on them.' He slowly extracted his hands from his pockets. They were crooked, deformed, and he seemed unable to straighten his fingers.

Rudolf drew in a long breath and felt bad for staring at them.

'They look a lot worse than they are,' said the man. 'I was taken to the hospital when I got here and given my own room. I practised holding a pen and writing again. It was slow going at first, but I was determined they wouldn't beat me.' He gave a short laugh, then replaced his hands in his pockets.

'How long were you in the hospital?' asked Rudolf, who was finding it hard to comprehend what torture the man must have suffered at this other camp. He'd heard rumours about how brutally the prisoners were treated at Kamp Amersfoort and this man was living proof that the rumours were true.

'Eight... no, nine months. But after a week they transferred me from the main hospital into the barracks for recuperating patients. So, no more special privileges. But I got to know the doctors in the hospital. They bought me time until I was well enough to leave. It's ironic.' He paused reflectively. 'They look after you until you're well enough to leave the hospital, but once you're out you're immediately at risk of being put on the next transport to a far worse camp. Which I intend to avoid at all costs.' He gave Rudolf a searching look. 'I know you. You're Rudolf Breslauer, from Amsterdam. Your portrait photography is famed. I'm sorry you've had to stoop so low as to land this job. But I suppose you didn't have any choice.'

Listening to this bleak appraisal of life inside Westerbork, Rudolf felt discomfited. He knew only too well that his status meant that he and his family had certain privileges not afforded to other prisoners and that they were safe from the transports. For now, at least. 'No, I don't suppose any of us do. And my fame, though I don't like to call it that, didn't help me one bit. It wasn't hard for Schlesinger to single me out. He turned up one day at my studio in Amsterdam. I didn't know at the time, but it was a snare. He made me an offer I couldn't refuse.' The words didn't come out as he intended and he realised they sounded as if he'd been richly rewarded to come and work here. Nothing, of course, could have been further from the truth.

Their eyes met in understanding over the hopelessness of their respective situations.

'I don't know what's worse,' said the man. 'Being forced to work for the Germans or imprisoned and tortured for no apparent reason.' He shook his head sadly, then introduced himself. 'I'm Philip Mechanicus.' He held out a crooked hand. 'Foreign editor and journalist for the *Algemeen Handelsblad*. Please call me Philip.'

'Rudolf. Very pleased to meet you.' Rudolf gingerly took his hand, taking care not to press too hard. He suddenly thought he could grow to like this man who seemed to sympathise with his predicament. 'I'd offer you a drink, if I had one,' he said with a tentative smile. 'But let's take this portrait of you. You can stand with the white wall behind you.'

Philip moved into position and tilted his face slightly to one side so he wasn't square on to the camera. He looked altogether more confident, more poised than when Rudolf had first set eyes on him.

'You've done this before, haven't you?' Rudolf smiled as he adjusted the camera.

Philip laughed. 'When I was travelling for my job we always had a photographer with us. I've attended quite a few conferences with heads of states over the years. I got used to seeing how he worked with his subjects.'

'Well, unfortunately, I have to ask you to stand straight on to the camera and keep a solemn face. It's not the way I would do it, but Schlesinger...' He left his sentence hanging as he bent over the camera and snapped the photo. 'It'll have to do,' he said, standing up straight. 'If you don't mind, I need to get a few details from you to go with the photo.' He moved over to the desk and found one of the cards from the stack David had prepared. It didn't take long, but when he'd finished the other man didn't seem in any hurry to leave.

'Listen, there's something I'd like to discuss with you,' Philip said evenly, holding one hand in the other and massaging it gently. 'You and I are in complementary professions. We are both observers of people and situations. I do it through my writing and you do it visually through your photography. We record – if you like interpret – what we see for others. I think that's a powerful thing.'

Rudolf had to agree. He was intrigued that Philip understood his desire to capture the truth from a single frame that was often part of a bigger story. He knew he was in a fortunate position because his work enabled him to preserve a moment in time for the future.

Philip seemed to talk to himself as he spoke. 'I feel compelled to write what I see is going on around me. All my life I've been a writer and I feel it's my duty to put things down in words. It's what I've been doing these past nine months inside the hospital. I write everything in exercise books. What I see all around me and my impressions too. I often write all day. Then I stow my books safely away.'

He turned his head to look Rudolf in the eye. 'A friend of mine bought one of your prints of two cyclists crossing a bridge over a canal in Amsterdam. It was a reminder of how normal life used to be before the war.' He sighed and looked away as if the memory of that time was too painful to contemplate. Then he seemed to compose himself as he said, 'What I mean to say is you have in your possession the means to record the truth in here that no one has any idea about on the outside. We both have.'

There was no denying that what he said was true. Rudolf understood exactly what he meant and found his argument powerful and compelling. But then he remembered that Bella and their children were his priority and that he wasn't prepared to put them in danger under any circumstances. 'Forgive me if I'm wrong in thinking that you're suggesting I should go around the camp taking photos of the prisoners. I know the Germans would pounce on me the moment I got my camera out. I can't imagine what good could possibly come of it. I'm afraid I can't agree to it,' he said finally.

Philip gazed at him, disappointment evident on his face. 'You're right. It was stupid of me to expect you to think the way I do. I spend so much time inside my own head. I sometimes forget about the dangers of what I'm doing. But thank you for listening. I'd better be going.'

Rudolf felt a rush of anxiety that if Philip were to walk away now there wouldn't be another chance to talk together so candidly. He needed to say something. 'Wait – I'm here every day, so please drop by again. I may not be able to do what you ask, but I am interested in what you have to say and would very much like to talk to you again.'

TWENTY-FOUR

It was only after Philip had left that Rudolf reflected on their conversation and started to come round to his way of thinking. A duty to put down what he saw around him. Philip's words kept swirling round his head and often kept him awake at night. If only he could find a way of providing photographic evidence of the misery and cruelty inflicted by the Nazis without the kommandant finding out. And if he committed to recording the truth as Philip was doing, he wouldn't be doing this alone – that was, if it wasn't already too late. But how? Time and again he felt himself on the brink of taking his camera out and shooting what he saw, but how could he be so reckless when his family's safety was at stake? The decision was taken out of his hands because Philip didn't come by the studio again, and Rudolf began to wonder if his injuries had put him back in the hospital. Or worse, that his name had come up and he'd left Westerbork for one of the prison camps over the border. That had to be a distinct possibility. Every week an ominously long clanking cattle train left the camp with thousands of people heading for Auschwitz, Theresienstadt and Bergen-Belsen. All anyone knew was that these were Nazi-run camps, and some clung on to the belief that life had to be better there than at Westerbork. But Rudolf was convinced that something much darker was at play, that anyone bound for these camps would never return, even though he had no proof of this. Perhaps Philip knew, or, if he didn't, he was sure to have an opinion one way or another.

Rudolf put all thoughts of Philip to one side as the drudgery of his day-to-day existence took precedence over all else. It was all he could do to keep satisfying the demands of the kommandant. Life was tedious and monotonous, except on the day before the names came out of those to be deported that week. It was always a lottery whose name was on the list. Some were transported almost as soon as they arrived, while for others it could be weeks or months before their time was up. Rudolf tried his best to reassure Bella that his job offered his family protection, but the longer this waiting game went on the greater were their chances that they could be next.

One morning, after they'd been at the camp for several months, Rudolf realised his circumstances were about to change. He had taken a longer walk to his studio so as to avoid the crowds on the boulevard of misery, and he encountered the kommandant riding purposefully towards him on his bicycle. Instinctively he tensed up when he saw the German lift a hand in greeting. He slowed to a stop and dismounted to walk beside him.

'Just the man I was hoping to see. How are you, Herr Breslauer?' The kommandant seemed to be in a cheerful mood.

'I'm fine, Herr Kommandant,' said Rudolf, always careful never to say too much.

'Good, because I have a new project for you. Why don't we go to your studio and I can tell you more. I think what I have in mind will suit you very well.'

'Of course,' said Rudolf, attempting to muster some enthusiasm while trying to ignore the ominous feeling of creeping dread.

The kommandant chatted amiably, as if talking to an old friend, but, as soon as they stepped through the door of the studio, he came to the point. 'I'm very proud of what we have achieved at Westerbork and I want the world to know about it. In fact, I'd even go as far as to say that this is a model camp that others can learn from.'

Rudolf tried to keep the consternation from his face. If this was a model camp, then how much worse could the others be? When the kommandant glanced at him to gauge his reaction, he thought he'd better nod in agreement.

'And you are just the man to show the world,' the kommandant blithely went on. 'I want to document how we do things here with photographs of the best we have to offer. We have an excellent school, so I understand, so let's see the children at work. Our prisoners are making a great contribution to our local community. I want you to go into the factories and show everyone how industrious the workers are. You mustn't forget the workshops – they were my idea.' He patted his chest and seemed to glow with pride. 'We have talented carpenters whittling away making delightful wooden toys.' He spoke in that sickening sing-song tone of voice Rudolf remembered from their first meeting. Revulsed, Rudolf noticed he even had a tear in his eye. 'I'm sure you agree it's a wonderful idea. What do you think, Herr Breslauer?'

'I think—' Rudolf began, and was relieved when the kommandant interrupted him, so eager was he to talk about his vision.

'I want you to start right away. And please don't hold back. Take as many photos as you need to.'

Rudolf was unable to show any enthusiasm, so instead he said, 'I will need more film, as well as chemicals to develop the pictures. Photographic paper too.' He hated himself for implicitly accepting what the kommandant was ordering him to do.

'Details, details.' The kommandant waved a hand airily. 'Speak to Schlesinger to sort things out. I'll come back in a week. I know you won't disappoint me.'

'I don't suppose he's going to pay you for it,' said Bella. Rudolf had gone straight back to tell her of his troubling conversation with the kommandant.

He'd expected her to be relieved that he was buying them extra time. 'Of course not. What were you thinking?' he said, exasperated.

Bella clasped her arms round herself protectively, her face drawn with worry. 'I don't know, but I can't see any good coming of it. It's a big thing he's expecting of you. Everywhere I see people living a miserable existence, just getting through each day. How can you possibly show this place in a good light?'

Their eyes met and he shook his head. 'I've no idea right now, but I'll have to find a way.'

'I know how I can help,' she said suddenly, and her face softened in sympathy. 'You can start in the schoolroom. There are bound to be happier scenes there. I know the teacher well and can tell her what this is all about.'

Relief flooded through him. It felt good to have her on his side and helping him with this disagreeable task. 'Would you? And you can help me sort through the photographs before I decide which ones to show him.'

She nodded, but her expression hardened. 'On one condition. Please don't include our children in any of the photos. And especially Mischa, who's far too young and innocent to be caught up in this awful charade. I don't think I can bear the idea of that man poring over pictures of our children.'

Of course it was unthinkable. He already despised the fact

that his precious innocent children were part of this nightmare through no fault of their own. He would not, could not entertain such a thought. 'I absolutely agree. I promise I'll be extremely careful they don't appear in any of the photos I take.'

TWENTY-FIVE

The children whispered excitedly amongst themselves and the teacher had to clap her hands to bring order to the proceedings.

'Try and forget Mr Breslauer is here with his camera and settle down to your work, children.'

A hum of disappointment went up from the class as she read out the page number of the book they were working from and waited for them to quieten down.

Bella squeezed Rudolf's hand and whispered that she would see him outside. He went to the back of the class, where he checked a few settings on his camera, then moved quietly round the edge of the room, snapping what he saw. A row of children, all with their heads bent over as they wrote in their exercise books; a boy talking behind his hand to a girl, who was trying hard to suppress a giggle; a girl staring into the middle distance as she sucked the end of her pencil in thought.

Ursula was sitting next to her friend Bekkah. They were sharing a book and their heads were touching. As her father walked past, Ursula gave him a secret wave and smiled. He smiled back, thinking how at ease she looked in this setting. He was sorely tempted to take her photo, but Bella's words were still ringing in his ears, so he gave her an apologetic shrug and went on past.

The session took no more than a few minutes. Rudolf thanked the teacher and excused himself. Bella was waiting for him outside.

'How was it?' she asked, linking her arm in his and leading him over to the other classroom block for younger children.

'Fine, but I could tell Ursula was desperate for me to photograph her. Did you tell her I'd be coming?'

'No, I haven't said anything to either of them. I thought it best not to draw attention to what you're doing.' She looked at him curiously. 'You didn't take her photo, did you?'

He snapped his head round, surprised that she would doubt him. 'Of course I didn't.'

'Good,' she said, and seemed relieved. 'They'll never see the photos, will they?'

'No. They won't.' Then he was struck by a new unnerving thought of his photos circulating amongst the kommandant's cronies to be pawed at and picked over for reasons he couldn't begin to understand.

'Rudolf? You've gone quite pale. Are you all right?' said Bella, gently pulling on his arm.

He blinked back to the present and saw the concern in her eyes. 'I'm fine. Let's get this finished.'

He was packing his camera away into its ancient leather case when he heard his name being called. He looked up and saw Philip come striding towards him looking casual, with his hands stuffed in his pockets.

'I thought it was you. Keeping busy?' Philip nodded with a questioning look at Rudolf's camera.

'You could say that.' Rudolf laughed. Compared with when he'd last seen him, he noticed that Philip was less gaunt and actually looked quite well. 'I thought something must have happened to you,' he added.

Philip shook his head. 'Let's walk. Which way are you going?'

'Back to my studio. I have some photographs to develop. Why don't you come along and see for yourself?'

'I'd like that,' said Philip and they fell into step, remaining silent as they passed a group of German guards who were keeping a close eye on everyone.

Rudolf waited till they'd gone past them. 'It's strange how they try to appear threatening but then let us walk freely around the camp. Is it my imagination or are more out patrolling these days?'

Philip shrugged. 'It's just for show but also to demonstrate who's in charge. They want to remind us how good we've got it in here.' He spoke sarcastically, then said nothing more until they arrived at Rudolf's studio.

Once inside with the door shut, Philip was first to speak. 'The reason you haven't seen me is because I've been working hard at stopping my name appearing on the transport lists. Being in hospital gave me immunity, but since I came out my name's come up five times.'

'Five! That's unbelievable. How do you avoid being put on the trains?'

Philip laughed. 'Before I left Kamp Amersfoort, I had **S** for *strafgeval* stamped on my identity card.'

'What's that mean?' asked Rudolf.

'Punishment case. Normally it means you're put on the next transport out of Westerbork, but I made friends with one of the Jewish doctors who arranged for the **S** to be removed from my card. Even then, I wasn't exempt. So that's when I made friends with Schlesinger. Not through choice, obviously, but necessity. He's the man with the lists. But he's also Jewish, so that makes him one of us. He has to watch his own back, just like we do. And I suppose I can be quite persuasive when I want to be.' He gave a small smirk.

Rudolf shook his head in admiration at this man's nerve at standing up to the thugs in authority. He wasn't sure he'd have the courage to do the same.

'Tell me about what you're doing with that camera.' Philip pointed his finger, which was bent at an odd angle.

Rudolf let out a long sigh before answering. 'I'm doing a job for the kommandant. He wants photographic evidence of how well he runs this camp.'

Philip let out a harsh laugh that was devoid of any mirth. 'You've got to be joking. Have you ever watched the scenes when the trains are about to leave?'

Rudolf felt uncomfortable; he'd deliberately avoided going to see the transports out of the camp. It wasn't that he was unaware the deportations were happening, just that he'd convinced himself it wasn't right to watch let alone film people in such misery. If he didn't go, it wasn't quite 'out of sight, out of mind', but it helped him believe that he could still keep his family safe. 'No, I've always been too busy with the arrivals to go and see.' It was a weak excuse and he could tell Philip wasn't taken in by it, but the other man replied without judgement.

'Not many people go along to watch. But I have a compulsion to go and see things for myself. It starts off around six in the morning, the long procession of humanity traipsing in rows along the boulevard of misery. They're not put on passenger trains, but in animal wagons intended for horses or cattle. You'd think they'd at least have put down straw for them to sit on, but they provide nothing. It's shocking to see these poor unsuspecting people climb up with their bags of food and all their possessions and then have to scramble for any available space to sit down. And then it's just bare boards.'

Rudolf's heart started to race at Philip's lurid depiction of the deportations. He knew that what he said could so easily apply to any of them – to Bella, to his children.

'The sick are also being sent away,' Philip went on as if compelled to tell Rudolf everything. 'It started not long after I came out of the hospital. They're cramming everyone on to trains, everyone in together, even the sick who need constant care. It's a terrible sight.' Philip paused, then apologised. 'I'm sorry, it's all rather upsetting. I haven't been able to tell anyone about what I've seen. You're the first person I've said a word to. But I am writing it down.'

'I hope you're careful where you put your notebooks,' said Rudolf, feeling worried for his friend. Suddenly, an idea came to him. 'I can stow them here in the back room if you like. I'm the only one with a key and here's as safe a place as any.'

'Would you really do that for me?' Philip looked surprised at the offer, hopeful even.

'Yes. Let me show you.' Rudolf walked to the inner door and unlocked it, and the strong odour of chemicals pervaded the room. 'Sorry about the smell. I usually air the place before I start work.' He snapped on a light switch, lighting up the tiny space, the shelves containing bottles of developing fluid, the stacks of blank paper for photographs, the clothesline with pegs strung from wall to wall. A tripod, neatly folded, was stowed at the back.

'Over here,' he said, pointing to a small cupboard, low to the floor and barely visible. 'It's messy – full of odds and ends. I don't think anyone would be interested in the contents and I can hide your notebooks at the back. Do you want to take a look?'

'No thanks. Let me think about it, Rudolf. It's a generous

offer, but I don't want to put you in any unnecessary danger. I've managed so far on my own.' Philip gave a tight smile.

Rudolf nodded, disappointed he'd rejected his offer, then thought perhaps he'd been too forward in asking. 'The offer stands. You know where I am.'

They stood awkwardly for a few moments. Rudolf didn't want Philip to walk away as he had the last time, so he ended up blurting out what he'd been struggling to come to terms with these past weeks.

'I've given much thought to what you told me the first time you came here. About using my camera to show the truth about this place, like you do with your writing.'

Philip's interest seemed piqued. 'You have?'

'The longer I'm here, the more I see how hopeless things are. When the kommandant asked me to show the camp in a good light, I hadn't realised quite how difficult it'd be. All around me I see people struggling to comprehend why they are here. It shows on their faces. I understand I'm in a privileged position going around with my camera because of my job. I need only show the kommandant the photos that paint the rosy picture he believes in. He never needs to know about any other photos I take, which I'll store in here. They'll never find it.' He turned his head to look at the small store cupboard and was surprised when Philip moved forward to see for himself, crouching down and peering into the dark space.

'It's bigger than I thought,' Philip said, reaching inside and feeling around.

'Exactly,' said Rudolf.

Philip slowly got to his feet. 'You're right. I need to hide my writing, not just to save myself but because I don't want them destroying these records if they find them. I'll bring you the notebooks of my time in the hospital. I've numbered them in the order I've written them. I don't suppose I'll ever see them again, but hopefully someone with good intentions will find them after the Nazis are defeated.' He gave a slow, sardonic smile. 'It won't just be my word against theirs. Your photos will corroborate everything I have written.'

Their eyes locked in reciprocal understanding as they shook hands on their decision. Rudolf wasn't entirely sure what he was about to let himself in for, but he knew he had to record the truth.

TWENTY-SIX

Rudolf became a familiar sight around the camp, with his camera hanging from a leather strap round his neck. The German guards ignored him most of the time, though he was sometimes stopped and interrogated, and received the occasional request to take a photo. He always politely refused, saying he had a specific job to do for the kommandant, which was usually enough to stop anyone from pestering him.

At first, he wandered around without taking any photos. He wanted to gain an outsider's impression of what went on in the camp. What surprised him was that life for the prisoners wasn't all misery and despair and that many were able to lead a reasonably normal life despite being coerced to work in the camp factories and workshops. Sports activities and even entertainment laid on by the Germans gave people a sense of normality and calm, even if the reality couldn't have been further from the truth.

The camp extended far beyond the length of the boulevard of misery. He timed himself walking round the perimeter and reckoned it was at least a mile and a half all told. He still marvelled at how much had been achieved in this camp, which had many of the facilities one would expect of a small town: the shop selling a few basic provisions, a medical centre with a doctor and dentist, a school and operational hospital, which was as large as any he'd seen in Amsterdam. There were factory buildings where shoes were made and scrap metal reclaimed, along with various workshops, and so it went on.

He walked between the endless rows of accommodation huts, which seemed to stretch for miles until they finally thinned out. Then, to his surprise, he came upon a large green area for recreation, including a field marked out for football.

He doubled back along the boulevard and arrived in the centre, where he stopped to look up at a two-storey building he hadn't noticed before.

Just then, a young man in a long overcoat fell into step beside him. 'Are you waiting to go in the theatre? I can let you in,' he said.

Rudolf saw he had a key in his hand. 'I didn't know there was a theatre, but I would like to see it.'

'You're the camp photographer, aren't you? I remember you took my photo when I first came here,' said the young man, unlocking the door. 'I'm Ernst.'

'Rudolf. Pleased to meet you.'

They stepped inside and Ernst switched on a light. 'We put on performances once a week,' he explained. 'Mainly cabaret, but a group of us actors are working on a play, which should be ready by the end of the month.'

Rudolf looked around and was impressed by the size of the place. It was a proper auditorium, with seating for several hundred people in front of a wide stage.

'Come up and see.' Ernst went to switch on more lights that lit up the stage. He led the way up the wooden steps and walked to the centre of the stage, where they could look out over the seating. Rudolf regarded the sea of empty seats, imagining what it must be like to be an actor performing here in front of hundreds of prisoners.

'The kommandant calls us the Kamp Westerbork Theatre Group. It was set up by Max Ehrlich. Have you heard of him?'

Rudolf was shocked to hear that this well-known actor was here in the camp. 'Of course I know Max Ehrlich. I've seen him perform in Berlin. How long has he been at Westerbork?'

Ernst shrugged. 'Several weeks. Most of us were brought here after our theatre in Amsterdam was shut down by the Nazis. We're determined to carry on with what we do best. Naturally, the Germans love it that we provide them with free entertainment. Particularly the kommandant, who brings all his cronies to the performances.' He scoffed and reeled off a list of well-known Jewish actors and artists who had all arrived at the camp around the time Ernst himself had arrived.

'Unfortunately, we have no control over how long anyone is kept here. It's quite common for actors to be replaced with new prisoners coming in all the time. I suppose it keeps us on our toes.' He smiled, but there was a sadness in his eyes.

Rudolf wondered how many of the people Ernst had worked with had already disappeared, but stopped himself from asking. 'Thank you for showing me round and telling me about your work. It's very inspiring. And courageous, if you don't mind me saying.'

Ernst shrugged again. 'Like everyone here, we don't really have much choice. Refuse, and you'll be put on the next transport to Auschwitz or Theresienstadt, and no one wants that. At least if you're an actor you can prolong your time here. Would you like a cigarette?' He held out a crumpled packet, but Rudolf declined. While Ernst lit up, Rudolf told him about his photographic assignment for the kommandant.

'He's asked me to document life in the camp using photos as proof of how a camp should be run. I now understand that setting up a theatre with well-known actors is all part of his scheme. I'd like to come to your next performance and take a few photos. When is it?'

'Always on a Monday evening,' said Ernst. 'Do you know why that is?' He gave Rudolf a sideways glance as he blew out a plume of smoke.

Rudolf thought for a moment. 'Tuesday mornings are deportation day...' he began, then faltered, shaking his head.

'It's a ploy. Putting on entertainment the night before the transports leave for Poland is a distraction. Everyone is terrified it'll be their turn next.' Ernst dragged deeply on his cigarette, as if his life depended on it. 'Anyway, if you don't mind, I need to get started on the set before the others come in.' He walked to the back of the stage and disappeared behind a screen painted to look like a forest scene.

Rudolf retraced his steps outside, where the sun had broken through. As he stood squinting against the bright sunlight, he became aware of the sounds of a scuffle and loud insults being shouted up ahead. A prisoner was being wrestled to the ground by two guards, who began kicking and hitting him with wooden batons. The young man, no more than sixteen or seventeen, tried to protect himself by covering his head with his arms.

An older man came running out of nowhere and began remonstrating with the guards.

'Leave my son alone! He's done nothing,' he wailed, then lunged at one of the guards and tried to drag him away from the boy, who lay whimpering on the ground.

'Stay out of this,' growled the guard and roughly shoved the older man, who fell backwards and hit his head on the ground with a sickening crack. When the guard saw what he'd done, he muttered words to his accomplice and the two of them made off in a hurry.

Rudolf was first to rush forward to help – the man lay still with blood seeping from a head wound. Several other prisoners turned up, some crying, others talking at the tops of their voices.

The younger man staggered to his feet and seemed visibly upset when he saw the prone body of his father.

'He needs medical help. I'll go and fetch someone from the hospital,' said Rudolf.

'It's too late for that,' said one of the onlookers as the younger man laid his head on his father's chest and began moaning pitifully.

Rudolf gasped in horror. All he could do was stand by, powerless to help.

Eloise

It was a bitterly cold but gloriously sunny wintry day when all seemed right with the world. Eloise and James were out for a walk in the University Parks, admiring the stark beauty of the majestic trees that stood out against a perfectly blue sky. They skirted the edge of the park where the River Cherwell curved round, ending up at the duck pond, where a few moorhens were pecking around in the rushes at the water's edge.

'Let's stop here for a moment,' said James, leading Eloise to a wooden bench next to the pond. They sat down, arms entwined, and Eloise leaned her head on his shoulder, savouring the moment. Across the pond something must have disturbed a duck – it quacked loudly, flapped its wings and took flight. She wasn't sure why, but it suddenly made her think of her grandmother and the promise she'd made to her. She'd been so wrapped up in being back with James since the Christmas break that she'd clean forgotten about it. In an instant, her feeling of peace shattered. She stiffened and pulled away from him.

'What's up?' he said, turning to her with a frown.

'I'm sorry but I need to go. I said I'd go and see my grandma this afternoon. I can't possibly let her down.'

'What about our Sunday lunch? It's all booked. Can't you go afterwards?'

Eloise shook her head. She couldn't bear the thought of breaking her promise to visit.

'I'm sorry, James, but I can't. I promise I'll make it up to you.' She traced the contours of his face with a finger, then a thought occurred to her. 'Why don't you come with me?' she asked tentatively, though she didn't really expect him to agree.

He held her gaze for so long that she was convinced he would say no. Then he broke into that smile that always made her insides melt. 'Yeah, why not? Then I can still be with you.' He kissed the tip of her nose. 'We can do lunch another day. She won't mind if I come with you, will she?'

Eloise was amazed that he'd accepted so readily. She hadn't really thought he would. 'I'm sure she won't mind. She loves company,' she said happily and leaned in for a kiss. 'It's really nice of you to say you'll come.'

'Anything to be with you. And maybe you can get her to show me those photo albums you've been telling me so much about.' The corners of his mouth lifted, and she wasn't sure if he was teasing her. But what did it matter, she thought, enjoying the feeling of snuggling up against him.

After a quick sandwich at the Summertown deli, they bought an assortment of pastries to take out. Eloise filled him in on a few details about her grandma, saying how she liked to be addressed and that she could come across as rather direct at times; James wasn't to take it personally. She assured him that her grandma would take to him.

They arrived at the flat and Eloise pressed the bell, which loudly buzzed.

'The door's open. Come in!' called a voice from inside.

Eloise squeezed James's hand and led the way into the small hallway. 'It's me, Eloise. And I've brought a visitor.' She exchanged a quick look with James, who nodded for her to go through. She found her grandma standing beside her armchair and went to give her a kiss on the cheek.

'Lovely to see you, my dear. But who is this?' She peered inquisitively at James, who was standing behind Eloise.

He stepped forward and held out a hand. 'It's a pleasure to meet you, Mrs Moses. I'm James and a friend of Eloise. I'm also a student at Oxford.'

She gripped his hand in both of hers, scrutinising his face. 'And what are you studying?'

'I'm taking a BA in history, focusing on European and world history this year.'

'Is that so?' she said, still perusing him. 'How long have you known my granddaughter?' Her question came out quite sharply, making Eloise squirm, but James didn't seem to notice.

'I met Eloise on her first day at Oxford, but we didn't get to know each other properly till just before Christmas.' He caught Eloise looking at him and gave a little laugh.

'Well, you seem a nice young man.' The old lady relaxed her gaze and nodded with what appeared to be approval. 'Let's all have a cup of tea.'

Eloise had warned James not to offer his help, so he politely accepted.

'We popped into the deli and bought some pastries to have with the tea,' said Eloise, holding up the paper bag.

'That's nice of you. Why don't you fetch plates from the sideboard and make yourselves comfortable.' The old lady was already feeling her way across the room towards the kitchen.

There were only two armchairs and one was Grandma's, so

James drew up an upright dining chair that looked as if it may once have been part of a set. Eloise arranged the pastries on an ornately patterned plate, then sat down next to James. As they waited, they whispered quietly and listened to the old lady moving about in the kitchen – to the sound of the kettle coming to the boil, the clatter and chink of china and the sudden tinkle of a spoon or something similar falling to the floor.

Eloise couldn't help herself from springing up and going to her assistance. Grandma was holding on to the kitchen counter and seemed flustered. 'That spoon just slipped out of my hand. Would you pick it up, my dear?' Then, more quietly, she said, 'I like the look of your new boyfriend. Make sure he looks after you.'

Eloise felt herself redden as she retrieved the spoon. 'I've only known him a few weeks,' she said in a loud whisper so her grandma could hear.

'That doesn't matter. I can see from the way you look at him that you're smitten. Now, hurry up and take the tray through or he'll think we're gossiping about him.' She gave Eloise a twinkly smile.

Aware she was still blushing, Eloise picked up the tea tray, took it through and placed it on the coffee table.

'Everything all right?' said James with an amused look.

'Couldn't be better,' she whispered, as her grandma appeared in the doorway and moved slowly back to her chair. She lowered herself down with an audible sigh. 'I'm sorry it took so long to make the tea. Small things do these days,' she said. She waved a hand at Eloise to pour the tea.

It wasn't long before she was asking James about his course and what elements of the Second World War were on the syllabus. 'It always surprises me how little is taught about the Netherlands during the Second World War. Have you heard of Westerbork?' She gave him a penetrating stare. Unfazed, he said he'd read much about the spread of Nazism in Europe, but that Westerbork wasn't a name he'd come across.

She glanced to the side and sighed. 'I thought not. It's not your fault, but the way history is taught these days. The English have no idea that the Netherlands was occupied by Germany for the duration of the war. The Dutch suffered terribly and many thousands died of starvation. It was such an awful time for everyone. I should know... I was there. At least for a time.' She gazed into the middle distance.

'Do you want to tell me about it?' James asked carefully with a quick glance at Eloise, who nodded her approval.

'Perhaps I will,' she said, adjusting herself in her chair. 'My family and I were living in Amsterdam and led a normal peaceful life, but it all came to a stop in 1942 when the Germans sent us to Westerbork with hundreds of other Jews. No one knew what went on in that camp after the Germans took it over. You see, it used to be a refugee camp for Jews. We were considered lucky because we stayed for almost two years, which was unheard of.'

'Two years?' said James in a horrified voice. 'That must have been terrible for you. What happened then?'

Eloise too was shocked by her grandmother's revelation and wondered if she would want to speak further about it. After all, she'd never talked about what went on in Westerbork before. No wonder she hadn't, she thought, judging from the stories Eloise had read about the concentration camps like Auschwitz. Could Westerbork have been as bad?

Her grandmother took her time speaking, and Eloise noticed she avoided James's question. 'The majority of prisoners were deported on cattle trains within a week or two of their arrival. We didn't know that in the beginning. My father, Rudolf Breslauer, was given the job as the camp photographer. No, that's misleading... he was *forced* to take up the position by the German kommandant. A nasty piece of work he was.

Gemmeker, his name was.' She spoke the name with pure hatred.

As she continued to reminisce about her father, her expression softened. 'I used to help him sometimes in his studio. Not often, but he showed me how to develop the photographs. I was fourteen at the time. I had a pretty good idea of what the Germans were up to and that my father's photos were to show Westerbork in a good light.

'One day, I was sorting through some photos and two caught my eye. The first was a portrait taken when I was thirteen. I simply couldn't bear the idea that Papa was going to give it to the kommandant, so I took it. Then I came across another of the children in the schoolroom. I wasn't in the photo, but my best friend Bekkah was. I don't know what came over me, but when Papa wasn't looking I slipped that one into my pocket as well. It was a bad thing to do and I still feel guilty about taking them to this day.'

'Did you keep the other photo?' asked Eloise, hoping it were true, for she hadn't seen any photographs taken inside the camp.

The old lady shook her head sadly. 'I hid it under my mattress and had to leave it behind when we left Westerbork in a hurry. I always thought that was my punishment for stealing it.'

'But you kept the one of yourself,' said Eloise.

Her grandmother nodded. 'I managed to save that one. Your father put it in an album of family photos.'

'And he gave me it on my thirteenth birthday. I must have been intending to use it as a bookmark, but I didn't realise the significance of it till it recently dropped out of my book. I'm glad I have it and I'll always treasure it,' said Eloise, with a break in her voice.

James, who had been listening quietly, changed the subject. 'Rudolf Breslauer... he made a film. I think I've seen it. You say he was your father?'

The old lady's eyes brightened at this. 'You've heard of him?' She looked pleased.

'I've seen footage of the films he made, which are on You Tube… the internet. I know how important these films were in providing evidence that the transports to the concentration camps really did take place. These films are now part of UNESCO's Memory of the World Programme. They're so important for future generations. You must know that, though.'

'No,' she said with a hint of sadness. 'I don't know anything about that, but then why would I? Computers are a mystery to me. But I'm glad to hear his work hasn't been entirely forgotten.'

The light was starting to fade and her grandma asked Eloise to turn on the standard lamp behind her chair. Her face looked drained and Eloise suspected all this talk had taken it out of her. She mouthed at James that they should go, and stood up to clear the tea things on to the tray.

'Grandma, it's getting late. James and I should be going. Is there anything we can do for you before we go?'

'Just take the tea things through and I'll do the rest,' the old lady said with a tired smile.

'Are you sure? It's no trouble washing up,' said Eloise. She picked up the tray and took it through into the small kitchen. She heard her grandma saying to James how much she'd enjoyed meeting him, which made her smile. When she went back in, her grandma was still talking and seemed reluctant for them to go.

'Thank you for listening to an old lady. Will you promise to come again? I haven't even shown you my photo album.'

She held out her hands, which James took in both of his. 'I'd like that very much, Mrs Moses. It's been such a pleasure meeting you.'

TWENTY-EIGHT
SPRING 1943

Rudolf

After witnessing the brutal treatment of the young Jewish man at the hands of the Nazis, Rudolf resolved to go out of his way to photograph the reality of life inside the camp. He knew he must be careful not to overdo it, but once he started his eyes were opened to the number of people being maltreated. He simply couldn't let it go unrecorded. But he also had a job to do for the kommandant, and couldn't be seen to use too much film and photographic paper in case his secret project was found out.

One morning, Rudolf was walking down the boulevard of misery when he heard a barely audible noise coming from one of the barracks. It sounded like a child sobbing quietly. He went to investigate and couldn't see anyone at first inside the darkened room, so he called out softly. The crying stopped. He pushed open the door. As his eyes adjusted to the gloom, he saw a young girl sitting on the bare floorboards with her arms clasped around her knees. He crouched down and asked her what the matter was. She peered at him suspiciously with huge dark eyes.

'My name is Herr Breslauer. Will you tell me yours?'

'Marianne,' she said, so softly he almost missed it.

'Are you by yourself?' he asked, convinced she was all alone.

She sniffed several times, then glanced up at the bunk she was leaning against. Rudolf followed the direction of her gaze and saw the outline of someone lying under a blanket. He had parted his lips to ask who it was, but then she whispered, 'My mama is very ill. I don't know what to do.' She moaned softly to herself.

He didn't want to upset her more by asking any questions about her mother, so he told her he would go to fetch a doctor, but when he arrived at the medical centre there was a notice on the door announcing it was closed. What were people meant to do if they needed urgent medical care? Fury overwhelmed him as he realised there was nothing more he could do, but he knew he couldn't leave the little girl by herself. He returned to the barracks and found several people crowding round the bed attending to the ill mother, with Marianne still hunched miserably on the floor.

He decided it was best not to interfere, but just as he was turning to go he stopped. His hands went to his camera which hung round his neck and was half hidden inside his jacket. He quietly adjusted the settings to take account of the low light. Click. It was over in an instant, but, as soon as he'd taken the photograph of the distressed group, with Marianne staring at him with large, scared eyes, he regretted what he'd done. He had intruded on an intensely private moment. Not only that, he felt he'd taken advantage of their sorrow.

Later, he was in his studio, developing the photos he'd taken that day. He wasn't proud of his actions, but he'd been unable to ignore this growing compulsion to document what he saw. Only after the image had gradually revealed itself on the wet paper did he fully understand that this was what Philip had meant when he'd talked about having a duty to record the truth. No sooner was this print dry than he quickly locked it away at the back of the cupboard. He simply couldn't afford to make a slip in case he was found out.

Bella sifted through the dozens of official photographs that Rudolf had laid out on the table, making little sounds of approval each time she moved one aside into a new pile. It was easy to discern that Westerbork was a place of constant activity where people were occupied in a variety of jobs. It could be construed that the jobs were fulfilling. He'd photographed people making wooden chairs, tables and colourfully painted toys, shoemakers hammering soles onto shoes and the impressively large facility that employed dozens of people salvaging scrap metal for reuse. The unspoken fact that all of this industry was for the benefit of the Germans was only too evident to Rudolf when walking round observing this activity. No one working here, or indeed any of the prisoners with minimal possessions or whose only pair of shoes had worn thin, would ever gain from the fruits of their labour. Nevertheless, Rudolf was quietly pleased that he had managed to achieve what the kommandant was clearly looking for, while not shying from the terrible reality.

He glanced down at the shots he'd taken of the amateur football team, smiling broadly for the camera before their Sunday afternoon match. Several of the men had told Rudolf how they were members of a successful team before coming to Westerbork and how pleased they were to be able to continue playing. Rudolf had been there with his camera to capture their exuberance and joyful abandonment on film when one of their own scored a goal. You could almost hear the roars of excitement erupting from the crowd of spectators from the photo. It was one of the few times that the prisoners and guards came together to forget about their misery and deprivations for an hour or two.

Rudolf became aware that Bella was giving her approval to only some of the photos he'd taken. She'd made a selection showing scenes in the factory and workshops, a couple of the football match and those he'd taken when she'd gone with him to the schoolroom. Frowning at the perceived slight, he asked her what was wrong with the others she'd left strewn across the table.

She gave a small smile. 'Nothing at all. In fact, you've done such a thorough job that I'm sure the kommandant will be delighted.'

'So what's the problem?' Sullenly, he began flicking through some of the photos she'd rejected. He'd taken them in the schoolroom and been so careful to exclude Ursula and Stefan. What could she possibly object to?

She stood beside him and laid an arm on his back. 'I know you want to do your best, which is a good thing. But the kommandant only cares about having enough photos to show what a great camp he's running. Once he's got what he wants, where will that leave you... or us?'

Her words hit a nerve and he felt he needed to justify himself. 'This project isn't the be all and end all, you know. I still have my other work photographing new arrivals. And he's holding a big dinner on Thursday and wants me to photograph the guests. He said there'll be more occasions like that.'

Bella nodded, but didn't look convinced. 'What I suggest is you give him some of these photos and leave him wanting more. You don't want to give him any reason to think you've done your job and are now dispensable. Rudolf, please don't be angry with me. It's not just about doing your job well, but what happens to us, your family.' She reached up and gently touched his face.

'I know that. I wrestle with it every day,' said Rudolf, moving away from her. He felt taut with anxiety and was desperate to unburden himself. He was on the verge of telling her about the photos that he had deliberately avoided showing her. He didn't want to give her any further cause for worry. In particular, the one of that poor innocent girl whose mother was on the point of dying. He felt sick at what he'd done but he knew he could never show her it. He decided it must stay hidden in the cupboard of his darkroom, along with Philip's diaries. It was essential he did so if he was to keep his family safe.

He turned to Bella, aware that telling her would only create more tension between them, and that was the last thing he wanted. 'You're right, Bella. The kommandant doesn't need to know the full extent of what I'm doing. I need to keep him satisfied – that's all that matters for now.'

TWENTY-NINE

After Philip brought the first of his diaries to Rudolf for safe keeping, he became a regular visitor to the studio, where they swapped notes about what they'd seen around the camp. Philip knew much about the Westerbork theatre and wrote candidly on the plays they'd both seen and the fate of those who went to watch it the night before the transports. One day he read Rudolf his diary entry:

'The peerless Max Ehrlich reprised his role as Schmidt Kapellmeister in the romantic comedy Der Hochtourist *along with some of the original cast from Berlin. It had the audience in stitches. Was I the only one who found the production ineffably sad, knowing how many actors had already departed Westerbork for Auschwitz? How many more will be gone tomorrow on the next long mangy snake of old, filthy wagons? Many people on the train don't even know that Amsterdam is being emptied of Jews. Herded together and taken away like cattle. From hearth to home to foreign parts – oh, the misery these people must be going through. Separated from their wives and children. How can the Good God allow this?'*

He paused. 'Is it too much?' he asked, frowning.

'No. It's the truth. You're stating what people fear but daren't voice themselves.'

Rudolf felt sobered by Philip's account as he shuffled through the photos he'd taken of that evening. He'd stood at the back of the auditorium throughout the performance, where he could take photographs unnoticed. He'd been careful to give a good representation of the production and the actors, but was more interested in recording the reactions of the audience. No one noticed the shadowy figure with a camera moving about unobserved. He had wanted to capture the stark contrast between the Germans and camp inmates, so he'd taken two shots of Germans in uniform laughing uproariously. One focused just on the group, clearly showing the Germans' enjoyment, but for the second photo he angled his camera so that a man and a woman could be seen sitting several rows behind. Despite the fact that they were facing the action like the Germans, they weren't laughing or even smiling. There was no mistaking the haunted expressions on their faces.

Rudolf pushed both photos over to Philip. Philip gazed at them, then turned over the one showing the couple. 'This is exactly what we need and more powerful than any words. But I do think you should sign it on the back. When these photos are discovered, people will want to know who took them. Rudolf Breslauer will forever be associated with what actually went on in the camp.'

Rudolf felt an icy chill run through him. 'I'd rather not put my name to what we're doing. Call me a coward, but it's costing me a lot even to do this. I want you to understand that if I'm caught it won't just be me who is punished, but my whole family too. I'm already convinced the authorities are watching my every move and looking for any way to catch me out. I managed when it was just the kommandant coming here to check the photographs. He was only interested in the finished prints and seemed satisfied. But now he's handed over to Schlesinger to keep an eye on my work. I wish he hadn't.'

'Surely that's a good thing. You forget Schlesinger is one of us.'

Rudolf sighed in exasperation. 'He works for the kommandant. I don't trust him and have every reason not to. The last time he was here he insisted on scrutinising the negatives. No doubt on orders. He's never asked to do that before, but I could hardly refuse. The only reason I was able to hide this one from him was because I'd separated it from the rest. I told him it hadn't come out because the exposure was wrong.'

'Well, there's your answer. Keep doctoring the negatives before Schlesinger has the chance to see them.'

'It's not that simple. I get all my photographic supplies from the Nazis. They note down every last sheet of photographic paper I use, so I have to be extremely careful to account for every print I produce for them. It doesn't leave me with much opportunity to do anything else.'

He went over to the cupboard and retrieved a folder containing the stash of secret photographs. He leafed through them, then handed them across. 'I'm afraid I've only taken ten in all, including the one I've just shown you. It's not enough, is it?'

Philip flicked through each one. 'These are ten more than anyone will have seen. I don't want to force you to do anything you don't want to. I understand if you want to stop.'

Rudolf felt torn about what he should do. There was still so much that had gone undocumented that would complement the detailed diaries that Philip had compiled. But the more pictures he took, the greater risk he ran of being found out. The sensible thing would be to stop in order to protect his family. Wasn't that what really mattered? He glanced down at Philip's pile of exercise books, which lay on the table. With Rudolf's pictures, they formed compelling proof of people's suffering at the hands of the Nazis. He took the top one, a faded blue colour and dog-eared, and began turning the pages, which were closely covered in Philip's handwriting – his testimony of everything he had witnessed over the past twelve months. He noticed Philip watching him and wished he'd the strength to say he would agree to signing his work, but he couldn't bring himself to do so.

Philip seemed to sense his discomfort. 'Let's leave it for now. Let me know what you decide when you're ready.'

The following morning, Schlesinger turned up as Rudolf was finishing up taking the identity photos of the last of the new arrivals. Four hundred and eighty-eight men, women and children he counted, down on last week, but still it was a shockingly high number. He had the feeling that the Nazis weren't prepared to stop until every last Jew had been eradicated from the Netherlands.

But Schlesinger was in an ebullient mood, which immediately put Rudolf on his guard. From his encounters with the kommandant's right-hand man, he'd learned never to take his moods at face value.

'Good morning, Rudolf. Everything in order here today?' He rubbed his hands vigorously and let his small dark eyes roam around the studio before coming to rest on David.

'David helps me with the photographic records, Herr Schlesinger.'

The boy, sitting at the small desk, glanced up at Schlesinger, his cheeks flushing dark red. He murmured a greeting.

'David, I think we're finished for today. Thank you. You can go,' said Rudolf, squirming in sympathy at the boy's unease. David hurriedly tidied up his things and left the room.

Schlesinger turned to Rudolf. 'I saw you at the theatre this week. May I see the photographs you took?'

'Of course,' said Rudolf, inwardly shaking to hear that he'd been spotted without realising it. Then, with a sudden rush of terror, he remembered he'd absently put the photo of the haunted-looking couple in with the rest. His heart began to thud. With his back turned, he took down the folder from the shelf and opened it. The damning photograph lay on top. How could he have been so careless? There was nothing he could do about it, so he quickly shut the folder and passed it into Schlesinger's outstretched hand.

'I'm looking forward to seeing these,' said Schlesinger with that insincere smile of his. He placed the folder on the desk. Taking out the top photo, he frowned at it for a few moments, then put it aside. He examined the next one and the next until he'd seen them all.

Rudolf watched him, feeling increasingly sick and unable to gauge his reaction. It was impossible to know if Schlesinger had noticed the couple just out of shot.

'Are these all the photos you've taken?' Schlesinger said, when he'd seen them all.

Rudolf swallowed hard, sensing an implied criticism. 'Everything I've taken so far. I've been busy photographing the new arrivals,' he said by way of an excuse. He hoped that Bella's suggestion to keep some back wasn't about to come back and haunt him.

'The kommandant is expecting you to photograph people *enjoying* themselves. I don't see much of that here.' He jabbed at the offending photo, making Rudolf wince. 'That can't be too hard for a man of your exceptional abilities, can it?'

'No, Herr Schlesinger,' Rudolf replied, relieved at his response but still annoyed at the backhanded compliment.

'Good. I'm glad we understand each other. Can I rely on you to deliver the rest of the photos by the end of the week?'

Rudolf detected a note of anxiety in Schlesinger's voice and wondered if he was also worried about his position in the camp. If Schlesinger didn't do the kommandant's bidding, then might he also find himself on one of the lists? For a very brief moment, Rudolf felt sympathy for the man's position.

Then Schlesinger's expression hardened. 'I said I want you to have the photos ready by the end of the week.'

Rudolf's mind was in turmoil. How could he achieve this in such a short space of time? There was no doubt that Schlesinger's ultimatum carried a threat, even if he was trying to save his own skin. Rudolf thought back to the many soirées he'd been ordered to attend and the kommandant's precise instructions to photograph all the guests enjoying themselves – the SS officers in their uniforms with their polished medals and their wives in all their finery. Rudolf had known all along that these elaborate evenings were a charade organised by the kommandant to show himself in a good light, perhaps even to safeguard his own position in the Nazi hierarchy. That had been easy in comparison to what Schlesinger was asking him to do now. Feeling panicked, Rudolf knew he had no choice but to obey orders, which could mean only one thing. What had been unthinkable only moments before was suddenly his only way out. He must compromise all his principles and break his promise to Bella – although it caused him deep pain, he knew he had no choice but to photograph his own children.

THIRTY

MAY 2023

Eloise

It was a warm May afternoon after Eloise's last exam and James wanted to celebrate by taking her punting on the River Cherwell. She couldn't have been happier with his suggestion and was looking forward to lying back amongst the cushions, glass in hand, with James at the helm. But despite his protestations that he'd done it before, it took him several botched attempts at manoeuvring the punt out of the dock before they were able to get going. It was busy out on the river and James made slow progress, but Eloise was grateful that he managed to avoid bumping into any other punts. She sat back and relaxed, enjoying the sound of the soft splash every time James brought the pole out of the water and the distant chatter and laughter from people enjoying themselves on the far riverbank.

She must have been dozing under the brim of her sunhat when she suddenly became aware that they were stationary on the water and James was trying to drag out the pole, which was anchored in the river mud. Suddenly, the pole came free and they were on their way again. 'Well done,' said Eloise, relieved she wouldn't have to help; she pulled her sunhat down over her eyes against the sun.

They made slow progress until Eloise recognised a favourite walking path of theirs inside the University Parks. 'Why don't we stop here? We can get out and have our picnic on the grass.' She squinted at him from under her hat, before adding, 'Do you want any help?'

'No, leave it to me,' said James, as he wrestled to extract the pole from the riverbed again and gingerly brought the punt towards the bank. He secured it by wedging the tall pole in the mud close to the river's edge. He jumped onto the bank and asked Eloise to throw him the rope, which he looped around the pole.

None too elegantly, Eloise clambered out, thankful to be on dry land. She spread out a white and yellow checked blanket she'd brought along and unpacked the picnic. After making sure the punt was secure, James lowered himself beside her with a sigh and stretched his long legs out in front of him.

Eloise handed him a plastic tumbler of Prosecco. 'Here's to the end of our exams.' She clinked her glass against his.

'To the end of our exams,' said James and took a deep drink. 'And us,' he said, lifting his glass again.

'To us.' She smiled fondly at him, savouring the moment. No more exams, the peaceful sunny afternoon and delicious prospect of several weeks without constant deadlines and stress.

She leaned towards him, but before she could kiss him he took her empty glass, tossed it on the grass and pulled her, giggling, onto the rug and into a passionate embrace. She felt light-headed, maybe a little from the wine, but also from sheer happiness that they felt the same way about each other.

After they'd consumed the food and finished off the bottle, Eloise said she felt sleepy and was in no hurry to get back. James murmured his agreement and they lay dozing in each other's arms, allowing the afternoon slip by.

A distant church clock struck five. A breeze had whipped up and Eloise suddenly felt chilly. She propped herself on one elbow so she could look down at James. 'I don't wish to be a spoilsport, but don't you think we should get this punt back?'

'I was hoping we could forget all about it and walk back,' he said lazily.

'I can try my hand at punting,' she offered, though she didn't really mean it. She was sure she'd make a mess of it.

'It's a lot harder than it looks.' He gazed out at the river, then suddenly sat up on his forearms. 'Eloise, I've been meaning to say – let's go on a trip this summer.'

Her heart gave a flip of excitement at this unexpected announcement. 'Really? What sort of trip?'

'I thought we could get an Interrail ticket and travel round Europe for a couple of weeks. Stop off wherever we feel like it. It's something I've been wanting to do for ages, but it'll be even better together. Please say yes.'

'I... I'd love to,' said Eloise, momentarily overwhelmed. 'But where will we go?'

'Well,' James said thoughtfully. 'I thought we could start by going to visit the memorial centre at Westerbork where your grandmother and family were taken.'

'Not taken,' corrected Eloise, slightly perplexed by his choice of words. 'My grandfather was given a job as the official photographer and he had no choice but to take the family with him.'

'I know,' James said quickly, then went on, 'When I saw your grandmother's album, I must admit I was slightly disappointed. I was expecting there to be photos of the camp taken by her father. It got me thinking about what might have happened to them. So, I've been doing some research and found out that the Westerbork museum has the original photographs taken by your great-grandfather in their archives. They might give you some clues about your family.'

'Do you really think so?' said Eloise, excited by his announcement, but also a little taken aback to hear that James had been digging into her past without telling her. It seemed wrong given how little her grandmother was prepared to talk about her own experiences in Westerbork.

'I do. It'll be a real chance to finally see his work, which your grandma thought hadn't survived the war.' He tilted his head and regarded her eagerly.

'I'd love to go, but I wonder what Grandma would have to say about it. She's always been so reticent about what her father did. When I showed her the photo I had of her as a young girl, she almost brushed it aside after telling me her father had taken it. It's like there's some dark terrible family secret that she doesn't want me to know about. I would need to approach this sensitively as I would hate to upset her.' As she thought of her grandmother, who seemed both frail and at the same time so determined, she hesitated before agreeing to his suggestion. 'How did you find out about these photographs?' she said.

'Actually, it was my tutor who put me onto it after I told him your grandma's amazing story. He has a contact who works in the archives of the museum, who told him they've discovered boxes of photographs that are all attributed to Rudolf Breslauer.'

Eloise was stunned. She knew she should have been glad but couldn't understand why he hadn't already thought to tell her what he'd been up to.

'What's the matter?' James frowned. 'I thought you'd be pleased.'

'Don't get me wrong, James. I'm just a bit surprised you're telling me this now and not before. How long have you known about all this?'

He gave a curious look. 'Not long. The photographs have been lying in storage for decades and have only just come to light. They're a real find. I thought you could tell your grandma before we go. There will be photos her father took that she will never have seen. She's bound to be thrilled.' James took her hands in his, his eyes bright with excitement.

Eloise allowed herself a laugh. 'Thrilled might be stretching it. She's always been so reticent to talk about her father's work – she might think it's a terrible idea. In fact, I'm worried it'll dredge up painful memories she's been trying to forget.'

James looked thoughtful. 'That doesn't mean you can't go and see for yourself, does it?' He kissed her lightly on the lips.

'You're right. Seeing as you've gone to all this trouble I should go. I'm sorry if I overreacted, but you did rather spring it on me.' She tapped him playfully on the arm, which he took as an invitation to kiss her again. Unable to resist him, she realised how lucky she was to have him, even if he did vex her at times.

James became serious as he said, 'We don't need to make any plans straight away. We've got the whole summer.' He sighed. 'Let's forget about it for now. Besides, I need to get you back home in one piece.'

THIRTY-ONE
SPRING 1943

Rudolf

'Now come towards me holding hands. And smile,' Rudolf instructed Ursula and Stefan. He'd taken them over to the path that ran just inside the fence so he could photograph them with the kommandant's residence in the background. It made for a more interesting composition, he convinced himself, though he hated putting his children through this charade and having to lie to them. He'd already made up his mind that these would be the last of the photos he would take of them. Just enough to satisfy the kommandant. But he had another motive – this secret endeavour was the only way he could think of to protect his family from almost certain deportation to a place where he might not even receive the same dubious privileges he had here.

It was a warm Sunday afternoon and he had already photographed the children under the trees beyond the barracks. He'd chosen it because it was peaceful here amongst beautifully scented purple lupins. It was also the one place inside the wire fence where people could catch a glimpse of nature, a veritable balm to the soul for those who had almost given up hope.

Although it was strictly forbidden to pick the blooms, bunches of lupins kept appearing in tin cans on roughly hewn wooden tables and on windowsills in the barracks. Their fragrance helped to disguise the smell of unwashed clothes and bodies. In another week, the lupins would be over and this brief respite from misery would become a distant memory.

Rudolf had laid out an artfully placed rug for the children to sit on and had taken several photos of them laughing over some joke he'd made. He'd felt bad about making them promise not to tell their mother, but what else could he do? The photos would be a surprise for her birthday, he'd said, conscious that he wasn't telling them the entire truth.

Resolving to stop after these last few photos, Rudolf caught Stefan's happy, carefree expression on camera as he ran along the path in plain sight of the kommandant's villa. He knew the kommandant would approve, he thought grimly. Stefan's fair hair gleamed and his round metal-rimmed glasses glinted in the sunlight. Ursula walked self-consciously beside him, looking as if she wanted to be anywhere but here. With her dark wavy hair and her adorable heart-shaped face, she took after her mother in looks. When she smiled, her whole face lit up, but he could tell her heart wasn't in it.

'Please smile, Ursula. Do it for Mama.' Rudolf stood poised with his camera.

Ursula pursed her lips as if she needed to think about it. Suddenly, Stefan took her by surprise and tickled her in the ribs. Caught off-guard, she couldn't help bursting into peals of laughter with her head thrown back, while Stefan kept on tickling her with a mischievous look on his face. Rudolf was ready. Click, click. He stopped there, unwilling to subject Ursula to more of this ordeal.

'All finished now,' he said brightly. 'Now you can both go off and play.'

Stefan immediately rushed off to play ball with a friend, but

Ursula hung back. He could tell something was bothering her. 'What's the matter, Ursula?'

She scuffed the toe of her shoe against the loose stones on the path; she seemed reluctant to say, when she blurted out, 'What's the real reason we can't tell Mama about the photos?' She put her head on one side and looked up at him.

'I told you. It's a surprise for Mama's birthday.'

She glanced at him disbelievingly, but Rudolf was determined to stick to his story even if it were only a half-truth. He could hardly reveal that Bella had begged him not to take any photos of the children. 'I tell you what, why don't you come back to the studio and you can help me develop the photos. Would you like that?'

'Can I, Papa?' Ursula said in a breathless voice.

Rudolf smiled at her sudden change of mood. 'I don't see why not. You're old enough now to see what I get up to.'

She gave him her special smile and slipped her hand in his. With a sense of relief, Rudolf felt his heart swell with love for her.

Ursula was enthralled by the whole process of developing images from negatives, especially the wait while they gradually changed from a blurry misty grey into sharp black-and-white focus on the wet paper. Rudolf watched her at work, fascinated by how absorbed she was. He dared to dream a little that maybe one day she might become a photographer herself and join him in the family business.

As she pored over the photos of herself and Stefan, a small frown appeared between her eyebrows. 'Will you give all of these to Mama?' she said.

'No, I always take more than I need because you never know how they'll turn out. Look at this one. I didn't get the setting right and it's too dark.' He picked up a photo of the children sitting on the blanket under the trees, knowing it would actually do fine for the kommandant. 'Why don't you choose a photo of the two of you for Mama?'

She looked up at him and a look of pensiveness flitted across her face. 'What will you do with the others? Throw them away?'

It was a perfectly reasonable question, but not one he was prepared to answer honestly. He quickly shook his head, realising he was already in too deep. His daughter was smart and perceptive – he knew he couldn't fool her.

'As you know, my job is to take photos of people when they arrive for their identity cards. And because I'm a photographer, I'm also asked to take photos around the camp. You know, like the time I came into the classroom.' He forced a smile, but she looked unconvinced. 'But I don't like to throw away photos I don't use.' The words didn't come out as he intended and he despised himself for not telling the truth.

Ursula's frown deepened. 'But what is it all for? There's nothing nice about this place. My friend Anne showed me where she and her family sleep. They don't even have their own beds. There are so many people in there and it smells awful. She hates it. They all do. No one wants to be in this camp. Not one person.' She spoke forcefully and Rudolf saw tears pooling in her eyes. 'Everyone looks so miserable. Are the Germans so blind they don't see it?'

'Sometimes we have to do things we don't agree with, and this is one of those times. Like you, I can see misery everywhere I look, but they don't want to see that from the photographs I take for them. I have to give them a different version of this reality, even though I don't believe in it.'

'So instead you get Stefan and me to pretend that everything here is wonderful. Is that why you don't want Mama to know what you're doing? These photos are a lie.' Her eyes blazed with indignation.

'No, they're not, Ursula. They're very real. But if you feel so strongly about them, then I won't give one to Mama for her birthday.' Immediately, he regretted his words. It was unforgivable to put her on the spot when he knew it made no difference whatever she said. He knew he would go ahead and give the kommandant what he demanded.

Ursula hesitated as she fingered the photos again, then picked one out. 'I think she'll like this one,' she said quietly. She held out one of Stefan tickling her.

'I'm glad you chose this one because it's my favourite too. It can be from the three of us. And Ursula, I'd love it if you'd come and help me again with the developing.' He smiled and hoped to coax a smile from her, but instead her solemn eyes remained fixed on him, as if she were evaluating him.

'What is it?' he said, shifting a little under her gaze.

She looked away. 'Nothing. Don't worry. I won't tell Mama your secret.' Unexpectedly, she came to him for a hug, which he gratefully reciprocated.

'Good girl,' he murmured.

After she left, Rudolf reflected on their conversation. All she wanted was that he was honest with her. It hurt him that he couldn't be. He hated lying to her, as well as everyone else, because it completely went against his nature. But surely it was better to lie than to provoke the ire of Schlesinger and be condemned to leave the camp on a transport? With a heavy heart, he admitted to himself that to tell the truth now was far too risky – it could endanger all their lives.

The morning of Bella's birthday, Rudolf was up early putting the finishing touches to her present. He'd kept the brown wrapping from a consignment of photographic paper and smoothed out the creases until it almost looked new. It was a far cry from the beautifully designed embossed wrapping paper in rich red and blue hues he used to buy for all their birthdays from the high-class stationers in Leipzig. With a sad smile, he remembered how Bella had always carefully folded the paper and used it to line their drawers; he remembered with a rush of nostalgia the ease with which they went about their lives back then. He pushed the thought away as he concentrated on tying the faded red ribbon into a bow. He still had his family around him and that was all that mattered, he told himself. He laid the gift on the table just as Ursula and Stefan came in bearing birthday cards they'd drawn. Ursula put hers beside the present. 'Put yours next to mine, Stefan. Where is Mama? Isn't she up yet?'

Stefan bounced up and down with excitement. 'Can I go and get her?' he cried.

'What's all this noise so early in the morning?' said Bella, coming into the room followed by Mischa, who ran to his papa in excitement when he caught sight of him.

Rudolf kissed Mischa, then went to kiss his wife. 'Happy birthday, *Liebchen*.'

Bella looked from one to the other in surprise. 'I'd clean forgotten it was my birthday.' Her eyes moved to the cards and gift. 'Are these for me?' she said delightedly.

'This is from me,' said Stefan, grabbing his card and thrusting it into her hands. He'd drawn a picture of the five of them holding hands with each name carefully spelled out above their heads.

'It's perfectly lovely,' said Bella. 'And this must be from you, Ursula.'

Ursula had drawn a picture of a large birthday cake with candles burning. Inside, she'd written something that brought tears to Bella's eyes. She nodded, saying quietly, 'I love you too, Ursula. In fact, I love all of you. And thank you for remembering my birthday.'

'What about your present?' said Stefan impatiently.

'Ah, yes, my present. How could I forget?' Bella laughed

and drew the rectangular package across the table towards her. Mischa was waiting impatiently for her to open it, so she let him pull the ends of the ribbon, which slid away. Before she could object, he'd torn the paper in his excitement, making them all laugh.

Then she lifted Mischa onto her lap. 'Lovely paper and ribbon,' she said, with a quick glance at Rudolf.

But as he watched, Rudolf suddenly felt a twitch of anxiety that she would be angry when she laid eyes on the photograph of Ursula and Stefan. Would she see straight through his gesture, just as Ursula had?

Bella peeled back the paper and gave a gasp. She looked up at Rudolf, a questioning look in her eyes, then back down at the slim black leather photo album. 'I'd completely forgotten about this old album. And you brought it with you. How did you manage it?'

'I slipped it into my suitcase at the last minute, right at the bottom underneath a flap. I forgot I'd done it, until now... turn the pages, Bella. There's more.' He was suddenly impatient to see her reaction.

Bella's cheeks turned pink as she turned each page, pointing out pictures of Ursula and Stefan when they were little, frequently letting out a little cry of delight at each memory. 'It's perfect,' she declared, but seemed sad as she shut the album and looked up at Rudolf.

'What is it?' he said.

'I'm just sad that there are no photos of Mischa as a baby in this album. It feels incomplete without them. His baby photos all went into the album I had to leave behind in Amsterdam.' She glanced anxiously at Mischa, who was now on the floor absorbed in the torn paper and ribbon and oblivious to their conversation.

Rudolf nodded sympathetically. 'I know. But look, you've missed a photo,' he said, and couldn't stop himself taking the album and turning to the last page. 'Do you like it?' he said apprehensively. He'd made a larger print of the photo Ursula had chosen, which filled the entire page.

Bella gasped and put her hand to her mouth. 'You must have taken this only a few days ago. I can still see the lupins,' she said, peering closely. Then, brightly, she said, 'It truly is the best present I've ever received. Come here, Ursula, Stefan, and let me give you a hug.' She opened her arms to let Mischa in too.

If she suspected, she certainly wasn't showing it, thought Rudolf, as he watched Bella squeeze the children to her. Then she looked up at him with tears in her eyes. 'Thank you, *Liebchen*,' she mouthed. He felt his heart constrict with love... or was it guilt?

Then Ursula twisted her head round and gave him an unreadable look. A sharp pang of remorse shot through him. He'd lied to her the day he'd taken the photo, not just once, but repeatedly, and it was painfully obvious that she'd seen straight through his deceit. His daughter Ursula had opened his eyes to the fact that every day he was living a lie, but there was nothing he could do to stop.

THIRTY-TWO
JUNE 2023

Eloise

Before she left Oxford for the summer, Eloise needed to speak to her grandmother about her travel plans. She was excited and a little apprehensive about them, but there was another reason. After having listened to the old lady's reminiscences for so long, Eloise had realised how little she knew about the family after Westerbork. She'd learned from her father that they had all been put on a train to Auschwitz, which was shocking enough, but what she didn't understand was why her grandma had survived when the rest of her family had perished. Eloise didn't hold out much hope of persuading her to open up, but she owed it to her to at least try.

Once her grandma had her beloved photo album open in front of her, she brightened up – she always enjoyed describing everyone in each of the photos, but soon a sadness descended on her face like a veil.

'This must be you and your brother, right?' asked Eloise, pointing to one of the photos she'd been shown on several previous occasions. They both gazed at the earnest fair-haired boy with wire-framed glasses sitting next to an older girl with short dark hair who was wearing a checked jacket. They were sitting under a tree and all around them flowers were growing, though it was impossible to see what kind they were from the black-and-white image. The photograph had been taken inside the camp, this much she knew.

'That's me and darling Stefan. And the flowers all around us were the most beautiful purple lupins. It was one of the last photographs our father ever took of the two of us.' The old lady ran a finger over the outline of the boy in the photograph. She seemed to be trying to remember what he looked like. Eloise wondered if she often sat alone with the album on her lap making this same gesture.

The old lady carefully turned the page and gazed at the final photograph, which showed Stefan tickling Ursula, whose face was a picture of unbridled joy. She sighed.

Suddenly, a thought occurred to Eloise that hadn't struck her before, which might help explain why her grandmother refused to speak much about her family. 'Grandma. Did you have any other brothers or sisters?'

'Why do you ask that?' her grandmother asked sharply, her eyes darting around anywhere but at Eloise.

Eloise felt uncomfortable, but still she pressed on. 'I was just wondering if there were any other photos. Didn't your father take any more of the family?' she asked carefully.

Her grandma glanced at her and frowned; Eloise had the feeling she was expected to know the answer, but how could she when this album of photos was all she'd ever seen of her great-grandfather's work? Eloise became very still as she waited for her to continue.

After drawing a long breath, she said, 'I can't answer that. My father was always too busy with his work to take family snaps. That's all I have to say on the matter.' She closed the album and put it down next to her armchair, then looked up at

Eloise. 'Please don't think I sit here dwelling on the past. I don't. These days, I live for all my descendants, who mean the world to me. In the end, that is all that matters. Now tell me something cheerful about yourself. How is that nice young man of yours?'

Eloise felt a thump of disappointment but tried not to show it. 'James – he's doing fine. We've both passed our end-of-year exams, which is a big relief. And we're going travelling to Europe by rail over the summer. In fact, he's arranged for us to visit Westerbork.' She glanced at her grandma and waited for her reaction.

'Really? I doubt there will be much to see. I heard that the entire camp was dismantled after the war.'

Eloise gazed at her a moment and wondered why she was disinterested in what had happened to the camp. 'Yes, it was,' she persisted. 'But since then, there's been a lot of interest in preserving the past for future generations. It's a memorial centre now and apparently you can walk round with a guide. And there's a museum too. In fact, James has arranged for us to speak to the curator, who's going to show us photographs from the archives. They've only just been discovered, and, would you know... all of them are attributed to your father.' She was unable to keep the excitement from her voice, even if her grandmother wasn't enthused by the news.

Grandma stared at her, shaking her head in disbelief. 'Astonishing. I thought that all of his work had been destroyed and that this album was all that was left.'

'I thought you would mind if I went,' Eloise said tentatively.

'Why would I? You have every right to go. After all, Rudolf Breslauer is as much family to you as he is to me.'

Eloise hadn't thought of it like that, but was pleased at what seemed like a change of heart. The connection to the man she'd never known gave her a warm feeling and a resolve to find out everything she could about her relatives who'd died so needlessly at the hands of the Nazis. Emboldened, she asked if she could take a couple of photos from the family album.

Her grandma quickly shook her head. 'I'm sorry, my dear, but I can't possibly let any of these out of my possession.'

'No, I didn't think you would let me. That's not what I meant.' Eloise hurriedly took her phone out of her bag before her grandmother could refuse even further. 'I'd like to take a few photos on my phone. Here, let me show you.' She swiped the screen and held it over the photo of the two children they'd been poring over earlier. She held up the screen for her grandma to see.

'Did you just do that? How remarkable,' the old lady said with a chuckle. 'Do that again, will you?'

Eloise obliged, and took great pleasure in her grandma's delight at each photo she took. In all, she must have ended up with eight or nine on her phone.

'Does this mean people don't use cameras any more?'

Eloise shrugged. 'Most people don't these days, but camera enthusiasts still do.'

'Well, I'm glad my father never lived to hear about this newfangled invention. I'm sure he wouldn't have approved. He loved his Leica camera and I remember how he took it everywhere with him. He had his own studio inside the camp where he developed his photos. I think I mentioned that occasionally I helped him. They were special times.' She pursed her lips and sniffed in a deep breath. Eloise hoped she was about to make an announcement and was gratified when she went on, 'For years, I had my regrets about that time. I only wish I'd had the nerve to speak out to my papa.'

'What kind of regrets?' Eloise asked, leaning forward in anticipation.

'Nothing. It's nothing,' the old lady said and waved a hand across her face. 'But there is something you can do for me.' She pointed to Eloise's phone. 'I would very much like to see the photos you are shown. The ones I never got to see. Would you be able to do what you did just now with that thing?' She waved her hand around as she grasped for the right words. 'And bring back pictures to show me?'

Eloise nodded enthusiastically to hide her disappointment. What were these regrets that clearly still upset her? 'Yes, of course I will. I can't wait to see the photos for myself.' Relieved to have her grandma's blessing over this important issue, she felt a ripple of excitement. She was sure that what she was about to discover at Westerbork would be quite extraordinary.

Bella

It was one of Bella's days to work in the kitchens and she was on the serving section along with four other women. She'd been on her feet since seven in the morning, having taken Mischa to the small nursery run by volunteer female prisoners. She hated leaving him, even though she trusted the women, who took great care of their charges; she worried that the German guards could get it into their heads to close it down on a whim when she wasn't there to retrieve her precious son.

Once in the kitchen, she set about peeling mountains of turnips, onions and carrots, which would end up in a tasteless watery soup for the masses. It saddened her to work with so few ingredients, which simply weren't enough to constitute a decent meal. It didn't matter how many chunks of vegetable she threw into the vat, it never seemed to suffice for the growing number of inmates, whose only source of nourishment was this meagre ration from the canteen. Looking around to make sure no one was watching, she went to the store cupboard for a few scoops of beans from the sack that was designated for the German staff, who always enjoyed proper meals consisting of chunks of decent meat and plenty of potatoes and vegetables covered in a rich gravy. Bella's mouth watered at the thought of it, though she'd only ever caught a whiff of the enticing aromas that often wafted through from the other kitchen, where she and her fellow workers were forbidden to go. Surely a few beans wouldn't be missed, she thought, as she poured as many as she dared into the pocket of her apron. It wouldn't make much difference to bulking out the soup, but it was the principle that mattered.

She returned to her workstation, relieved that the burly German ex-soldier in charge of the kitchen wasn't about. Not much escaped his eye, though she'd never seen evidence of any culinary expertise on his part. He spent more time shouting at the staff for any perceived misdemeanour, and kept a beady eye out for anyone seen pilfering food for themselves. Ensuring there was enough food to go round was the last thing on his mind.

It was almost the end of service and Bella was concentrating on scraping up the last of the vegetables that had cooked down and were stuck to the bottom of the soup pot, making sure she didn't waste any. She deposited a ladle of the thick liquid into a bowl and looked up, hoping to see a child who would benefit from this little bit of goodness, but instead found herself gazing into the eyes of her best friend, Rachel. She caught her breath, for she almost didn't recognise the deathly-white face with dark bruises smudged beneath her eyes. Her beautiful wavy hair, which Bella remembered always shone with copper highlights, now hung limply around her face.

'Rachel... I can't believe it's you.' Bella's gaze dropped down to Max and Klara, looking terrified as they clung to their mother. 'Where's Jozef?' asked Bella quietly. Her heart began to pound.

'I don't know,' Rachel whispered and quickly glanced at her

children. She looked devastated, broken, but Bella didn't dare ask for any more information within earshot of the children. Just then, Max tried to get his mother's attention by tugging on her hand.

'I'm hungry, Mama,' he whined.

'So am I,' piped up Klara.

Bella's heart went out to these children. She so wished she could scoop them all into a warm hug and whisper that everything would be all right, even though it so obviously wasn't. Instead, she pushed the bowl towards the boy with a bright smile and told the small family group to wait a moment while she fetched more soup. But, on hurrying back to the stove, she found that all the pans had been removed. The other women had already finished serving up and were taking their empty pans to the sink to wash them up.

Confused, Bella looked around the kitchen, convinced there had been another full pan of soup. She rushed over to Sonja, one of the workers. 'I left the last of the soup on the stove,' she began, as the German orderly came striding towards her, his round ruddy face set grim. Undeterred by his demeanour, she said boldly, 'There are people still waiting for soup, but the pan I left on the stove has been moved. What am I supposed to do?'

'Too late,' he said, looking pointedly at the kitchen clock. It wasn't yet half past twelve. 'I want this kitchen cleaned up right away.'

'But—'

'You heard what I said. Do you want me to report you for slacking?'

Bella frowned, indignant at being addressed in this manner by a man who couldn't have been more than twenty. 'I'm trying to do my job and there are hungry children here who will have to go without food. That can't be right, can it?'

His expression changed and suddenly he didn't look so sure

of himself. 'Then give them bread instead. One slice each only, mind. And hurry up. You heard what I said about clearing up.'

Bella was seething but bit her tongue. No good would come of arguing with someone who held power in a place like this. She'd seen how easily a rash word could result in someone's name appearing on the next transport list.

She was full of apologies when she went back to Rachel's small family with three thin slices of stale grey bread smeared with the merest scrape of poor-quality margarine. 'I can't understand how it happened but I'm afraid the soup is finished for today. Do you think you can share your soup with Klara?' she said to Max, but he looked crestfallen. She handed him a slice of bread as compensation, which he immediately began stuffing into his mouth. Klara did the same, and they both kept their eyes fixed on Bella, making her feel as if all this were somehow her fault.

'Where are your manners, children? Say thank you to Mrs Breslauer,' scolded Rachel.

'Thank you, Mrs Breslauer,' the children mumbled through mouthfuls of bread.

Then Rachel tore her piece of bread in two and handed half to each child.

'Let me get another piece,' said Bella hastily, and cast an eye around the kitchen in search of her boss.

'No, I don't need any. I can wait,' said Rachel, turning her sorrowful eyes on her. 'But you can do one thing for me. Let me know when you're finished here. I need to talk.'

THIRTY-FOUR

It was with a heavy heart that Bella walked the length of the boulevard of misery in search of hut number 163. In the few short months she'd been in the camp, dozens of new barracks had sprung up to accommodate masses of new arrivals. Many wandered about the camp in a state of bewilderment, unable to comprehend why they were here, let alone for how long. For most, their stay would be short before they were herded onto another far worse transport than they'd arrived on to take them to some grim place they'd never hear of.

Bella weaved in and out of the crowds, wondering what the Nazis were intending by bringing in so many more prisoners when it was obvious there wasn't enough space for them all. If she was shocked by this spectacle, she could only imagine how terrified Rachel must be feeling after being thrown into this chaos completely alone with her two children. Thank goodness for their chance meeting at the canteen, she thought, and vowed to do all she could to support her dear friend.

The crowds had thinned out at this end of the camp, which was small consolation. She let out a sigh as she arrived at the hut she'd been searching for. A few children were playing hopscotch in the dirt. An elderly man watched from a rough wooden bench; his hands were clasped over the top of his walking stick. He lifted his rheumy eyes to Bella as she approached and she nodded a greeting.

'Come and sit next to me for a moment,' he said in a gravelly voice and shuffled up to make space for her.

'Thank you,' she said, feeling sorry for the old man as she lowered herself onto the bench. 'Are you by yourself?'

He gave her a sorrowful look. 'My wife passed away a year ago. She was spared all of this.' He waved a hand across the rows and rows of barracks and people milling on the avenue.

'I'm sorry,' said Bella.

'Don't be. I'm old. But look at all these young people and children who don't deserve to be here.' He turned his head to look at her again. 'Why are you here?'

Bella gave a short laugh. 'Why are any of us here? I'm here with my husband and children. You might have met my husband when you arrived. He's the camp photographer.'

He stared blankly in front of him for so long that she thought he'd forgotten she was there. 'Rudolf Breslauer,' he said at last.

'Do you know him?' Bella asked in surprise.

'Oh yes. I knew him in Amsterdam. I owned the jeweller's in the same street as his photography shop. There were a lot of rumours about your husband after that Nazi came visiting. And then he suddenly shut up shop and came here – but I don't believe a word of what people were saying.' He gave her a quick glance as if he'd said too much.

Bella felt herself tense up. 'What sort of rumours?'

The old man coughed, then cleared his throat, before answering. 'People believe what they want to believe,' he began, and dropped his gaze to his feet. 'Some think he was paid to come and work for the Nazis.' He paused, then went on in a quiet voice, 'And that he became one himself.'

Bella grew hot with indignation. 'I've never heard anything so ridiculous. My husband had no choice but to accept the job here. And he would never become a Nazi. He's Jewish,' she said firmly.

The old man slowly nodded his head. 'Like I said, I never believed it.' And his face softened into the ghost of a smile.

The door to the barracks creaked open, causing Bella to look up. Rachel stood with a woollen shawl round her shoulders, holding it tightly with one hand.

'There's my friend.' Bella stood up. 'It's been nice talking to you,' she said out of politeness, though the truth was she felt unsettled by the old man's remarks. What else were people saying about Rudolf and their family? She was all too aware how they must appear, a privileged family with their own accommodation. Did people also think that Rudolf was doing special favours for the kommandant? As absurd as it sounded, no sooner had the thought occurred to her than she began to wonder it herself. She'd noticed how preoccupied Rudolf was these days, and whenever she'd asked him about his work he'd brushed her off, saying he didn't want to talk about it. She was absolutely sure he hadn't secretly become a Nazi, but was there something else he wasn't telling her?

'I didn't mean to upset you,' said the old man as if he could read her thoughts.

'No, of course not,' said Bella brightly and smiled.

He nodded and went back to gazing at the children, who were now taking it in turns to play with a skipping rope.

'Let's walk,' said Rachel, coming to Bella's side. 'You don't want to see inside there.' She pursed her lips as she glanced over her shoulder at the door that had swung shut.

'Where are Max and Klara?' asked Bella, suddenly anxious for them.

'They've made friends with the other children. I'm amazed at how adaptable they are.'

They carried on in silence, walking away from the barracks to the tall trees at the back of the camp.

'Do you want to tell me what happened?' said Bella, as they came to a halt to gaze out at the softly undulating purple heathland visible through the wire fence.

'Days after you left Amsterdam, Jozef came home in a state of panic. He'd heard they were planning a major raid on Jews in our area. We only had hours to escape. You remember Hendrik and Annemarie, the couple who are looking after your valuables?'

'Of course,' said Bella, with a sharp twist of unease.

'They're the only ones we knew who could help us, so we packed as much as we could into two suitcases and left home immediately. We were so worried about turning up on their doorstep and were sure they would turn us away, but they were so kind and let us stay in a small room at the top of the house. I was frightened that someone might have seen us ringing the doorbell, but Hendrik reassured us that we would be perfectly safe. He'd constructed a door into a room through the back of the wardrobe and said he'd been expecting something like this to happen.'

'And that's where you've been all this time?'

Rachel gave her a pained look and nodded. 'Most of the time it's been just me and the children. Jozef went missing not long after we moved there. He was so anxious that he hadn't had a chance to tell anyone about the shop and didn't want to leave it unattended. I begged him not to go back but he insisted. He left one day at midnight and I waited up all night for him, but he never came back.' Rachel turned to Bella, her wide eyes filling up with tears. 'Of course I couldn't leave the children to go looking for him. Hendrik and Annemarie did what they could, making discreet enquiries, but no one seemed to know anything about Jozef. He just disappeared.'

'That's so terrible for you,' said Bella, wishing there was

something positive she could say to alleviate her friend's distress. 'How are the children taking it?'

Rachel gave a small hopeless shrug. 'I lied to them and said their papa had to go away on business for a while. And now this.' She turned back to gaze at the squat rows of dismal wooden barracks. 'You can probably guess I'm still in shock,' she said, glancing at Bella. 'It came out of the blue late at night. The first thing I knew was being jolted awake by the sickening crack of wood splintering. Three men in uniform came thundering up the stairs and in seconds were dragging us from our beds and ordering us to get dressed. I was more frightened for Max and Klara than myself, but they've been so good, so quiet. The van was waiting in the street outside. I didn't get a chance to say goodbye to Annemarie and Hendrik.'

Bella hugged Rachel and felt her body shake with sobbing. How the tables had turned from that time when she'd been the one sitting in Rachel's kitchen being consoled.

'What do you think will happen to us?' said Rachel in a small voice.

Bella looked into her face and hesitated, wondering if she had any idea about the lists and the Tuesday transports. Most arrivals hadn't. 'I don't think anyone who's landed up here knows,' she said, not untruthfully, but there was something in Rachel's face that made her want to share what little she did know. 'Every week on Tuesday, a train leaves Westerbork with thousands of people on board. We know they are taken to Auschwitz, but someone told me they're starting to take people to Theresienstadt too, which is an old fortress in Czechoslovakia. They say it's not really a camp at all and people can move freely about without being constantly watched over. It's a proper train with seats that takes people there. Maybe there's some truth in it.' She was aware that her words must sound hollow to Rachel, who was already experiencing such misery.

Rachel looked stricken as she listened. 'Does anyone get any warning about where they are being sent?'

Bella shook her head. 'I'm afraid none of us knows if our names are going to be on the list when it's issued. If you're called to the station there's a fifty-fifty chance your name is on it.'

'Surely you and Rudolf are safe?'

'As long as Rudolf is employed as the camp photographer, then yes, I suppose we are. But neither of us have any illusions – it could all change in an instant.'

'Poland, Czechoslovakia,' Rachel murmured despairingly. 'Those countries sound so far away. How will Jozef ever find us?'

'Don't think about what may never happen,' said Bella, wishing she had something consoling to say. On the spur of the moment she decided to tell her friend a white lie. 'I've seen people released from this place and allowed to go home. We just have to believe it's true.'

THIRTY-FIVE

Rudolf

The day Schlesinger turned up with a thin bespectacled man bearing two black leather suitcases marked a significant shift in circumstances for Rudolf. His first thought when they walked through the door of his studio with the suitcases was that they were meant for him to pack up his few meagre belongings because Schlesinger had decided on a whim to make him board the next train. His heart began to thump wildly at the thought of being separated from Bella and the children.

'No need to look so worried, Herr Breslauer.' Schlesinger chuckled. He seemed to enjoy Rudolf's disquiet. 'This is Herr Schmidt who is visiting from our Berlin headquarters. He has brought something I'm sure you'll find interesting.'

The thin man murmured a greeting. He lifted the suitcase onto the desk and flicked open the clasps. He brought out a rectangular metal box, which Rudolf recognised to be a cinecamera, the type he'd seen used for newsreel footage. His nerves gradually calmed.

'Have you used one of these before?' said Schmidt, holding it for him to see.

'I'm familiar with it. May I take a look?' said Rudolf, unable to suppress his curiosity. Anything to do with photography interested him, especially the different kinds of cameras that came onto the market. But this one was unlike the model he'd used to film his family on holidays. He carefully picked it up and examined it, noting that it was well used, with black paint peeling off in places.

Schmidt explained the workings with great enthusiasm. 'It's called the lunchbox, because it's portable and easy to use. It's a marvel. Devised by a German inventor called DeVry. It takes twenty-four frames per second, which provides a minute of filming. Why don't I set up the projector for you to see an example of what it can do? That white wall will do just fine.'

He spent some time setting up a spool of film into the projector, which he took out of the other suitcase. It took several attempts to get the contraption to work, because the film kept jamming. It made terrible squealing noises, but eventually the images crackled into life on the white wall. A series of blurry white letters appeared on a shaky black background, followed by several disconnected images of large groups of German soldiers marching in formation; then it switched to men wearing long coats and trilby hats talking and smoking in some café or other, while an educated German voice cut in to describe what they were discussing. It was hard to make out the words. The clip lasted barely a minute before it came to an abrupt halt.

'I'm afraid it's only a short sequence, but it should give you an idea of what we can do with this. I took it from a longer film of the returning troops marching to the Brandenburg Gate in Berlin after they'd taken Poland. It was a proud moment.' Schmidt took a handkerchief from his pocket, wiped his eyes and noisily blew his nose, emotion clearly getting the better of him.

'Thank you for the demonstration,' said Schlesinger. 'I'll take it from here. You can pack up the projector and leave us to our discussions.'

Schmidt clicked his heels together and lifted the palm of his hand up. 'Heil Hitler!'

After he'd left, Schlesinger turned to Rudolf. 'Impressive, isn't it? Do you think you can handle it?' He pointed to the cinecamera.

'It doesn't look too difficult. I'm sure I can get the hang of it. What is it you want me to do?'

'The kommandant is keen for you start a new project to make a documentary film of life in the camp. Similar to what you've been doing for him, but this project will be much bigger and more important. It will put Westerbork up there as an example to other camps. Your work will be seen across the whole of Germany. Just think, the story of Westerbork told through the lens of Rudolf Breslauer. It has quite a ring to it, don't you think?' Schlesinger guffawed, evidently pleased with his assessment of the task.

'If you say so,' said Rudolf remembering to smile, though he was beginning to shake inside. He didn't like the way this conversation was turning out.

'Come on, now. Where's your spirit?' said Schlesinger. 'Can't you see we're offering you a fantastic opportunity to make your mark and be remembered for your work?'

What glory was there to be had in filming the inside of a Nazi-run camp? was what Rudolf really wanted to say, but instead he replied, 'You seem to forget I'm a portrait photographer. And you want me to switch to becoming a film-maker. There's a world of difference between the two.'

Schlesinger looked uncomfortable and nervously rubbed his hands together. 'Herr Breslauer. Be reasonable. The kommandant has specifically requested that I put you in charge of filming footage of this camp. It really wouldn't do to refuse. I'm sure an intelligent man such as yourself can see that.'

There was no arguing with a man like Schlesinger, but Rudolf wasn't going to accept without some assurances. 'I need to know some details about the making of this film. Will I have any say over what happens to the raw footage and the final film?'

I wouldn't worry about any of that,' said Schlesinger quickly, and went on as if everything had been agreed between them. 'All I'm asking you to do is to go out and film what you see. And remember, we only want the positive stuff, but you know that already, don't you?' He proceeded to dig out several sheets of folded paper from his breast pocket, along with a fountain pen. 'One more thing. I just need your signature on this form. It's to confirm that you are in receipt of the camera and will return it in the same condition you received it.'

Rudolf took the pen and glanced through the closely typed wording, but was unable to make sense of it. The typeface seemed to swim in front of his eyes. 'Is this a contract?'

Schlesinger avoided Rudolf's eye, and said, 'As I said, it's for the receipt of the camera. It's just a formality. Please, your signature.' He jabbed at the place where he wanted him to sign.

Rudolf hesitated. Why was Schlesinger so eager for him to sign? Did his own job depend on it? But if he refused to sign, he was in no doubt that Schlesinger would turn against him in an instant. Unlike Philip, Rudolf knew his relationship with Schlesinger was complicated, and that no amount of persuading would keep the Breslauer family's names off the lists.

'It seems rather long,' he said doubtfully. 'Would you give me a moment while I read it through?'

Schlesinger huffed out a breath. 'All right. But I can't wait all day.'

It was a contract, and a lengthy one at that. He noted the date of completion of the project, which was one month from now. 'What happens after I've finished the work?' he made himself ask, though he suspected he already knew the answer.

'Listen, Rudolf,' said Schlesinger, who hadn't used his first name since that time in his Amsterdam studio. 'I'm doing you a favour. As long as the film is in production, neither you nor your family will be put on the transport list. I will personally guarantee that. Thereafter... I'm afraid it's out of my hands.'

THIRTY-SIX

Things came to a head when Ursula arrived back from school in tears saying that three of her classmates hadn't come in that day.

'The teacher won't say, but everyone knows they've been put on today's transport. Mama, I'm so scared they'll come for us next. Please say it won't happen,' she wailed.

Mischa, who was playing with a jigsaw puzzle on the floor, looked at her with big round eyes. His little face crumpled and he began to cry too. Meanwhile, Stefan stood stiffly beside his sister, his chin trembling as he tried to hide his own emotions.

Bella watched her children with a growing sense of dismay. How could she be expected to come up with a reasonable explanation as to why their names wouldn't appear on the next list?

She crossed the floor, scooped up Mischa and kissed his wet cheek, muttering soothing words until his sobs subsided, then turned to Ursula and said, 'Papa is doing everything he can to make sure it won't happen to us. The Germans respect his work as the camp photographer and that accounts for a lot. Please don't worry.'

'That's all very well for Papa. But they can still send us away, can't they?' said Ursula in that way she had of voicing uncomfortable truths.

Bella cast an anxious glance at Stefan and ventured a smile. 'No. We're a family and I won't allow them to split us up.' She meant to be reassuring, but it only made Ursula cry. Stefan remained rigid, his eyes fixed on her, disbelieving.

The door suddenly flew open and Rudolf came in, holding a small leather suitcase. At the sight of it, Stefan became inconsolable. 'You're leaving us, Papa, aren't you?' he cried out.

Rudolf put the case down and went straight over to Stefan and hugged him tight. 'I'm not going anywhere. I promise.'

Mischa still clung to Bella, who was watching Rudolf. She saw his eyes were filled with anguish as he looked at her over Stefan's shoulder. 'The suitcase?' she mouthed, anxious that it signified something sinister – she couldn't picture anything worse than Rudolf being taken away from them. She wondered whether she was mistaken, as she watched him ruffle Stefan's hair and tell him the suitcase was to do with his work.

All three children stopped crying as he brought out the cinecamera. 'This camera records moving images,' he said, and went through how it worked.

Curiosity got the better of Stefan as he moved in for a better look. 'Have you used it yet?'

'No touching,' said Rudolf with a gentle smile. 'I've only just been given it – well, I've been lent it to make a film of life in the camp.'

'Don't you already do that with your own camera?' asked Ursula sharply.

'I do, but this will be for a different purpose.'

'You mean like when you used to make holiday films of us... will it be like that?' Ursula kept on.

'Something like that,' Rudolf replied.

Bella watched their conversation and wondered why

Rudolf didn't elaborate. Was there something he was hiding from them?

But Ursula wasn't finished. 'Will you come into the classroom and film us like the last time? You didn't take my photo then, so will you now?'

'That's enough questions, Ursula,' said Bella quickly. 'This isn't about who will or won't be on the film.' She gave him a desperate look, willing him to agree with her, but the way he dropped his gaze made her even more convinced there was more to this business of the cinecamera than he was letting on.

Ursula shrugged her shoulders and suddenly seemed to lose interest in the whole idea. 'I need to go and talk to Bekkah,' she announced, before turning to stare at Rudolf. 'About things.'

It wasn't until later, when the two of them were alone, that Bella broached the subject again. She'd been brooding over the conversation between Ursula and her father when the reason for her daughter's strange behaviour suddenly hit her. Bella had been so flattered by Rudolf's thoughtful birthday gift that it hadn't occurred to her that the photo must have been one of several he'd taken of their older children.

Rudolf was studying the workings of the cinecamera; he looked up in surprise when she confronted him.

'Why did you lie to me?' she asked him, her voice dangerously quiet.

'What are you talking about?' he said in a startled voice.

She watched his face carefully, wondering if he was feigning surprise. Always, she'd believed she knew and understood him, but now she wasn't so sure. 'Admit it – you've been taking photos of the children against my wishes. For the kommandant.'

He shook his head in a gesture of irritation and opened his

mouth to speak, but she silenced him by lifting a finger in the air.

'Rudolf, you're better than this. You broke your promise to me. Please don't pretend you didn't. I know that you've been getting the children to pose for you. When did it all start?'

He took in a long shuddery breath and gave her a desperate look. 'I've been under such pressure from the kommandant. Schlesinger too. They want so much more from me, but I couldn't see how I can manage it. You know what it's like here... I tried my best to film people looking happy, but it's become impossible.' He ran his hands through his grey-streaked dark hair, which she noticed had grown long. He looked older, and with a shock she realised she probably did too. And who wouldn't in this dreadful place? All at once she felt a swell of sympathy for him, but almost as quickly it vanished as she thought of the kommandant examining photographs of her children.

'But we discussed it. You promised to keep them out of it.' She moved away from him, unable to face him. 'Ursula knows what you're up to, doesn't she? Is she complicit in what you're doing?'

Rudolf came to her side and gently leaned his head against hers. He spoke haltingly, his voice starting to crack. 'No, *Liebchen*. Ursula's just angry with me, and I can't blame her. Even though my intentions were harmless about wanting to make a nice photograph for your birthday, she saw right through what I was doing. I want you to know I haven't been left with any other choice. If I don't deliver what the kommandant is demanding it'll be all over for us.'

'I know it's hard for you,' she said wearily. 'Are you going to tell me what those evil men want from you now?' She looked askance at the cinecamera lying in the open case.

'To make a propaganda film showing how well run this camp is. You know I don't believe in it. But I suspect the kommandant is coming under pressure from Nazi high command to show that he's capable of running this place, to prove he's up to the job. Bella, there's something else you should know.'

He gazed into her eyes with an intensity that made her nervous. All she'd wanted was for him to be truthful to her, but she wasn't sure she was ready to hear what he was about to say. 'Go on,' she made herself say.

'Schlesinger has forced me to sign a contract. As long as the film is in production, our names won't appear on the Tuesday list.'

'I don't understand. What does that even mean?' Bella went rigid with cold as she realised there was no way out for them now, however much Rudolf had been trying to avoid the inevitable.

Rudolf was still gazing at her. 'It means they will do what they like when they like. I have to give them what they want, but I will keep on at Schlesinger to keep our names off the list. I honestly think he's our only hope.'

THIRTY-SEVEN
AUGUST 2023

Eloise

Any misgivings Eloise might have had about James's intentions in visiting Westerbork quickly disappeared when he presented her with the details. He'd arranged it all, the date and time of their appointment with the assistant curator, who said she would be delighted to show them the photographs and discuss what other material had come to light from the archives.

Their journey took them by boat to the Hook of Holland, where they spent several days on the coast before travelling to Amsterdam and visiting the main sights, all prearranged by James, who had booked them a delightful hotel in a converted tall townhouse on one of the canals.

'I think I could quite easily live in Amsterdam,' she mused over breakfast one morning. 'Everyone's so easy-going here, and you don't even need to speak Dutch.'

James nodded. 'Shame really everyone speaks English,' he said. 'You know, I even learned a few Dutch phrases I was hoping to impress you with.'

'You learned some Dutch for me?' said Eloise with a laugh and laid a hand fondly over his. She knew very few words of Dutch herself; it had never occurred to her to learn. How typically sweet of James to do that, she thought, and was touched by his gesture.

'Well, yes, but that wasn't the only reason,' he admitted. 'I thought it might come in handy when we're looking through documents at Westerbork.'

'Oh,' she said, feeling deflated. 'I thought the purpose of the visit was mainly to see my great-grandfather's photographs. Or did you have something else in mind?'

'No, of course not. But you know me, I like to be prepared.' He smiled, but Eloise wondered if there was something he wasn't telling her. She was sure he meant nothing by it and had to remind herself that he was making an effort to make their trip a success.

They left Amsterdam Central station on a train travelling east, which gradually emptied out the further away from Amsterdam they travelled.

For most of the journey, James had his head in a book about the history of Westerbork, but Eloise was unable to settle as she stared out of the window at the countryside flashing past. It was the first time since they'd arrived in Holland that she'd fully appreciated the flatness of the landscape, the endless green fields, farmhouses with deep thatched roofs and the occasional old-fashioned windmill with slowly turning sails. As the train passed through small towns she was much taken with the unusual design of the houses, the geometric shapes and roofs at odd angles and the way the Dutch liked to fill their large picture windows with house plants. Eventually, the scenery changed and soon they were travelling through extensive beech and pine woods; she glimpsed people on bikes just visible through the trees. She noticed the train was stopping more frequently now and more people left the train than got on.

'Two more stops after this one,' said James, smiling, as he looked up from his book to check the name of the station they'd just pulled into.

'Tell me what you've been reading,' said Eloise, glancing at the cover, which depicted a black watchtower beside a broken rail track. In one corner was a smaller black-and-white image showing crowds of people with what looked like sacks slung over their shoulders as they waited to board a train.

James put the book down with a sigh. 'It's about the history of Westerbork and how it was once a refugee camp set up by the Dutch for German and Austrian Jews fleeing from the Nazis. That was in 1939, before the Germans occupied the Netherlands. During the war, they took over the camp, which is near the German border, and turned it over to a transit camp for the deportation of Jews from all over the Netherlands. More than 100,000 people were taken from there on ninety-three transports to Auschwitz and other concentration camps.'

Eloise took a sharp intake of breath. 'So it switched from being a place where Jews felt safe from persecution to something more sinister that was the complete opposite? My family must have been absolutely terrified not knowing what was about to hit them.'

James frowned, nodding his agreement. 'The worst of it was that the Germans hid their real intentions by creating the impression that Westerbork was still a place where people could lead normal lives. No one had any idea what was in store for them when they arrived. Any hope they might be spared deportation proved entirely false.'

Eloise felt a rush of despair as she grabbed the book and flicked through the pages, expecting to see photos of human suffering. But what she discovered was something quite different. She stopped at a chapter entitled 'The Westerbork Theatre' showing pictures of an orchestra, a pianist and actors with joyful expressions on their faces putting on a revue. She kept turning the pages and saw a picture of a farm with workers, another of a group of women doing gymnastics, children at work in a classroom. It was extraordinary. People looked happy. With a dawning realisation, she turned to James. 'These were taken by my great-grandfather, weren't they?'

'I'm almost certain they were,' said James, 'but we'll need confirmation.'

'He must have hated pretending that everything was fine when there was so much suffering all around him. No doubt the kommandant made sure he didn't film the awful truth.'

'That's the interesting thing. Rudolf Breslauer was an intelligent man who walked all over the camp with his camera and must have realised what the Germans were up to. Did he take other photos in secret? I'm certain he did. And if that was the case, whatever happened to them?' He rubbed his hands together. 'I'm hoping that's what we're about to find out.'

Eloise sighed. 'I don't think it'll be that simple. It would have been too risky for him to take incriminating evidence out of the camp when he was deported to Auschwitz. He knew he could have been searched before he boarded the train. But if he'd managed to smuggle his photos with him, the Auschwitz guards would have immediately removed them along with all his other possessions. And if they had discovered any photographs that put them in a bad light, they would have surely destroyed them. He must have known he was taking an enormous risk, but why?' She shook her head sadly. 'Perhaps we'll never know.'

'Let's not jump to any conclusions just yet,' said James as the train pulled into the next station. 'This is where we get off.'

He got up and lifted their backpacks off the rack. 'What we're about to find out is so exciting.'

Eloise laughed at his enthusiasm but couldn't quite match his mood. She so wanted to be optimistic, but it didn't feel right to get her hopes up just yet. Not just because the whole mystery over Rudolf Breslauer directly concerned her, but because what she really wanted was to bring back good news for her grandma.

THIRTY-EIGHT

SPRING 1943

Rudolf

It was early morning and already there was a warmth in the air and the sound of joyful birdsong promising a beautiful spring day ahead. Yet Rudolf barely noticed. Having kissed Bella goodbye, he was on his way to shoot footage of the dreaded Tuesday transport. Philip had told him the details of what happened on these occasions, how people were callously ordered onto the platform to find out if their names were on the list. It was a complete lottery as to whether they'd been spared or not. Rudolf could barely imagine just how terrified they must feel.

He'd been meticulous about keeping the spools of film for Gemmeker separate from those he'd earmarked for his own purposes. It took some doing, but he managed to persuade the kommandant to allow him to go in person to the Agfa photographic shop in Arnhem for supplies, saying that only he could discuss the details of the types of film and papers he needed. By chance, Rudolf knew the owner of the shop, who used to supply materials for his studio in Amsterdam, so they came to a private arrangement over the additional canisters of film he needed to carry out his secret documentary. He'd been careful not to tell the owner the specific purpose of his request in case it got back to the kommandant. As he set out to start filming, he was beset with nerves.

People were beginning to gather nervously in groups on the platform. The train was ready and waiting. The beast loomed larger and was significantly longer than in his imagination. Not a regular train with carriages for passengers, but wooden cattle wagons without windows and doors, with iron bars to lock the cargo in place that could only be opened from the outside. Rudolf glanced up and read the destination board nailed to the side of the train. It read:

BERGEN-BELSEN

He looked away quickly with a wave of nausea, and was unable to rid himself of the claustrophobic feeling that crept up on him as he tried to envisage being crammed inside there for hours on end. If the rumours were true, the terrible journey would last for days. He made himself concentrate on what he had set out to do. Something that was not included in his brief from the kommandant and that would land him in deep trouble if he were found out. But his mind was made up. The cinecamera in his hands gave him the power to do what no other man was able to. He was determined to carry it through at all costs – even if it meant putting his precious family at risk.

Rudolf strode down the platform, hoping to reach the front of the train so he could get a view looking back, but after five minutes of walking there was still no end to the line of carriages stretching away like a menacing snake about to pounce. He'd never witnessed anything of such scale. Wearily, he retraced his steps.

He took himself over to a copse of trees by the side of the platform where he could position himself out of view. He opened his leather bag and took out the rectangular cinecamera, which he set up ready for use.

By now, the platform was filling up with men, women and children dressed in their winter coats and wearing hats and woollen scarves, despite the gathering warmth of the day. They held on to their possessions, an assortment of leather and cardboard suitcases, or wore haversacks strapped to their backs or carried large, overstuffed bags. He saw that many pieces of luggage had crudely written names in thick black or white lettering. Given the hundreds of people congregating here, this was the only thing distinguishing them from the next person.

The idea of filming suddenly sickened him, despite the promise he'd made to himself. He gazed around at these stoical faces: an elderly gentleman, dapper in his black coat and grey trilby hat, with a neatly trimmed white goatee beard. He wore a yellow star, like the majority of the others. What can he be thinking, feeling? Rudolf wondered. Close by, a man was kissing a woman in a dark red coat with great passion, the two of them oblivious to the sea of people circulating around them. Nobody, except Rudolf, seemed to notice this tender moment.

His hands shook as he forced himself to start filming. He tore his eyes away and saw a young man, cleanly shaven and in a beret, upright and proud, trying to hold his emotions together; a mother fussing over her twin boys and making sure the collars of their coats were straight. All of it was unbearable to witness. He tried to push from his mind that these people could so easily be Bella, Mischa, Ursula and Stefan. He had a job to do, he told himself. He mustn't let his emotions get the better of him.

Gemmeker arrived in full uniform riding his bicycle, which he handed to one of his people. He looked confident; he was clearly the man in charge. He consulted his clipboard and strode up and down issuing instructions to his officers, who were gathering in large numbers to police the crowds.

And then Schlesinger turned up and marched straight to

the kommandant. Rudolf watched the two of them in heated discussion. Gemmeker was jabbing his finger at the clipboard and Schlesinger looked distinctly uncomfortable. It seemed to Rudolf that he was being given a telling-off over the lists. Then it occurred to him that he and Philip weren't the only people Schlesinger had made promises to about keeping their names off the list, and that Gemmeker wasn't happy about it. He quickly suppressed this thought and what it meant for him and his family as he secretly let the film roll.

There was now a palpable tension building amongst the prisoners, who still had no idea whether their names were about to be read out. So many people were now crowding on to the platform that Rudolf realised no one would take any notice of him if he mingled amongst them. He went to stand with his back to the train. From here, he could observe every-one, their movements and interactions, and quietly record what he saw.

He was lost in concentration when he heard his name. He turned to see Philip sauntering towards him with his hands in his pockets. He certainly didn't look as if his name was about to be called.

'You're confident you're not on the list then,' said Rudolf, switching off the camera momentarily. Philip shrugged. He seemed nonchalant, as if he didn't care, but Rudolf guessed it was probably a cover for his nerves.

Philip replied, 'I check with Schlesinger every week on Monday evening and so far it's worked.'

Both men looked over at Schlesinger, who was still locked in conversation with Gemmeker. Was something amiss? Rudolf wondered.

People were now gathering in their hundreds. Philip watched impassively. 'It's the same every week – this enormous mangy snake will crawl away with thousands of people on board.' Then turning to Rudolf, he spoke in a flat monotone.

'Save some film for when they wheel in the sick and dump them like so much baggage into the carriages.'

At that moment, there was a crackle over the loudspeaker, and the whole platform fell silent. Rudolf had to strain to hear but quickly picked up that the list was about to be announced. There was a ripple of murmuring voices as the disembodied voice began to call name after name after name. A shiver shot through him, like an electric shock. He watched people wail, cry out or sob silently as they clung to their loved ones.

As soon as the loudspeaker fell silent, the SS officers surged forward and began herding people on to the waiting train. Rudolf's photographer's instincts kicked in and he set the camera rolling. No one noticed the man in their midst. They were all lost in their own personal story, their own grief and whether they were the ones boarding the train or the so-called lucky ones left behind this time.

Rudolf turned at a sudden loud clacking and grinding sound, to see a stretcher consisting of a flat platform in between two enormous wooden wheels being manoeuvred towards the train. The porter, Jewish judging from the yellow star on his jacket, was visibly sweating from the exertion. The poor soul who lay on this contraption looked so ill that Rudolf was convinced she wouldn't survive being loaded onto the cattle wagon with so many others.

He looked around for Philip, but he had gone. Still, he kept the camera rolling, documenting people's fear and distress, until an SS officer came marching as if heading towards him, slamming shut the doors and locking them. He stopped filming when the officer came close, briefly turning his back on him.

There were still people milling about on the platform, for all the world looking as if they'd come to see off a family member or friend on holiday. They stood watching and waving as the mangy snake shook and rattled into life, slowly taking its human cargo away.

Rudolf didn't care any more if he were seen with the camera in his hand. He stood gazing up as wagon after wagon rolled by.

Suddenly, his attention was caught by the face of a young girl wearing a blue headscarf – she couldn't have been more than fifteen – appearing between two wooden slats of one of the carriages. She was staring straight at him with a mixture of confusion and fear written on her young face. Surely she couldn't have been all alone? The idea that she had been separated from her family and forced to leave the camp with all these strangers, not knowing where she was being taken, was unbearable.

Their eyes met for the briefest of moments. Then, with a jolt of recognition, he realised he'd seen her before, with her own people, who lived in caravans at the edge of the camp. She must be a Sinti persecuted by the Nazis for no good reason other than the prejudice they held against her kind.

Rudolf looked straight into her eyes and her lips parted. She seemed to be about to shout out something to him.

In a split second, he was forced to make a decision: listen to her plea for help or record the scene unfolding before his eyes. With his heart in his mouth, he let the camera roll until the film ran out.

THIRTY-NINE
AUGUST 2023

'Liesbeth Hendrick. You must be Eloise, the great-granddaughter of Rudolf Breslauer. It is indeed an honour to meet you.' The woman's eyes shone as she warmly shook Eloise's hand. She was the assistant curator of Westerbork's museum, a tall Dutch woman, dressed elegantly in a beige trouser suit with a silk scarf tied at the neck.

Eloise nodded and flushed with embarrassment. She had no idea what to expect from this meeting, and just hoped it would go some way to explaining what really did happen to her family. 'I'm pleased to meet you, but I don't know a lot about him. My grandmother hasn't said much about her father or his work, apart from showing me a few photographs.'

'I hope we can rectify that.' The woman turned to shake James's hand. 'Thank you for getting in touch. We had no idea Breslauer had any living relatives before we received your email.'

James gave her a courteous smile. 'All thanks are due to my tutor. Without his contact at the museum none of this would have been possible. We're both excited to see what you have to show us.' He glanced at Eloise, who nodded a little uncertainly. She didn't want to admit that she was nervous about what she was about to find out.

'Please come through to our archive library, where we can talk undisturbed,' said Liesbeth, and led the way to the back of the building and into a long room housing row upon row of shelving containing neatly labelled cardboard box files. Along one wall was a stack of shallow drawers, the kind used for large documents, maps or photographs that needed to be kept flat. She motioned to the two of them to sit at a round white table with a stack of files in the centre. Before taking a seat herself, she offered them coffee, before going over to a smart chrome machine to make them all a cup. She then came over to sit between them. 'I'm sure you're impatient to see what material we have in the archives, but first I want to tell you what we do know about your great-grandfather. You must stop me if any of this is already familiar to you.'

Eloise was anxious to get started. Having come all this way, she didn't want to miss a thing. 'Please don't assume I know anything. Do tell us everything you know.'

'Of course.' Liesbeth smiled and Eloise felt herself relax. 'It was unusual for people to be taken to Westerbork unless they were prisoners of the Nazis. Rudolf Breslauer was brought here to take on the job of camp photographer and was forced to bring his family too. I think this is important if we're to understand his state of mind when he took on the job. This was a man who'd worked all his life in the family business. He'd entrusted his photographic shop and studio to a Jewish friend to look after in the belief that one day he'd return. He lost everything – his job, his home – except his family, which was the one thing he still had. He would have wanted to protect them at all costs.'

Eloise nodded. 'My grandma was twelve when they went to

Westerbork. She must have been aware of all this, but she's never talked much about it.'

'Survivors of the camps often find it difficult to talk about their experiences. Even in Westerbork, where no one died directly at the hands of the Nazis.' Liesbeth removed the top file from the pile in front of her and opened it. 'We're very excited by what we've discovered because his work is the only true visual record of events that occurred at Westerbork. What makes them unique is that there are no photographs or films taken inside any other Nazi-run camps, as far as we know. So when you see footage inside the camps in Second World War documentaries, they will almost certainly have been taken by Rudolf Breslauer. What excites us at Westerbork is that even more photographs of his are coming to light. They're giving us a more rounded, more complete picture of what life was like for prisoners inside the camp.'

She turned to the file in front of her. 'The photos we've collected will go into a special exhibition of his work, which we are holding next summer.' She spread a selection of black-and-white images on the table. 'Not all of these were from our archives. A few came to us later in donations to the museum.'

The photos she had laid out were of children and Eloise instantly recognised Ursula as a smiling little girl, her hand resting on a book. Next to it was another of a younger boy, grinning for the camera and in a similar pose – Stefan.

'School photos,' she murmured, then turned her attention to the next one. She paused, examined it carefully and frowned. There were three children in this photo: she recognised Ursula, Stefan, but there was also a boy who was not much more than a toddler. The three of them were sitting at a piano, their mouths open as they sang. Eloise turned it over and saw the date written there: 1942. That was the year before the family went to Westerbork.

'I don't understand,' said Eloise, looking up, puzzled. It

didn't make sense. In all their discussions, her grandmother had only ever referred to having one brother. Even though Eloise had long suspected she might have had more siblings, seeing proof of a second brother was startling. She could only think that something terrible must have happened to him for her grandmother to deliberately avoid talking about him. 'My grandmother only mentioned one brother, called Stefan.' She pointed her finger at the toddler. 'Never two.' She peered at the names written below the photo in pencil. Ursula, Stefan. 'Mish… I'm not sure I can read it. Is that his name?'

'I believe so. Mischa is written here,' said Liesbeth.

'Do you have any idea why my grandmother denied telling me about him?'

Liesbeth shook her head. 'It's hard to know. Perhaps you should ask her.'

'It's like this sweet little boy never existed,' Eloise said with tears in her voice. She felt James move towards her and put an arm round her shoulders. Grateful to have him next to her, she took a deep breath. 'Can you tell me how you came by these?'

'They were handed in to the museum some years after the war in a suitcase, which we believe the Breslauers had left with a friend. It often happened that Jews asked Christian friends to look after valuables before they were deported. The descendants of these friends found the suitcase when they were clearing the house, and wanted to donate it to us. These photos come from an album in that suitcase.' She slid across a small sepia-coloured photo of a young smiling Ursula wearing a crown of flowers on her head. 'This one is of your great-grandmother as a little girl. Ursula Breslauer, aged eight, is written on the back.'

Eloise smiled as she turned it over. She tried hard to put the revelation of a third child out of her head for now. 'I also have a couple of photos I'd like to show you.' She reached for her bag and brought out the photograph of Ursula aged thirteen that she'd found in her copy of *Pride and Prejudice*. Then she scrolled in her phone till she found the photo of Ursula and Stefan sitting outside on a rug. 'The children were older in this photo and you can see they look quite different to the earlier ones,' she said. 'Ursula's a teenager and wore her hair in braids. And Stefan wore wire-framed glasses.'

Liesbeth took her time examining the image, enlarging it with two fingers, then bringing it back to the actual size. Looking up she said, 'This is remarkable. We have a photo just like this one in our collection. Let me find it for you.' It took her a few minutes to locate it from one of the other box files. When she laid it side by side with the phone image, Eloise could see the two were almost identical.

'Incredible,' said Liesbeth to herself. 'We always assumed they were of other children in the camp. We never suspected they were Breslauer's own children. But wait, I have others, which must also have been taken at that time.' She removed a sheaf of photos from a separate folder and they went through them one by one. There were several of other children besides Ursula and Stefan, many taken in classroom settings. The two siblings were often photographed together, walking towards the camera or playing a ball game. Stefan featured in more photos than Ursula, and looked the perfect studious pupil as he bent over his schoolwork. Another was of him making wooden toys on a workbench.

'Mischa doesn't appear in any of the pictures,' said Eloise. It was the first thing she noticed and it made her wonder why.

'I suppose if we'd had other photos of the three siblings we would have realised these ones were of the Breslauer children,' said Liesbeth.

There was a knock at the door and a young woman put her head round. 'Your next visitor is waiting for you,' she said.

'Tell them I'll be a few more minutes.' Liesbeth turned back to Eloise. 'There's still so much you should see. I'd like to show you some of the raw video footage from the films Breslauer took. Can you come back tomorrow morning? I have a free hour at eleven o'clock.'

Eloise glanced at James, who nodded enthusiastically. 'We'd love to,' she said.

'Good. I'll expect you then.' She shuffled the photos back into the folders and replaced them in the box file, before showing them out.

As they stood in the lobby, she shook them both warmly by the hand. 'I can't tell you how exciting this discovery about Rudolf's children is for us. It will put the exhibition in a whole new light.'

After they had left the building, Eloise was unable to put the revelation of Mischa out of her mind. 'None of it makes sense,' she said to James as they went to wait for a bus to take them back to their hotel. 'I even asked Grandma if she had any other siblings and she just avoided answering my question. I believed her, but now I've seen these photos it makes me wonder why she didn't tell me the truth.'

James didn't have any answers, but at least he lent her a sympathetic ear. 'I doubt she meant to lie. I suspect something terrible must have occurred to Mischa that she's never managed to get over.'

'Yes, that's what I've been thinking.' Eloise looked up as their bus approached their stop. 'And if it's true, it's so terribly sad. I have to find a way of asking her about it.'

FORTY

SPRING 1943

Rudolf

The train slunk away at a snail's pace. It clunked and shuddered, the wheels grating and squealing as it pulled away. There were a few stragglers left on the platform, who stood with upturned faces in the hope of catching a glimpse of a loved one in between the wooden slats of the locked doors.

Rudolf kept his head down as he hurried along the platform in the direction of the Grote Zaal, the reception centre for arrivals where he had his studio. He was anxious to get back and conceal the evidence of what he'd just recorded. Part of him wished he hadn't come. He'd taken an enormous risk turning up to film what the Germans did not want the world to see.

Occasionally he glanced up at the train, and saw pairs of eyes staring out through the slats. Suddenly he heard someone cry out above the noise of the train.

'Please help me!' It was a woman's plaintive voice.

Rudolf's step faltered as he considered shouting out words of comfort, but the train suddenly sped up, and the woman in the wagon was gone. But as he watched the train disappear into the distance, he saw something flutter to the ground a little way ahead of him. He caught sight of something scrawled on a piece of lined paper torn from a notebook. Picking it up, he wondered if it was meant for him, then realised it was addressed to someone else.

Dear Mother,

By the time you read this I will have left Westerbork on a train. I don't know where they are taking us, but please don't worry about me. I can look after myself and will do all I can to get back home. As soon as I am able, I'll write you a proper letter.

Your loving daughter,

Sarah

Rudolf wondered if the woman he'd heard cry out had pushed the note through a crack, hoping that he would help. But it had no name or address and had clearly been written in a hurry. Rudolf folded it in two and two again and stuffed it into his pocket, knowing there was nothing he could do to reunite it with the person for whom it was intended. On top of everything else, he couldn't think what to do about it right now.

Rudolf was in his darkroom marking up the circular metal can containing the film when there was a knock at the door. He hurriedly hid it in a drawer under a sheaf of photographic paper and went to open up. He tried to look nonchalant.

'Philip,' he said, relieved. 'Come in and sit down. I managed to lay my hands on half a bottle of jenever, which was lying around after Gemmeker's last shindig. Would you like a nip? I know I would.' He thought Philip looked terrible, not that he would have said. He suspected he didn't look much better.

'You're good to me, Rudolf. Thank you. A drink would help steady the nerves. It doesn't matter how many times I do this, it always gets to me,' Philip said with a shudder.

'Please. Sit down.' Rudolf gestured to a chair next to the workbench, on which there were several developing trays next to a large sheet of white paper with strips of negatives pinned on to it. 'Do take a look. They're the last of the prints Gemmeker asked for. I haven't decided which ones to give him.'

Philip took his time, slightly frowning as he held the negatives up to the beam of light from a small desk lamp.

'Here. Drink up,' said Rudolf, after he'd poured their drinks and pulled up a stool for himself. 'What do you think?'

'I think you're a very talented photographer. And frankly, they don't deserve to have you.' Philip emptied his glass in one gulp, then turned to Rudolf with a rueful grin. 'If I were you, I'd hold back as many as you dare.'

Rudolf shrugged off his compliment. 'Which ones then?'

'For certain, this one.' He pointed to a photo of a young woman with a scarf tied at her neck, relaxing against a haybale with a basket of vegetables beside her. She was shielding her eyes from the sun and smiling at someone or something out of shot. It was one of a group of photos Rudolf had been allowed to take outside the camp, on Westerbork's own farm, where prisoners were put to work. Another showed a group of young men sorting potatoes into wicker baskets; then there was one of sheep grazing peacefully in a field; another sheep was looking towards the camera. There was also a striking image of a shirtless man stoking a fire in the metal foundry where old scrap metal was melted down to be made into ammunition for the Germans.

'I can see these attracting a great deal of attention in a future exhibition of your work,' Philip said. 'You have so much material here. You simply mustn't hand everything over. They'll never know what's missing.' He shifted himself in his seat so he could retrieve an exercise book from his jacket. 'I decided today this will be the last one I give you. I don't have the appetite to keep recording everyone's misery while I keep managing to avoid the inevitable. Can you put this one with the others?'

As he took it, Rudolf felt a well of sadness. Philip seemed to know it was the end of the line for him and was bearing it stoically. 'Has something happened to change your mind?'

Philip glanced to the side as he chose his words. 'As long as you're working for Gemmeker you'll be spared, but there's no earthly reason why my name won't come up for one of the transports now. I've run out of options, but I'm hearing that Bergen-Belsen and Theresienstadt aren't nearly as bad as Auschwitz. So I'm going to try for the lesser evil. Maybe that's just an illusion, but Schlesinger assures me he'll arrange a seat for me on one of the trains to Theresienstadt.' He gave a dry laugh as if he didn't quite believe it himself.

'What makes you so sure your name will come up? You've managed to avoid it so far.' Rudolf nervously fingered the notebook now in his possession.

'I'm not sure, but I have a strong feeling my time will be up soon. Please don't be sad on my behalf.'

But Rudolf was sad. In fact, he was bereft. 'If it wasn't for you, Philip, I couldn't have done any of this. I'm not sure I'll have the nerve to continue once you're gone. I want you to know – you're the only friend here who I can really trust.'

'I feel the same way, but it's time to face facts.' As Philip stood up, he held on to the edge of the table to steady himself.

'Let me at least show you where I've hidden our evidence,' said Rudolf quickly. He was reluctant to let Philip go, knowing it would be for the very last time.

He opened the drawer and retrieved the film can before going to the back of the room, where he unlocked the secret cupboard. He removed several cardboard boxes shielding the entrance so he could get at Philip's diaries, in their dozen or so exercise books in different colours. There was a stack of his own prints, and also film canisters containing negatives and several reels of film. The two men silently took in the spectacle before looking at one another. Rudolf then walked Philip to the door of his studio. Before opening it, he said, 'I wanted you to see it all. In case you're the one who comes back.' He so wanted to believe his own words, but in his heart he knew that neither of them would return.

Philip nodded unconvincingly, looking resigned. 'Well, we've done what we set out to do. The rest is now out of our hands.'

FORTY-ONE
AUGUST 2023

Eloise

Eloise spent a restless night turning over what she'd learned at Westerbork. The revelation that her relatives had been forced to relinquish everything dear to them was heartbreaking enough, but to have confirmation that they'd had three children and not two as she had believed was at least some relief. Why had Rudolf Breslauer taken photos of his children knowing they would be used by the Nazis in their propaganda for Westerbork? But what bothered her most was why her grandma had never mentioned she had a little brother and evaded the subject whenever Eloise had raised it. Why hadn't he appeared in any photographs after the family had left Amsterdam? Eloise had an urge to know more, even though she knew she shouldn't probe her grandmother for painful memories she wanted to suppress.

The next morning Eloise and James went back early to Westerbork so they could walk along a winding woodland path towards the former site of the transit camp. When they came to a long tarmac road flanked with tall wooden posts positioned all the way along its length, James consulted his map and told her it was the former railway track that ran all the way into the camp.

Eloise wandered off to look at the posts, which had brass plates nailed onto them. 'Auschwitz, Bergen-Belsen, Theresienstadt... these must represent the destinations of the trains. What do you think the numbers mean?'

James read out from the leaflet he was holding. 'Each post represents the name of a concentration camp and the number of prisoners who were taken there from Westerbork. There were 107,000 people who left Westerbork on transports.'

'Each train must have had hundreds of carriages,' said Eloise, moving into the centre of the road and gazing at the sight of all the wooden posts disappearing into the far distance.

Lost in thought, they walked on in silence until they came to a large green-and-white-painted wooden house with a balcony on the first floor. Strangely, it was entirely encased in glass.

'Was this connected to the camp in some way?' Eloise said, turning to James with a shudder.

James looked at his leaflet. 'It was built for the director of Westerbork while it was still a refugee camp. The German kommandant, a man called Albert Gemmeker, took over the running of the place when it became a transit camp. Apparently, his bedroom was on the side of the house with the balcony because it overlooked the camp. Probably to keep an eye on things.'

'That's so creepy,' said Eloise, wrapping her arms round herself. 'I wonder why they didn't just knock the place down. They seem to have got rid of everything else.' She stared up at it for a few minutes longer. She wondered if her great-grandfather had ever been inside. She imagined him standing on the balcony next to the kommandant as he proudly described everything to him. More than anything she'd seen so far, it was this thought that disturbed her the most. She turned away. 'Come on. Let's see what else there is.'

The camp was well laid out, with information boards in Dutch and English and an audio guide providing further detail. They walked along the former boulevard that divided the camp in two, giving a sense of how many barrack buildings there'd been. At the far end stood a solitary wooden barrack, the sole building to have been saved from destruction. As they moved towards it, the sun suddenly broke through from behind a cloud, creating the illusion that the building was large, light and airy. The truth couldn't have been more different, James explained, and read out how few facilities there were for the prisoners forced to share such limited space. Each barrack had housed seventy prisoners, with rows of bunk beds stacked three high. One chamber pot and twenty cold-water taps were provided for the whole hut.

'Thank goodness my family didn't have to endure this,' said Eloise with a shiver, though in her heart she knew that their lives couldn't have been any more tolerable.

They finished off their tour standing in front of a memorial to the different groups of prisoners: the Jews, Sinti and Roma and those who had been members of the Dutch resistance. They were represented by 107,000 stones laid out on the ground in the form of a map of the Netherlands. As Eloise walked in between the terracotta stones of differing heights, she noted that almost every stone had been stamped with a metal Jewish star signifying those who had perished here.

Back at the museum, they still had some time before Liesbeth was ready to see them. James was keen to go to the bookshop in search of more books on Westerbork, and Eloise wandered round the exhibits.

In the main exhibition space, she was immediately struck by

the large number of shabby cardboard and leather suitcases stacked on top of one another, with more lying open to display their contents. She realised these suitcases represented people who'd had the misfortune to spend time in Westerbork. On the inside lid of each suitcase was the name of its owner, with family photographs and a description of their lives before they were sent to Westerbork. She was surprised to see that Anne Frank's was amongst those shown and that her diary lay in her battered black leather suitcase. She thought it unlikely it was the original but it served as a poignant reminder of the heart-rending story of the brave and fearless young girl, who ended up at Bergen-Belsen, where she died.

Eloise moved from one display case to another and lost herself in these personal stories. One suitcase had belonged to a nurse and was filled with medicines, bandages and a few personal effects. Did this nurse imagine she would be able to treat prisoners inside the camp? Eloise deliberated. Another was a child's suitcase and contained a couple of well-thumbed storybooks, a photograph of two smiling young girls – sisters, or best friends, Eloise guessed – a pack of playing cards and a skipping rope. What struck Eloise was the optimism with which many of these people must have packed for a journey, fully expecting to return home. It was heartbreaking.

She carried on till she came to a large wooden structure, a reconstruction of part of a barracks similar to the one in the camp. Inside was a metal bunk, three beds high; a makeshift washing line was attached to a nail hammered into a wooden slat on the wall and there were open suitcases with clothing spilling out on all the beds. She noticed there were no bedclothes, only lumpy, stained mattresses. On the floor lay rows of shoes, boots and even a pair of clogs. In one corner stood a small black stove and next to it a wicker basket containing logs; a kettle stood on top of the stove, which she guessed must have been used to boil water for washing.

Sighing, she turned to see James walking towards her holding a carrier bag from the museum shop. He held it up with a sheepish grin. 'I couldn't resist buying some more books about Westerbork. Fortunately, they're in English,' he said, and planted a kiss on her cheek. 'Anyway, I came to get you. Liesbeth is ready to see us now.'

Eloise smiled and reached for his hand. 'I'm glad I had some time to myself to look round, but I think I've seen enough.'

Liesbeth greeted them warmly and took them through to a meeting room set up with a projector and screen. A young man was feeding a long spool of film into the projector and nodded a brief greeting.

'Paul and I have been examining closely some of the raw film footage in the light of what you told us yesterday. Why don't we take a look?' The assistant switched off the lights and they sat in darkness as the film began to roll.

Eloise put her elbows on the table and rested her chin in her hands. The screen lit up with a series of black-and-white images that were already familiar to her, but seeing the film filled her with great sadness. There was her great-grandmother, swinging Ursula and Stefan round and round. All three were laughing with joy. The camera zoomed in to a close-up of Bella's face, and kept filming her laughter for a good ten seconds, before the screen stuttered into blackness. Next came a close-up of Stefan bent over a wooden toy he was whittling with a small knife. He didn't seem to be aware that he was being filmed, and the camera lingered on him for a long moment. None of the sequences were connected but they all showed only the two older Breslauer children, never Mischa. She wondered if the reason he wasn't present in these shots was because he'd already died, perhaps succumbing to some childhood illness. The next few seconds of film showed Ursula and Stefan walking towards the camera and a man's voice could be heard urging Ursula to do something. Eloise shifted in her seat and leaned forward, but she couldn't catch his words. Then Ursula looked straight at the camera and gave a slight smile. All the while Stefan skipped beside her as if he didn't have a care in the world.

Eloise frowned as she peered at the backdrop. She immediately recognised the kommandant's wooden house. She gave a quiet gasp. 'What was Rudolf doing filming them in front of that house? It must have been deliberate.'

'OK, Paul, let's pause it there,' said Liesbeth, getting up to switch on the lights again. 'What you've seen is just a small part of the film Breslauer made for the German authorities. They were intending to turn it into a propaganda film, but it never happened. By then, the game was up and all the Germans could think about was saving their own skins.'

Eloise shook her head – it just didn't make sense. 'What was my great-grandfather thinking, using his own children as pawns?' It seemed such a callous, insensitive thing to do. She was close to tears again, as she'd been for most of the day.

James, who'd been sitting quietly, spoke up. 'I think he kept filming them to keep the kommandant happy, because if he didn't his whole family would have been put on the next transport.'

'But he didn't succeed, did he?' Eloise retorted. 'They *were* all sent to Auschwitz, and we know Ursula was the only one of her family who survived. How much more is there?' she said, desperate to drag the subject away from the morality of what her great-grandfather had done.

'There's more, but I'm afraid it's not in a format I can share with you just yet. We'll continue to work on it and the rest will be shown at the exhibition next summer. Which I hope you'll both attend.'

James looked up from the notes he'd been writing and said,

'You mentioned that the propaganda film was never completed. Where were the reels all this time?'

'That's a good question,' said Liesbeth. 'It wasn't until the camp was dismantled in the 1960s that they came to light. Breslauer had a studio above the Grote Zaal, which was a large hall the Nazis used for entertaining. The reels and photographs were found hidden in a cupboard in the back of the darkroom by builders. They also found a number of diaries written by Philip Mechanicus, a well-known Jewish journalist before the war.'

James looked surprised. 'I've read excerpts from Philip Mechanicus's diaries. I had no idea the two of them met at Westerbork. Will you be featuring any of his work at the exhibition?'

Liesbeth shook her head. 'Not on this occasion. This exhibition is all about Rudolf Breslauer's work.'

'I see,' he said, then added excitedly, 'What an amazing discovery that the two of them deliberately hid their work from the Nazis. They must have planned it together, maybe even made a pact that if their work was discovered after the war it would be made public to the world.'

'We have no definitive proof that they worked together,' said Liesbeth. 'But it's an interesting theory that cannot be ruled out.'

FORTY-TWO
SPRING 1943

Rudolf

It was Bella who broke the news to Rudolf, one Tuesday evening after he'd returned from his studio. She looked more worried than usual when she told him that Philip had left that day for Bergen-Belsen.

'That's not possible,' he said, in a state of shock. 'He told me that Schlesinger was arranging for him to go to Theresienstadt.' And then it came to him in a flash – despite everything Schlesinger had promised, the man had no more power over whose names appeared on the list.

'Schlesinger?' said Bella incredulously. 'What can he do? You know as well as I do that Schlesinger is Gemmeker's puppet. And Philip's always been a thorn in his side. He's always asking him for favours when the rest of us have to sit it out and wait to hear our fate. It wouldn't surprise me if Schlesinger had had enough of him.'

'That's unjust. Philip isn't like that. You don't know him like I do.'

'Well, that's because you never mention to me about what

the two of you discuss,' she retorted. 'I suppose he knew all about the photos you took of Ursula and Stefan for the kommandant?'

Rudolf had no answer for that, so changed tack and began to plead with her. 'Bella, please. Can't you see what's happening? Philip saw it coming, even if I refused to believe it. Now time is running out for us too. I've been working on the film for the kommandant for nearly a month and Schlesinger refuses to give me any assurances of my work continuing.'

Bella looked at him for a long moment, her eyes full of sorrow. 'I'm sorry for what I just said. I'm so scared we'll be next.' She went to him and laid her head on his shoulder, then slipped her arms round his waist. He closed his eyes as they clung together. He regretted the arguments they'd been having recently and wished he'd been more honest with her. Why hadn't he realised sooner that she was the only one he had ever been able to confide in? But it frightened him how close he'd been to losing her trust – and yet there was still so much he hadn't told her.

'Bella, there's something you should know.' He held her by her shoulders, wishing there was something he could say to allay her fears but suspecting he was only about to make things worse.

'What is it?' Her eyes flashed with worry.

'Philip and I made a pact. It was his idea, but I agreed. Ever since he came here, he's been keeping a diary and noting down what he sees around the camp in school exercise books. He started them when he was a patient and spent months bored in a hospital bed. Once he was out, he walked about the camp with his notebook recording what he saw. He used to be a foreign journalist for the *Algemeen Handelsblad*, so old habits die hard. He hopes that when his diaries are found the world will learn the truth about what the Nazis have really been up to.'

Bella listened without interrupting.

Rudolf kept eye contact with her as he went on, 'Philip asked if I'd be prepared to document what I see too, but through photos and film. At first, I refused because I knew it would put you and the children in danger if the Nazis discovered what we'd been doing. But eventually Philip persuaded me that I had a moral duty to record the truth.'

At last, Bella said, 'Why didn't you tell me any of this before?'

'Because I thought you'd try to stop me. You'd already made your views clear about filming the children, and you were right. But this was different. The photos I've made for Gemmeker don't show the reality of what it's like here. They're a sham, manufactured to make this place appear to be something wonderful, which it so clearly isn't. The ones I've taken and hidden away are damning evidence; they're the truth, especially the films. The last time I saw Philip was the morning I went to film the transports. What I saw there was truly terrible. It was the hardest thing I've ever done.'

'Where have you hidden all this material?'

'In a cupboard at the back of the darkroom behind some boxes. No one ever goes there but me. It's safe,' he said, hoping to reassure her that he hadn't been foolhardy.

'I'd like to see them, if you'd let me. Will you show me?'

'If you really want to. But I can only show the prints. I developed them myself. And then there are Philip's diaries. I'm sure he wouldn't mind you seeing them. But the films are still waiting to be developed and that can only be done outside the camp. It's not a risk I'm prepared to take. I only hope that whoever finds them knows what to do with them and is able to save the scenes I filmed.'

Bella squeezed his hand. 'I want to see it all, to understand what you and Philip have been trying to achieve all these months. Those photos you took of Ursula and Stefan...'

'I don't expect you to understand why I made them do it, and maybe I was wrong. But Gemmeker was putting such pressure on me that I feared he'd turn on me and—'

'Shh,' she said, putting a finger to his lips. 'I know. You were doing the right thing because you believed that only you could save us. And I love you all the more for it.'

FORTY-THREE

Rudolf pounded down the busy central boulevard, oblivious to the yells of annoyance and stares of those forced to step aside. His head churning with the devastating news he'd just received, it was all he could do to get back to Bella and his children to try his level best to reassure them. He was only dimly aware of the crowds congregating on the boulevard and that they were far smaller than usual. In a flash of clarity, he realised why. But he had no time to dwell on the reason – all he could think of was getting back to the small wooden building that stood apart from the grim rows of barracks and which his family now called home. He arrived out of breath and flung open the door. The place was in semi-darkness. He hit the light switch. Where was everyone?

'Bella?' he called out urgently, though the house was so small he would have known immediately if she'd been at home.

There was no time to lose. He moved quickly through the two rooms, picking up items, then hurling them aside, while muttering to himself, 'No, not that. Impossible. No point. Oh, God, what then?'

He slumped down on their bed, his head in his hands, paralysed by not knowing what to do. In front of him the battered suitcase that once belonged to his father lay open at his feet. It contained a few meagre items of clothing that he'd thrown in – a clean shirt, a change of underwear, his metal razor – and his precious Leica camera, all stuffed haphazardly into the tiny space.

He heard the front door opening. Bella's voice called out, 'Rudolf! What's going on?'

He leapt to his feet and rushed out of the room. Relief surged through him when he saw Mischa with Bella.

'Papa!' Mischa let go of Bella's hand and crossed the floor at a run. Rudolf lifted him into his arms and held him close.

'Tell me. Is it Ursula and Stefan?' Bella managed to say. He saw that she was shaking violently.

Rudolf put Mischa down and managed to distract him with his toy car while he whispered to Bella that the family had been ordered to go to the train station the next morning.

Some minutes later, Ursula and Stefan came through the door, and took in the sight of their parents sobbing. Rudolf turned his head to see the surprise and consternation written on their faces.

'Come here, children,' he said, as he tried to regain his composure and gather them round. 'I have news that will affect us all.'

But Ursula wouldn't let him carry on. Her voice rose in panic as she spoke. 'It's Monday today. That means tomorrow is transport day. I know what you're going to say – you've heard our names are on the list.' She broke down in noisy heaving sobs. Next to her, Stefan stood stock-still and also began crying loudly, big tears splashing down his cheeks.

Bella tried to console them. 'Save your tears. Everything's

going to be all right. Now listen to what Papa has to say.' She looked at him and indicated for him to speak.

Rudolf regarded his small family, the people he loved and cared about most in the world. He felt as if his heart would break in two, but somehow found the strength to give them the few words of encouragement they craved. 'We all have to pack a bag and go to the station at six o'clock in the morning. Nothing is certain, nothing at all, but there is a chance our names will be called out and we will have to board the train. But we might not be on the list after all, in which case we can come back here.' He forced a smile but had to keep his lips tightly shut to prevent himself from breaking down. He then crouched down to look Stefan in the eye. 'Now dry your tears. Mama will help you pack your suitcase.' It took an enormous effort on his part, but he managed to calm down. He wasn't sure how he'd managed it when only minutes before he'd been on the verge of a breakdown.

The hours before bed were filled with tears and arguments over what they could take with them. The children simply didn't understand that they must leave most of their possessions behind even though it was unlikely they would return. Rudolf couldn't bring himself to say anything about what might possibly lie ahead. He hardly knew it himself, but he did know that whatever they were about to encounter was likely to be grim.

After they'd all settled, Rudolf persuaded the children to carry on as if they were packing for a few days away.

Their bags lay open on the beds as they carefully chose the bare essentials – a change of clothes, several of underwear, a book here, a soft toy there. Bella went to a drawer and pulled out the photo album that Rudolf had given her for her birthday. She gazed at it longingly, page by page, then went to put it back.

Ursula was watching from where she was debating whether to take a favourite dress. Her only dress, in fact, although she'd almost grown out of it. In a fit of agitation, she tossed it aside and spoke indignantly. 'Mama. You can't leave the photos behind. They were a birthday present.'

Bella looked at the cherished family photo album, then exchanged a worried frown with Rudolf. He nodded for her to continue. 'We can't be sentimental at a time like this. There's not a lot of space in our suitcases, so we need to be practical about what we take,' she said, though she didn't sound as if she meant it.

Ursula pursed her lips in a gesture of defiance that Rudolf knew only too well. He was about to add his voice when she announced, 'There's a tear in the lining of my suitcase. I can put it in there and no one will be able to find it. Let me take it.' She thrust out the palm of her hand.

Bella hesitated, then turned to Rudolf. 'What do you think?' she said in a moment of uncharacteristic doubt.

Rudolf thought of his beloved camera, which would surely be more valuable to anyone wanting to rummage through their belongings. He was certainly not going to leave that behind. But would anyone be interested in something as worthless as a photo album? 'Let her have it,' he said, knowing his daughter was right.

Ursula's expression relaxed as she took the album and held it against her for a moment before putting it on the bottom of her small suitcase. She ripped the lining some more to push it through and out of sight, then laid a skirt and jumper on top.

'There. No one will find it,' she said, standing up. She had a small triumphant smile on her face, and Rudolf's heart filled with love for his spirited and brave daughter who already understood too much of the cruel and unpredictable world in which she'd been brought up.

FORTY-FOUR

Next morning at 6 a.m., the Breslauer family stood shivering on the platform along with several hundred other souls awaiting the announcement that would determine their future. Rudolf remembered Philip saying that more than a thousand were forced to congregate here each week to learn their fate. 'The thousand list' was Schlesinger's term, referring to the quota of prisoners he was tasked with reaching for each Tuesday transport.

Rudolf stood with Stefan and Ursula on either side of him, while Bella attended to Mischa, who whimpered softly in her arms. He looked around and noticed there seemed to be nowhere near a thousand people that day. The reason, at once obvious and sobering, was that the Germans' plan to empty Amsterdam of its Jewish population was working. Soon their job would be done and Westerbork would have fulfilled its deadly purpose.

Ursula tugged urgently on his hand. 'Do you have any idea where we're going? I hate not knowing.'

He squeezed her hand, struggling to offer any words of comfort. 'We'll know soon enough, *Liebchen.*'

But the minutes turned to hours and everyone began to grow impatient at the lack of information, until suddenly there was a burst of activity as dozens of uniformed Germans came marching onto the platform and began segregating people into groups in front of each of the carriages. The Breslauers found themselves being moved some way along the platform until they were positioned in front of a wagon whose doors were wide open. It was pitch dark inside – no windows, only bare dirty boards, with a small tin bucket just visible in one corner. The smell that emanated from inside that hellhole was putrid, causing people to shrink back and clamp handkerchiefs to their noses in shock.

Rudolf quickly ushered his family away from the cattle wagon to where he could keep an eye on a crowd gathering round one of the loudspeakers positioned along the length of the platform. The announcement would be any time now. Rudolf prayed silently that his family would be spared.

There was another long wait. People grew restless as the minutes passed. Children began to play amongst themselves and grown-ups fell into conversation as if they were simply waiting to board a train for a day trip. Was this some evil trick played by the guards to lull them into believing there wouldn't be a Tuesday list this week after all? Another wave of that terrible stench hit Rudolf and he knew they wouldn't have brought the train in unless they were intending to send it out of the camp crammed full of unsuspecting prisoners.

A single voice called out. 'It's started! Be quiet!'

The silence that descended was sudden and shocking. Rudolf grabbed Ursula and Stefan by the hand and moved closer to Bella. Mischa had fallen asleep in his mother's arms.

Name after name was intoned by a disembodied male voice, which paused from time to time, giving people reason to believe it was over. Each time it started up again, there was a collective groan of despair.

Would it never end? On and on it went.

And then it was over.

Bella burst into tears and each of their children joined in, not understanding what was happening. Mischa wailed the loudest.

'Mama, Mama,' cried Stefan, his cheeks wet with tears.

'Why are you crying, Mama? They didn't call our names,' Ursula sobbed to her mother in confusion.

'It's all right, my darlings. It's all right,' said Rudolf. 'We're going back home.'

Eloise

It was late August when Eloise and James reached the Hook of Holland, after visiting Paris, Marseille, Florence and Rome. She'd enjoyed winding down with James after their intense visit to Westerbork, although discovering the truth about her great-grandfather's work had taken its toll and made her immeasurably sad. Never far from her mind was the shaky black-and-white film of her great-grandmother playing with two, not all three of her children. She couldn't stop thinking about Mischa, the little boy who was so conspicuous by his absence.

The ferry was full of holidaymakers returning from their summer holidays. Before they set sail, they decided to go up on deck. It was empty of people and chilly for the time of year, with a blustery wind. It was a far cry from the balmy evening they'd experienced when they'd set out several weeks before. They moved to the back of the ship where it was more sheltered and watched as it slowly moved away from the port and the Dutch coastline gradually disappeared into the distance.

James stood behind Eloise and put his arms round her. 'Bye, Holland. It's been wonderful, hasn't it?' He squeezed her gently.

'Mm,' Eloise murmured, relishing his warmth.

They didn't speak as they watched two seagulls following on behind, their wide wings outstretched as they hovered on the wind, occasionally swooping down into the white foam in search of food.

'I couldn't have done any of it without you,' she said, leaning towards him.

'Do you mean it?' said James, and she nodded.

'I'm sorry I've been so distracted. I just can't seem to get everything I've seen at Westerbork out of my head. I honestly thought that going there would help me understand my family better, and that has happened now that I've discovered about Mischa. But I still don't have all the answers.' She let out a long sigh and held his gaze. 'I'm really not looking forward to telling my grandmother that I know about her little brother.'

'You don't need to apologise. But you can talk to me about it as much as you want to. There may be a perfectly reasonable explanation for why he wasn't in the photo. But admit it, the fact that your great-grandfather has made history through his work is nothing short of remarkable.' When she didn't answer, he changed the subject. 'Do you have any plans before the start of term?'

'To be honest, I hadn't really thought about it,' she said with a sigh. She knew that her second year at Oxford would involve even more reading and coursework. 'It's only a few weeks till term starts. It'll be nice to catch up with friends back home. What will you do?' She twisted her neck to look at him. He kept looking out over the waves and seemed pensive.

'I'm hoping to go back early as I really need to get started on my dissertation. We're expected to write twelve thousand words. That's more than I've written in my entire life.' He laughed nervously.

'I'm sure you'll be fine once you get into it. Have you decided on your topic?'

He pulled his gaze away from the horizon. 'I'm going to write about the rise of Nazism in the Netherlands. I've decided to focus on the events.'

'What was that you said?' She moved out of his embrace to face him so she could concentrate on what he was saying.

'I was saying about my dissertation. I've decided to focus on the events leading up to the Dutch occupation at the start of the Second World War.'

Eloise gave an involuntary shiver and wrapped her arms round her middle. The wind flapped her hair round her face.

James was watching the sea again as he went on, 'My tutor's been a great help in identifying some excellent source material. Of course, our trip to Westerbork has been invaluable, especially the discovery of all those photos and film.'

He didn't seem to have noticed that Eloise had moved away and was staring uncomprehendingly at him. She felt he was taking advantage of her by treating this holiday as a research trip for his own project.

'To actually go to Westerbork and see the evidence of what the Nazis were doing through the lens of Rudolf Breslauer's work is an absolute godsend.' He kept on as if he already had worked it all out. And all without a thought for how she might feel, it struck her in a moment of clarity. She couldn't believe what she was hearing.

He was smiling at her now, but she felt sick to her stomach. 'Stop it, James. Why are you're telling me this now? Do you not realise how this sounds?'

The look of surprise he gave her confirmed what she already knew. That he hadn't thought to consult her about what he was planning before they'd left. His interest in stocking up on books in the museum shop and how he'd sat making discreet notes in their sessions with Liesbeth Hendrick now sickened her. Her heart began to thump as she realised what he'd been up to under the pretence of persuading her to go to Westerbork for her sake.

James frowned and she saw a hurt in his eyes she'd never seen before. 'What do you mean? I thought you'd be pleased I'd chosen a subject that was so close to your heart.'

'You just don't get it, do you?' Eloise was appalled that he actually believed he was doing her a favour all this time. 'This subject you've chosen to study involves my family. People close to me who were innocent victims who perished at the hands of the Nazis. It feels like you've been using me.'

He gave a short, sudden laugh. 'Oh, stop being so melodramatic. I've never hidden from you that I was interested in Westerbork from a historical perspective.'

'Then why didn't you tell me about your dissertation sooner?'

He heaved in a deep breath but didn't quite meet her eye. 'It's not that I wasn't going to tell you. I just hadn't got round to it.'

Eloise shook her head in disbelief; she kept staring at him until he eventually looked at her.

'Eloise...' he pleaded, but she held up both her hands to stop him from talking his way out of this. He ignored her as he went on, 'I honestly didn't know it would upset you.' There was a slight break in his voice that, despite her reluctance to accept his explanation, tugged at her.

She glanced at him, trying hard to keep her own emotions in check. 'I don't know what to think right now. Perhaps it's for the best we don't see each other after we get back.' The words were out before she'd had a chance to consider them.

He nodded slowly, as if coming to the same conclusion. 'If

that's what you want, then I'll respect you for it. But if you change your mind…'

'Please don't make it any harder,' she said, shocked at how quickly their relationship had shifted in the space of one conversation. Or perhaps it had been coming for some time and she simply hadn't seen it.

FORTY-SIX
SPRING 1943

Rudolf

The agony of not knowing when their turn would come wasn't over. Another two Tuesdays went by without the Breslauers being summoned to the station. By the time the third Tuesday rolled round, Rudolf had become resigned to the inevitable. There was hardly any more work for him now, however busy he imagined himself to be. He'd been forced to hand back the cinecamera and completed several portfolios of photographs for the kommandant, for which he'd received little more than a curt 'thank you'. He sensed that, apart from registering a trickle of new arrivals, the kommandant had no need for an official photographer any more. He only hoped he was wrong.

Everyone was subdued, including his family, who seemed more accepting of what might happen. It was as if all their emotions had been depleted since that awful Tuesday morning and they had no more reserves to call upon. Or maybe it was because, having avoided fate once, they refused to believe they would be next. After all, it wasn't unheard of that people had been released from Westerbork and allowed to return home. There was still a chance they might be spared.

The second time the Breslauers were ordered to attend the announcement of the Tuesday transport list, there were fewer tears and no tantrums. They'd already gone through the motions of packing for a one-way journey once; somehow it didn't feel as poignant second time round.

There were even fewer people congregating on the platform than the last time, confirming Rudolf's suspicions that the Germans were almost finished with the transports. If that were true, Rudolf thought, could they perhaps avoid it one more time?

There was the same build-up, the same interminable waiting around for hours before anything happened. Only this time, Ursula and Stefan distracted Mischa with a wooden toy car, and their laughter brought a rare smile to their parents' faces.

And then Rudolf caught sight of Schlesinger marching along the platform with a group of uniformed officers. He appeared to be in a state of agitation as he flicked through the sheets of paper on his clipboard. Suddenly he broke off and came hurrying towards where the Breslauer family were standing. Rudolf stiffened but couldn't let pass the opportunity to speak to him. He told Bella to keep an eye on the children, saying he'd only be a moment, then stepped into Schlesinger's path.

'May I have a word?' he said, his heart pounding.

'Herr Breslauer,' Schlesinger said, surprised, then took in Rudolf's family standing behind him. He looked distinctly uncomfortable, then blurted out, 'I want you to know how much I value everything you—'

But Rudolf wasn't in the mood for pleasantries and quickly came to the point. 'Can you tell me if our names are on the list?'

Schlesinger didn't quite meet his eye as he muttered something about not being privy to the information.

But Rudolf knew he was lying. 'I'm thinking about my wife and children more than me. Is there anything you can do to prevent their names from being called?' He watched Schlesinger's face closely and noticed beads of sweat forming on his brow. It seemed to confirm everything he already suspected about the man.

'Believe me, these past weeks I've tried everything in my power to keep your names off the list. There's only so much I could do.' He turned his palms upwards.

Both men looked up to see the kommandant cycling along the platform towards them. He didn't appear to have seen Rudolf as he called out Schlesinger's name, then came to a halt and handed his bike to a passing officer. Only then did he notice Rudolf. His face broke into a smile. 'Our esteemed photographer,' he said without a trace of irony. 'I can't thank you enough for the excellent material you've produced for me. You should be very proud. But tell me, what are you doing here?' Frowning, he looked questioningly at Schlesinger.

'I had to fulfil the quota,' mumbled Schlesinger. All his old confidence appeared to have been knocked out of him. 'It's too late to do anything about it now. The announcement is about to start.'

'Ah, the quota.' Gemmeker frowned more deeply, then addressed Rudolf. 'I'm afraid it's the rules. But I want you to know you've done a fine job.' Satisfied he'd said the right thing, he went to speak to one of his officers, who was attempting to keep order amongst a crowd of people gathered round the loudspeaker. All at once, it burst into life with a loud hiss and crackle and the disembodied voice began to intone the list of names, one by one.

Defeated, Rudolf went back to his family. 'I tried,' he whispered to Bella, who gazed up at him with tears in her eyes. They all held hands as the voice moved from the As to the Bs until they reached their own.

'Rudolf Breslauer. Bella Breslauer. Ursula Breslauer. Stefan Breslauer. Mischa Breslauer.'

At first none of them reacted. The reality they had all been dreading was upon them, but all Rudolf could feel was numbness. He glanced up at the side of the cattle wagon, which he'd been so studiously avoiding looking at, and read the destination painted in bold on a board nailed to the side. He wasn't sure why he noticed that one of the nails was missing, but it distracted him for a moment longer.

He quickly looked away in the knowledge that he and his family were about to board one of the last transports out of Westerbork to a place he knew virtually nothing about. Perhaps that was for the best, he thought to himself, as he helped first Bella with Mischa, then Ursula, scramble up onto the bare boards of the wagon. Ursula disappeared inside to find a small space for them all to sit down, while Rudolf lifted Stefan up to Bella, who waited with outstretched arms. Only then did he climb aboard.

The destination board nailed to the side of the carriage read:

AUSCHWITZ

FORTY-SEVEN

Ursula

The Tuesday our names were called out was the worst day of my life. At least it was until I later discovered that there was far worse to come. Papa and Mama were convinced that we would manage to avoid the lists a second time, but now I realise they were just trying to hide the stark truth from us. I never spoke to them about how I felt – that too many of my classmates had been in the same position as us, called to the station only to be given a reprieve. They all believed they'd been spared. When they didn't turn up in class the following week, we all knew what had happened to them. I tried not to let it get to me, but I'd never quite got over the heartbreak of my best friend Bekkah disappearing in Amsterdam. I was overjoyed when she turned up at Westerbork, only for the same thing to happen all over again. By the time I arrived with my dear family on the platform a second time, there was an inevitability about what we were about to face and a sense of impending doom.

Distraction was the only way to get through the interminable waiting. I'd slipped Mischa's toy car into my pocket and his little face lit up with joy when I presented it to him. For a while, the three of us played with that car on the platform. Nothing else mattered in that moment.

I don't remember much about the announcement. One moment, Mama had lifted up Mischa and was pacifying him, the next she was in floods of tears. When I offered to hold him, Mama refused and held him tightly against her chest. I was confused and felt rejected. I'm not sure she even heard me. How was I to know that I would never have the chance to play with my darling little brother again?

I'd hardly taken any notice of the forbidding carriages that loomed above us on the platform, but now I realised it was no ordinary passenger train but a whole string of cattle wagons without windows. I had just begun to panic, when suddenly we were being jostled and pushed towards the open doors by the Nazi guards.

I stumbled onboard and crawled towards where Mama was calling me in the pitch black. The bare boards were rough and gritty. It was stifling hot and smelled terrible. Stefan was close behind me and I could hear him sobbing with fear. I didn't know where Papa was and I didn't care. I was still quietly simmering with rage at him, because I thought he was responsible for getting us into this situation. And I was angry with Mama too for shutting me out. The strange thing was that I didn't cry until I felt Stefan's small hand reach for mine. At that moment he seemed to be the only person in the world who understood me.

I wish I hadn't felt such hatred towards Papa and Mama. They knew as little as I did, but I'd convinced myself they should have done something to prevent the horror we were all subjected to. I was fourteen, but at that moment I was a small child who desperately wanted her parents' reassurance that everything was going to be all right.

I lost all sense of time, but I don't think it was long before my anger towards my parents dissipated. Of course I knew it wasn't their fault we were on that transport. How could it be? We were all victims and had no control over our circumstances.

We had no idea how long we would be cooped up with so many other desperate people. We all wanted to it end.

From time to time the train stopped for no apparent reason, and people wailed and shouted and banged on the sides to be let out. Occasionally, the guards opened the doors and threw in some stale bread, which we fought over. There was nothing else, not even water. I can't be sure if I remember this correctly, but I think they also pulled out the bodies of people who had died. And then the doors slammed shut again and there was the awful grating sound of the iron bars being dragged across to lock us in. We were thrust back into darkness and no one knew what lay at the end of it.

Was I relieved when we finally arrived? If I was, the feeling was short-lived and replaced with a new kind of terrible visceral fear I had never felt in my entire life.

Eloise

When Eloise arrived back in Oxford for the new term, her first thought was to visit her grandmother. She couldn't wait to see her and tell her about the photographs she'd seen at Westerbork, though she wasn't relishing asking about the little brother she still knew so little about.

Eloise arrived at the flat and pressed the bell. She heard her grandmother's faint voice call for her to come in. Half expecting to see her come cruising round the furniture to greet her, she stepped into the small hallway and put her head round the door to the living room. She was sitting in her usual chair and waved a bony hand for Eloise to come through. Her eyes were as bright as they'd ever been, but there was no mistaking how small and shrunken she looked amidst the cushions.

'How are you, Grandma?' Eloise tried hard to conceal her shock at her grandmother's appearance. She wondered if she'd been ill since she last saw her. 'I've brought you some dahlias to cheer you up. And our usual pastries.'

The old lady smiled, but Eloise could tell it was an effort

her for her to do so. Her voice was quieter than usual, but when she spoke she was as sharp as ever. 'I'm as well as can be expected for someone my age. Look in the sideboard for a vase. The flowers will look very nice in that. Would you mind putting the kettle on as well? I'm not as mobile as when I saw you last.'

'Of course, Grandma. Are you quite well?' she couldn't help herself asking.

Her grandmother gave her a sharp look. 'I didn't say I was ill, did I? At my age it's only to be expected I slow down, annoying as it is.' Her face suddenly erupted into a broad smile and Eloise felt relief wash over her.

The vase was at the back of the sideboard and was chipped, with a spider crack that ran all the way from the rim to the base. Eloise looked around for another, moving items of crockery that might once have been part of a dinner set. She couldn't find any other vases that would do the job, but the damaged vase was pretty, with its swirly pattern of rosebuds and leaves. She took it into the kitchen, snipped the ends of the stems off the flowers with a pair of scissors and arranged them as best she could. She then put the kettle on to boil and opened a few cupboards until she found an open box of teabags behind some half-empty jars of what could have been jam or chutney, well past their use-by dates. Eloise wondered where her grandma kept the cups and saucers as she carried on opening and shutting cupboard doors.

'The cups are in the right of the sideboard,' her grandma called out.

Eloise smiled. At least her hearing didn't appear to be a problem. She picked up the vase and went back into the other room, where she placed it down on a coaster.

'No, not there,' scolded her grandma. 'Here.' She gestured to the low table beside her chair. 'And hurry up. I've been waiting far too long to hear about your trip to Holland.'

Eloise glanced up to see a glint in her grandmother's eyes. 'I won't be a minute,' she said quickly, keen to take advantage of her grandmother's lift in mood before she grew tired.

She came back in with the tea tray and laid out the cups, saucers and pastry plates, before sitting down in the chair nearest her grandmother's. 'Going to Westerbork was a real eye-opener for me. I can't wait to tell you all about it.'

Her grandmother listened intently without touching her pastry or the cup of tea that sat on the table in front of her. Eloise wasn't sure if she was upset by her revelations about the discovery of the photos, or whether this quietness was something new. She'd heard how dangerous even a cold could be for elderly people, who might suddenly go downhill when anyone was least expecting it. Eloise tried not to brood on what might be nothing as she described her impressions of Westerbork, its layout and the information points helping people to imagine life inside the camp. She described going inside the only surviving wooden barrack, home to so many people, but stopped short of the details she'd learned about the terrible conditions prisoners had had to endure. There was no point in dwelling on what her grandmother would have remembered only too well.

Her grandmother shifted slightly in her chair so that she could lean forward for her cup and saucer.

'Let me get that for you,' said Eloise, half standing to hand it to her. 'Would you like a piece of the Danish? I've cut it up small.'

Her grandma took the cup and saucer but shook her head dismissively. 'Just tea for now. I might try a piece later. Please carry on. I want to hear everything.'

'We had two meetings with the assistant curator, who took us through the archive materials stored at the museum. I was surprised just how many boxes of photos they have in storage. So many, in fact, that we didn't have time to go through them all.'

Her grandmother smiled. 'It doesn't surprise me. I

remember Papa wore his Leica round his neck so he was always ready to take photographs of anything that interested him. And it meant none of the German guards ever bothered him. Everyone knew he was carrying out orders on behalf of the kommandant. Did I tell you that I used to help Papa develop the photographs?'

Eloise pretended she hadn't. 'Tell me about it.' She smiled.

'I used to look through all the negatives before they were printed, but never questioned what was on them. Papa simply said they were for his work and I accepted what he said. It was only when I was living in Israel and had a family of my own that I began to think about all those images again. In some the people were happy and smiling, but in others the people looked so miserable. Little by little, I realised my father was creating a record not just for the Nazis but for the future.' She directed her dark eyes at Eloise as she went on, 'Did you remember to take any copies with that instrument of yours?' She gestured towards Eloise's camera, which was lying on the table.

'Of course. I said I would.' Eloise's heart beat faster as she opened up the file she'd created for the photos. She wanted to gauge her grandma's reaction first, so decided she would keep back the ones that included Mischa. 'I meant to take more but I was distracted by seeing the originals.' She moved her chair closer and enlarged one or two of the photos on her phone for her grandmother to see. 'Some are very similar to the ones in your album.'

Her grandmother peered at each of them in silence; she sighed when Eloise came to the last one. 'I hadn't realised he'd taken so many of us. It's strange that the museum has them now. Do you have any idea why?'

'They were found hidden in a cupboard in the darkroom along with diaries from a prisoner they think must have asked your father to keep safe. There was also a stack of film reels, a mixture of stuff for the kommandant, but there was a film of people waiting to board trains. I imagine your father knew he was taking an enormous risk, but it didn't stop him. He managed to include footage of SS guards keeping order. He must have known that the only way he could keep the film from them was to hide it.'

Suddenly, Eloise became aware that her grandmother seemed to have stopped listening. Her eyes were shining with tears as she said, 'I should never have doubted him.'

Eloise frowned. 'What do you mean, Grandma?'

'My relationship with Papa deteriorated about the time that he started taking photos of Stefan and me. I always knew they were for the kommandant, but I thought it wrong that he was using us. I felt so ashamed because I believed he was willingly cooperating with the Germans. He'd always been so outspoken about how badly the Germans treated people like us and then suddenly he was happy to do whatever they asked him. I didn't know how to tell him how I felt, so I often refused to pose for him. He would plead with me and I'd deliberately scowl at the camera. Childish, I know, but then I was still a child.'

She searched in the pocket of her skirt and pulled out a lace handkerchief to wipe her eyes. 'I wish I could tell him what took years for me to realise. The fact I didn't still hurts me deeply to this day.' She pressed a hand to her chest in the region of her heart.

There was nothing Eloise could say, so she sat quietly with her eyes turned down to her hands, which lay clenched in her lap. When she looked up, her grandmother let out a deep sigh. 'I don't mean to upset you. It's why I've never spoken to anyone about it.'

'I'm glad you did, Grandma. It can't have been easy keeping something like that to yourself all these years. Did you never tell Dad any of this?'

'No. You're the first person in the family I've been able to talk about such things. It's always been too painful to rake up the past. And then you started to ask questions about our family history. It made me realise you have every right to know and that I'm the only one left who can tell you the truth about what happened.' She smiled tentatively, then out of the blue said, 'There are secrets I've been holding close to me for too long. When I'm ready, I think you, dear Eloise, should be the one to hear them.'

'There were several photos in the archive that didn't make any sense,' began Eloise, taking courage from her grandmother's decision to unburden her own secrets.

'Really? What could that have been?' Her grandmother looked genuinely puzzled.

'Let me show you.' Eloise went back to the photos on her phone and pulled out the one of Ursula, Stefan and Mischa singing together at the piano.

When her grandmother caught sight of the image she gasped and covered her mouth with the handkerchief she was holding. She caught Eloise's eye and began to nod. 'We only wanted to protect him.'

Eloise frowned. 'I don't understand. Your little brother was here in these photographs. Why didn't you keep any of him?'

Her grandmother let out a long sigh. 'I don't expect you to understand, but I will try to explain. It was about that time I started helping Papa in his darkroom. The kommandant was putting pressure on him to keep taking photographs for some secret project I wasn't told about. Papa said he would never take any photos of the three of us, but I saw he took photos of other children in the camp. But these weren't the only photographs he took – he made many portraits of the kommandant and a woman called Elisabeth Hassel who used to regularly visit him in his villa. I know it because I saw the photos with my own eyes. It didn't occur to me that she might be the kommandant's mistress. And then there were the big parties with high-ranking SS officials, when Papa was ordered to be present for the whole evening and photograph every person present. I hated the kommandant so much because of the demands he put on Papa. He was expected to develop the films overnight. It's how I got involved.

'I saw it all, Eloise. Not because I went into the Grote Zaal, where the men were all feasting and getting drunk, but because I was upstairs in the darkroom, which was right above it. One evening, I was moving some boxes and saw a light shining through a tiny hole in the floorboards. I put my eye against it and couldn't believe what I was seeing. I never told Papa that I watched him snapping photographs – it was the smile on his face that did it. I was convinced he was enjoying himself.

'Not long after, Papa started on about wanting the three of us to pose for photographs. But Mama absolutely forbade him to let Mischa be part of this charade, thank goodness. I don't know how much she knew about Papa's work, but I believe it was a mother's instincts that made her want to protect Mischa, who was barely more than a toddler.

'I was so angry with Papa. I couldn't understand why he needed us to be in photos he was taking for the kommandant. I knew that it was so wrong, but he didn't leave us with any choice. At least Mama made sure that dear little Mischa should never be implicated in this wrongdoing.'

She stopped, clearly exhausted by the effort of unburdening herself, but she still hadn't answered Eloise's question, so Eloise attempted to answer it herself.

'Grandma, I think I understand. You thought you could

protect Mischa by agreeing to your papa's request for photos and making sure he never included your little brother. But what you didn't know was that your mother had already kept these photos of the three of you when you were still in Amsterdam. If it hadn't been for her taking a suitcase containing the family photo album to a friend for safe keeping, they might never have come to light. But they did. That album was eventually discovered and given to the Westerbork museum.'

Grandma looked surprised. 'I'm glad it was found. It was wrong of me to pretend Mischa never existed all these years. He did exist and he will always be in my heart.' She closed her eyes and sank back into her cushions, then let out a long sigh.

Eloise glanced at her watch and realised they'd been talking for well over an hour. The effort had clearly taken it out of her grandma. 'Can you I get you anything... a drink, or something to eat? Grandma?'

Her grandmother looked as if she might have dropped off. Without opening her eyes, she lifted a hand and said in a weak voice, 'That's a good idea. I don't have the energy to get anything for myself. You'll find a tin of soup in the cupboard.' She sighed and still didn't open her eyes.

By the time Eloise had heated up the tomato soup and brought it through on a tray with a slice of bread and butter, her grandmother was deeply asleep, with her head falling gently to one side. Eloise stood contemplating her for a moment, unsure of what to do next; she put the tray down on the table next to her chair and sat opposite her. Still her grandmother didn't stir, so Eloise took out her phone to see if she had any messages. She glanced up every so often to check on her grandmother, but she remained fast asleep.

Eloise read an email from her tutor about a forthcoming assignment and made a mental note to start it when she got back; she deleted several others without reading them. Then, just as she was about to put her phone away, another email jumped into her inbox. It was from Liesbeth. She caught her breath, wondering if Liesbeth was contacting her with new photographs or documents from the archive. She remembered her saying that the process of sifting through the files was painstaking and that it was entirely feasible that something new might come to light. Could it be more photographs that her great-grandfather had been hiding from the Germans, or uncovered film footage exposing the brutality of the Nazi regime? But as tempting as it was to look, Eloise decided against opening the email – she might feel obliged to share it with her grandmother, and she didn't want her getting agitated in her current weakened state.

The old lady continued to sleep and Eloise was ambivalent about leaving now. Should she wake her and tell her she was going? She kept squinting at the email from Liesbeth and reread the first line; it told her nothing – it was just a greeting expressing hope that she and her grandmother were well. She had finally made up her mind to take a quick look when her grandmother stirred and her eyes flickered open.

'Oh! What time is it?' She looked flustered and her cheeks were flushed pink.

Eloise smiled, but the way her grandmother peered at her worried her. Did she even recognise her? 'Grandma,' she said in a firm voice, hoping to jog her memory. 'I made you a bowl of soup, but you were dozing, so I didn't want to wake you.'

Her grandmother blinked several times as recognition seemed to flicker across her face. 'Nonsense! I barely closed my eyes for more than a minute.' She shifted in her seat to try to sit up straight. 'Behind my chair is a tray for my lap. Would you fetch it, my dear?'

'Yes, of course,' said Eloise, still not entirely convinced her grandmother knew who she was. She hoped she wasn't mixing her up with one of the care assistants who regularly called in on the residents to see how they were coping.

Eloise found the tray, which had a cushion attached to the base, and placed it on her grandmother's lap. She suspected the bright orange soup was now cold from the way it congealed round the edges. Eloise chose not to make another comment, guessing that her grandmother might be feeling embarrassed to have fallen asleep in her presence. She placed it on her lap and handed her the spoon, but she didn't take any of the soup.

'Would you like me to help you?' Eloise couldn't stop herself saying.

'Why on earth would you do that?' her grandmother said sharply. 'I can manage perfectly well.'

Eloise retreated to her chair and picked up a television magazine that lay on the low table. It was two weeks out of date, but she flicked through it all the same. She stayed like that until she could be sure her grandmother had eaten at least some of the soup and a morsel of bread and butter.

'Eloise.' Her grandmother's voice was unexpectedly loud.

Eloise looked up with a start, both surprised and relieved to hear her name spoken.

Her grandmother was now wide awake. 'Eloise,' she repeated. 'You haven't said a word about that nice young man of yours. Remind me of his name.'

'James,' Eloise said, surprised by this sudden change of mood.

'Why didn't you bring him along today?'

Eloise didn't want to start a conversation about James, but she knew she wouldn't be able to escape her grandmother's stare if she didn't say something. She cleared her throat. 'I think he has a lot of work on at the moment. He's in his final year.'

'I see. Well, tell him from me that it's been too long since I've seen him. It's unusual to see young people take such an interest in old people's stories.' She paused and tilted her head on one side, looking pensive. 'Is everything all right between you?'

Instantly, Eloise felt herself dangerously close to crying, and that was the last thing she wanted to do in front of her grandmother. She steadied herself with a deep breath. 'We haven't seen each other recently. As I said, he's busy—' She hated the way her voice had suddenly come out high.

'Nonsense,' her grandmother interrupted, her voice sharp. 'You're not telling me the truth, are you?'

Eloise wished she'd stop going on about James. It just dredged up feelings she'd been trying to ignore for some time. With something not unlike a physical pain in her chest, she felt tears well up, and they began to spill down her cheeks as her breath came out in shaky sobs.

'Oh, my dear Eloise. Come, come. It can't be that bad, can it? Do you want to tell me about it?'

How could Eloise refuse after her grandmother had poured out her heart to her? She looked up through her tears as the old lady handed her a fresh lacy handkerchief to dry her eyes.

'Things always work out in the end and life goes on. I can attest to that.' Her grandmother's eyes were kind as she waited for Eloise to share her heartache.

FIFTY

Ursula

Auschwitz felt like we'd come to the ends of the earth. There was nothing to see, only the long platform; it was bleak, the buildings were stark, and a viciously cold wind penetrated my very being. I already sensed in my bones there would be no escape.

The guards had wasted no time in opening up the doors and yelling at everyone to get out. There were hundreds of us, although not everyone had survived the journey. I tried to ignore the shapes huddled in the corners of the wagon as I concentrated on staggering down the metal steps onto the platform. It was so bitterly cold, and Mama crouched down to button our coats. I can still remember the worry in her eyes as they locked onto mine. 'Be brave,' she said, just as a guard came up behind her and prodded her in the back with the butt of his rifle. She fell forward, but didn't cry out. Papa, who was holding Mischa, rushed to her aid. She managed to get to her feet and pretended she was fine, though she couldn't have been. It was a vicious, needless attack on a defenceless woman and it made my blood boil. I didn't realise then that there would be far worse to come. Ever since that terrible day, I've held on to the knowledge that it was Mama who was the brave one.

The platform was packed and it was impossible to form any kind of orderly queue. We were jostled from all sides as we shuffled forward, still completely unaware of what we were about to endure. The guards kept marching up and down, yelling at the tops of their voices. I held on to my small suitcase, but it took all my might. Every time a guard strode past, slapping his thigh with a leather strap, I gripped harder on to the handle, determined they wouldn't take it away from me.

Some of the guards had vicious German shepherd dogs straining at the leash. The guards seemed to take great delight at frightening us by urging the dogs to growl, bark and bare their teeth. As we moved slowly towards the end of the platform, I kept close to Mama, holding tightly to her hand. Mischa clung to her neck, his dark eyes wide with incomprehension as they darted around, taking in the scene. He was always so alert, so observant. Every so often, Mama bent down and whispered to me and Stefan to be brave.

It took a long time for us to reach the point where a group of smartly dressed SS officers directed which way the prisoners should go. One man's boots were blacker and shinier than the others. It wasn't until years later that I discovered this man was the infamous Josef Mengele, who was in charge of who should live and who would immediately be sent to their death. Our little family group stood as close together as we dared, not understanding why this man with the cruel smile made some go left while others went right.

And then, everything happened so fast. We were next in line and Mama, holding Mischa, Stefan and Papa were already being marshalled off to the left. I was still holding on to Mama's hand, but the SS officer wrenched it away. He stood like an immovable wall between me and them and yelled in my face to turn right. I tried to follow Mama, stretching out my arm and yelling her name, but she had already gone. Someone pushed me from behind to keep moving. Sobbing, I managed to glance over my shoulder, and saw my family all being led away. I never saw them again.

In an instant, I found myself completely alone. There were others around me who all seemed as bewildered as me. I later learned they too had lost members of their families on arrival.

The brutes thought they could take everything from us, our loved ones, our names, our dignity and humanity. But from that day forward I was determined that the one thing they wouldn't take from me was my life. Nor would I let them take the only thing that I had left of my family – the small photograph album that I had hidden in the tear of the lining of my suitcase. I managed to keep it hidden all the time I was in Auschwitz, thanks to the friends I made, who all looked out for one another. It's a miracle the brutes didn't find it, because they tried to take every one of our possessions away from us.

I now know I have my papa to thank for that. He taught me the importance of keeping a secret and how to hide it from those who tried their utmost to strip us of everything and anything that was dear to us. I believe it's what helped me survive, when countless others didn't. I clung on to my memories and would often go to check the small gap in the wall behind one of the barracks to make sure the photo album was still there. I would turn the pages and gaze at the photos of Mama, Papa, Stefan and me, tears streaming down my face. There were none of Mischa, so I only had my own sweet memories of him to hold on to.

Like I said, it was a miracle I was never caught, but then it was a miracle I survived those wretched weeks and months in squalid conditions and virtually nothing to eat. But I did. And I lived.

FIFTY-ONE
OCTOBER 2023

Eloise

Eloise had just left her grandmother's flat and was walking towards the bus stop when her mobile phone rang. She kept on walking as she retrieved it from her bag, but stopped dead when she saw who was calling her.

'James,' she said in surprise. It seemed too much of a coincidence after just talking to her grandmother about him. They hadn't spoken in weeks, so why now? Her cheeks grew hot as she accepted the call.

'This is a surprise. How are you?' she said, trying to sound normal. She ignored the banging of her heart.

'I'm good. How are you, Eloise?'

She could hear he was in a public place from the voices and laughter in the background. 'Fine, thanks. I've been with my grandmother all afternoon.'

'Ah, your lovely grandma. Say hello from me if you're still with her.' Eloise heard a peal of laughter in the background. 'Just a minute,' James said, and she heard his muffled voice saying, 'I'm calling about the email.' He paused, then said, 'Did you see it?'

'Are you speaking to me?' said Eloise, confused by the voices she could hear at his end. 'I don't know what you're on about.'

He laughed. 'Course I'm asking you, silly. Let me move somewhere quieter. While I'm doing that will you read the email?'

She didn't reply. Instead, she made a couple of swipes on her mobile till she was in her inbox. The only email that was marked unread was from Westerbork. Did he mean that one? She opened it up and saw James's address cc'd in. So that was why he was calling. She glanced down to the bottom to Liesbeth's sign-off, then went back up to the top. She read it quickly.

I hope you and your grandmother are well. I wanted to tell you that we have a date for the exhibition of Rudolf Breslauer's work, which will open to the public on 15 July next year. I would very much like to invite you and James to the preview evening on 14 July. We would regard it a great privilege if your grandmother could attend as well. We would be pleased to cover your travel expenses.

After your visit, we curated a selection of photographs and film footage from Breslauer's time at Westerbork. I want to thank you for your help and input in identifying some of these images, particularly of his children. These have contributed greatly to our understanding of the events that took place in 1942–44.

In our discussions we have come up with an idea involving your grandmother. At the entrance to the exhibition, we would like to feature a current portrait of her, and if she agrees we can arrange for a photographer to come to England to meet her. Can you please put this idea to her and let me know if she agrees?

All of us working on the exhibition are very excited to bring Rudolf Breslauer's compelling images to the public visiting Westerbork. We are confident that his important body of work will also attract much interest from outside the Netherlands.

I very much look forward to hearing from you.

My very best wishes

Liesbeth Hendrick

Eloise thought of her grandmother, small and birdlike in her nest of cushions, suddenly a diminished version of her former self. She shivered at the image in her mind's eye, then remembered how easily her grandmother had been able to keep up a monologue about her past memories without showing any signs of weakness. Her grandmother was a lot stronger than she looked and maybe this news was just the tonic she needed to get back to her old self.

A little way away, she saw her bus pull up to the stop. She could run and catch it, but decided against it. Instead, she switched back to phone mode. 'James, are you still there?'

'At last. I thought you'd given up on me.' He sounded amused and she smiled at his choice of words. It was the truth – she had given up on him, for no good reason other than that he'd taken a deep interest in her grandmother's history. Why shouldn't he have, she thought, suddenly feeling ashamed of herself. She knew she'd been impetuous in breaking things off, believing him to be selfish without having any real grounds for it. But pride prevented her from apologising, at least for now, so she decided to keep things neutral between them.

'Liesbeth seems to have made a lot of progress with the exhibition. I'm glad I was able to help.'

'Isn't it tremendous news?' said James, ignoring her

comment. 'I'd love to come to the preview, but I quite understand if you don't want me to.'

Eloise wasn't expecting him to say that. 'Don't be silly. You must come, especially as you were the one to introduce me to Liesbeth in the first place. But I'm not sure if my grandmother is up to coming. She's been poorly recently, so going all that way might be too much for her.'

When James didn't answer, she kept talking to fill the silence. 'James, she asked after you today. She called you a "nice young man" and wondered why you haven't been to see her.'

He burst out laughing. 'I'm glad she hasn't turned against me...'

'You mean like I have?'

'Now, would I say that?'

'Perhaps not, but you sounded as if you might.' She smiled. She'd missed their banter and it felt good to be joshing with him again. No hard feelings, she wanted to say, but she managed to stop herself. She hadn't entirely forgiven him for what he'd done, but it would be nice if they went to the preview together.

Just then, the next bus arrived at her stop, but she was in no mood to run for it.

'If it's OK with you, I would like to visit your grandmother again,' James said. 'With you, of course. We could tell her about the exhibition and see if she's willing to have her portrait done. You know, I find her so interesting, and not just because of my research. Anyway, you should know that I've taken a different angle for my dissertation. The Westerbork material I've decided to use is available in the public domain and represents only a small amount of what I'll be covering.'

Eloise drew in a deep breath. 'James, I shouldn't have reacted the way I did when we parted. To be honest, I felt overwhelmed by everything I'd learned at Westerbork. It all felt so personal and I didn't know what to think. And you calling now... well, it seems such a coincidence seeing as I've just been with my grandmother. She opened up to me in a way she's never done before. James?'

'Yes?' He sounded hopeful.

'You're the only person who understands what I've been through and... can we still be friends?'

'Yeah, of course we can.'

She detected a hesitation before he spoke, maybe even disappointment in his voice. 'I know you're busy, but shall we meet for a chat?'

'I'd like that,' James said casually. 'The wine café in Walton Street is good. Shall I meet you there at seven?'

FIFTY-TWO

James was waiting for her at a window table with a bottle of white wine cooling on ice.

'I hope you don't mind me ordering without asking you first,' he said, getting to his feet. There was a moment of awkwardness between them as he moved to kiss her on the cheek, then seemed to think better of it and gave her a clumsy hug instead.

'Not at all. You know how I like a nice cold Sauvignon Blanc,' she said, pretending not to notice, and took a seat opposite him.

He poured the wine and their eyes met as they chinked glasses. 'Cheers,' he said.

'Cheers. Thanks for agreeing to see me at such short notice.' She took a big sip of wine to cover her nerves. She wished she hadn't left it so long and was grateful that he'd contacted her first.

He shook his head dismissively. 'It's just lovely to see you.'

As they continued to make small talk, she kept sipping her wine, and knew she was drinking too quickly when he refilled her glass before his. It took a couple of glasses of wine before she began to relax.

'Tell me what your grandmother said to you today,' he said at last.

James listened intently as she told him her grandmother's story about her pain over losing the little brother she'd never mentioned before. And her guilt at having doubted her father when he was trying his level best to look out for his family. 'She still doesn't talk about what happened after they were sent to Auschwitz, but I bet the loss of her younger brothers hit her especially hard. She'll never get over it.'

James nodded sympathetically. 'Sadly, guilt was all too common amongst Holocaust survivors and many found it too painful to talk about it to their families. I recently read about survivor guilt syndrome in an article by an American Jewish psychiatrist whose own parents survived the Holocaust. It must have taken a great deal of courage for your grandmother to speak to you.'

Eloise was only half listening. 'I only hope it's not been too much for her. She's not been well for some weeks, James.'

'All the more reason to tell her about the exhibition. It'll give her something to look forward to.'

She eyed him doubtfully. 'Do you really think so?'

'Yes, I do. I can't see any harm in asking her. Even if she thinks it's too much now, by the summer she'll hopefully have recovered and will feel differently about it. Let's do this together. Shall we?'

Eloise smiled, realising how much she'd missed James's cheerful optimism. She felt as if a great weight had been lifted from her, and she let out a long sigh. 'All right, let's do it.'

They made plans to visit her grandmother at the weekend, but nothing beyond that. James didn't push her and she was quite happy to continue as they were. Eloise was relieved, knowing that if they were to get back together she would need time to trust him again.

FIFTY-THREE

'Remember what I said. She's quite frail, so we mustn't overexcite her.'

James's face was just visible over the top of the enormous bouquet of yellow chrysanthemums he had insisted on buying. He looked comical and seemed to know it. 'Understood, nurse,' he said with a chuckle.

Eloise shook her head and smiled as she pressed on the bell, then waited a moment before she opened the door. 'Hello, Grandma! It's Eloise. I've brought you a visitor.' She turned her head to give James a warning look, then moved through the narrow hallway into the living room. She didn't see her grandmother in her usual seat and immediately thought something was wrong. She worried that she'd had a fall and been unable to work the alarm she wore round her neck. Where was she?

'Grandma?' she called at the same moment the old lady appeared at the door to her kitchen. Eloise noticed that she was gripping a handrail she hadn't noticed before. She supposed it must have been recently installed to help her get around more easily.

'Ah, Eloise... did you say you were coming?' Her grandmother looked surprised; then James appeared behind her, half hidden behind the flowers. She broke into a wide smile when she saw who it was. 'Well, this is a nice surprise.'

'It's lovely to see you. How are you, Mrs Moses?' said James, presenting her with the bouquet.

She put a hand on her heart and gasped. 'For me?' Her voice was girlish and she smiled coquettishly. 'You really shouldn't have,' she said, sounding delighted, and buried her nose in the blooms.

Eloise watched with amusement the show her grandmother was putting on, and marvelled at how easily impressed she was by James's gesture.

She turned her head to Eloise. 'Will you put these in water for me? You can get rid of the flowers in that vase over there. They need throwing out.' She waved her hand dismissively in the direction of the vase on the low table next to her chair.

Eloise had to stop herself from saying anything. She knew her grandmother wasn't being intentionally hurtful about the flowers that she'd given her only a few days earlier, but she couldn't help feeling stung by her remark. Had James always had this effect on her? She tried to remember, as she cleared away the wilting flowers.

Eloise had already agreed with James that he would broach the subject of the exhibition and then play it by ear with regard to the portrait. After she'd made them all a cup of tea, she let James do the talking. Her grandmother listened attentively and showed great interest in James's studies and the research he was undertaking for his coursework.

'I'm sure you will have heard all about our trip to Westerbork in the summer,' he said at last.

The old lady nodded with rapt attention.

'The photographs taken by your father were extraordinary

and quite unlike any other I've seen from the Second World War. The museum obviously think so too and they're going to put on an exhibition of his work next July. They've been in touch with you, haven't they?' He turned his head to Eloise for confirmation.

Eloise nodded. 'They've invited the three of us to go to the preview evening. It's not until the summer, but I do hope you'll come with us,' she said expectantly.

'They want me to go all that way just for one evening?' Her grandmother frowned as she looked from one to the other, then slowly shook her head. 'It'll be too much for me. But of course you two must go.'

Eloise didn't think her grandmother would listen to her if she tried to change her mind. She knitted her brow at James, hoping he'd speak on her behalf.

'It's not for another nine months, so you don't need to make up your mind about it just yet,' he said. 'We can take you and I'm sure I can borrow my mother's car, so you won't need to worry about the journey.'

Eloise widened her eyes at him. Had he even passed his driving test? He winked at her with a look that urged her not to interject.

Her grandmother must have seen the wink, for her expression shifted. 'All right. I'll consider it. But I won't give you my answer just yet. It would be like tempting fate.'

'Of course,' said James smoothly, and proceeded to tell her of Liesbeth's plans to send a photographer to take her portrait, which would be featured in the exhibition.

'What a lot of fuss over nothing.' But she was smiling and was clearly flattered by all the attention.

'Not at all,' he said. 'Especially if you pose like that for the photographer. Leave it to us and we'll arrange for him, or her, to come here to your flat.'

Eloise and James left not long after. 'That went better than I was expecting,' she said, tilting her head towards him. 'You had her round your little finger.'

'Do you think so?' he said, feigning surprise, then went on, 'But I think we should sort out the portrait before she changes her mind.'

FIFTY-FOUR

Eloise had just completed the last essay of term and was looking forward to going out with friends later that evening when the doorbell rang. 'Anyone getting that?' she called out. She didn't want to be disturbed at that precise moment, for she was saving her work and writing an email to her tutor. With half an ear, she heard the front door open and the murmur of voices. She assumed it wasn't for her and so she was surprised when there was a knock a few moments later.

'Come in,' she said vaguely and pressed send on her email. She looked up as the door opened, and saw James standing there holding up a bottle of wine.

'May I?' he asked tentatively. He was wrapped up in a long overcoat and maroon scarf and his cheeks glowed. He didn't wait for her reply, but came straight in, bringing with him the evocative scent of a cold winter's evening.

Eloise snapped shut the lid of her laptop. 'Are you going somewhere with that?' Amused, she tilted her head towards the wine bottle.

'This?' he said and glanced at it as if he'd forgotten he was holding it. He edged towards her and placed it next to her laptop. 'I happened to pass Sainsbury's and they had a special offer on French wine. It occurred to me I haven't seen much of you lately. So I thought I'd come and surprise you.'

Eloise laughed, delighted to see him. It had been several weeks since they'd last met, though they'd kept in touch by text and the occasional phone call. She was still unsure of her feelings towards him and had used the pressure of work as an excuse not to meet. With her last essay of the term out of the way that particular excuse now melted away.

'Well, you've certainly done that. You may as well stay now you're here,' she said casually. She got up and went to the bookcase, where she kept a collection of glasses on one of the shelves, and picked out two. When she turned round, James had shaken off his coat and dropped it in a heap on the floor. He unwound the scarf from round his neck and let it drop too. He then sat down on one end of the bed and waited.

Neither of them spoke, but she knew that if she went straight to him now she wouldn't be able to stop herself from falling into his arms. And if she did, there'd be no turning back. Playing for time, she put the glasses down on her desk and moved a few things around, acutely aware that his eyes were on her. When she couldn't stand it a moment longer, she picked up the bottle and glasses and moved towards him.

'Will you pour?' she said as she sat down next to him.

He shuffled closer. She watched him pour, making sure he didn't spill any wine on the bed.

'Eloise,' he murmured.

For a moment, she wondered if he'd been drinking before he'd come, but she couldn't detect alcohol on his breath. 'What?' she said, knowing full well what was about to happen.

'I've missed you,' he said and planted a lingering kiss on her lips. She closed her eyes and succumbed to the feeling she'd been trying to ignore for so long.

Reluctantly, she pulled away, saying, 'I've missed you too.'

'Let me take those,' he said, first putting the bottle down on the floor, then carefully placing the full glasses beside it. He then kicked off his trainers and drew her on top of him. He held her head with both hands so he could keep kissing her. It felt just like the first time and she wondered why she could ever have thought of rejecting him.

Afterwards, they lay side by side gazing into one another's eyes. 'Do you forgive me now?' he said, his voice so deep it was almost inaudible; he ran a finger sensuously over her bottom lip. She nodded, unwilling to break the spell by saying something inadequate.

'I've been thinking a lot about us,' he went on, propping himself up on one elbow. Eloise's heart skipped a beat.

'What you said last summer about me using you wasn't entirely untrue,' he admitted.

She frowned. She wasn't sure she wanted to hear this, but he silenced her with another kiss.

'Hear me out, Eloise. I just want to explain what was going through my head at the time. I was under pressure from my tutor to settle on the topic of my dissertation. We had several long discussions, and I just couldn't come up with an angle that I knew would satisfy him. Even though it's my work I realise now that he was driving my narrative – I shouldn't have let him. But then he played his trump card by giving me his contact at Westerbork. He said I should go and visit. When I mentioned that your grandmother had been interned there during the war, he persuaded me that this would be the unique angle I was missing. You don't have to believe me when I tell you that the whole idea made me uncomfortable, but I was desperate to make it work. And then when we were on the ferry coming back and you confronted me about using you and your family, I simply didn't have an answer. I should have defended myself, because deep down I knew you were right.'

Eloise knew she should have been relieved at his admission,

but all she felt was guilt. 'There's no reason you can't discuss Rudolf Breslauer's work inside the camp. After all, it's all out in the public domain.'

'True, but I ruled it out because I wanted you to be happy with the idea rather than find out after the event. So I changed my approach and my tutor actually thinks my dissertation is stronger for it.'

'Oh, James. I'm sorry for all the trouble I caused.'

'No, you shouldn't. It was all my own making. I was devastated when you said you didn't want to see me. Ironically, being apart gave me the clarity I needed.'

'I'm glad...' Eloise began, but from his expression she guessed he still had something he wanted to say. 'Is there more?'

James nodded. 'I've had an idea. Nothing to do with my dissertation,' he added hastily. 'It might not work, but I really think we should try and see if it does. It's about the preview evening – I need your help in persuading your grandmother to come, but on no account must you tell her anything about what we're planning.'

'James, you're talking in riddles.' Eloise laughed and slapped him playfully on the arm. 'I have no idea what you're talking about. Tell me, please.'

'Patience,' he said teasingly with a knowing smile. 'Why don't we drink our wine first and then I'll explain.'

On the day of the shoot, Eloise woke with nervous excitement. Everything had been arranged for Westerbork's own photographer to travel to England for the portrait and she'd agreed with James that she should go to her grandmother's alone. The old lady had been flattered by all the attention and Eloise had noticed a change in her. She was almost back to her old self, apart from her mobility, which the doctor said was to be expected for someone of her advanced age.

Eloise stopped at the deli for cinnamon pastries and three takeaway black coffees. She'd only ever seen her grandmother drink tea before, so she hoped she'd make an exception on this occasion.

She arrived early to find that the photographer, Stefan Eggers, was already setting up his equipment, while her grandmother watched with great interest from her armchair. Eloise noticed that she was wearing her best navy cardigan and a thin gold chain lay in the hollow of her neck. Eloise approved of the fact that she'd made an effort with her appearance. 'Hello, Grandma. You look nice today,' she said, leaning down to kiss her on the cheek.

The old lady scoffed but didn't seem to be able to keep the smile off her face. It was obvious that being the focus of attention was doing her the power of good. 'Mr Eggers has been telling me that he specialises in portrait photography. Just like my own father did.' She gave a chuckle, then went on. 'This is my granddaughter, Eloise. She's studying at Oxford,' she said proudly.

Mr Eggers looked up from his camera to give Eloise an appraising look. He must have been somewhere around her father's age, Eloise guessed, taking in his thick silver hair and his clear blue eyes.

'It's a pleasure to meet you, Eloise.' He spoke good English, but with a strong Dutch accent.

'Thank you for coming all this way, Mr Eggers. We very much appreciate it,' she said with a quick glance at her grandmother, who was still beaming with pleasure.

'I've been looking forward to coming. I'm sorry I wasn't around when you came to Westerbork, but now I meet both you and your grandmother, which is a great honour. I'm sure I don't need to tell you that we hold Rudolf Breslauer's work in very high esteem. The exhibition has been years in the making, but, until we heard from you, we had no idea there were any living relatives.' He cleared his throat. 'As you know, so many prisoners died in the camps along with their entire families.'

Eloise looked at her grandmother, but she didn't seem in the least perturbed by his comment. 'It was terrible, but that's all a long time in the past,' she said, sitting up a little straighter. 'I want you to know that Eloise is not my only granddaughter. I have eleven other grandchildren living in Israel, Canada and the United States. Oh, and Switzerland. Danny's a scientist working for a medical company in Zurich.' Her dark eyes twinkled with pride.

'Eleven grandchildren! I didn't know that, Mrs Breslauer,' said Mr Eggers.

'Mrs Moses-Breslauer,' she corrected and pursed her lips at his mistake.

Eloise remembered the coffee she was still holding in the cardboard tray supplied by the deli. 'I bought some coffee and pastries. Let me decant the coffee into decent cups. Do you take milk and sugar, Mr Eggers?'

'Just sugar, please,' he said with a smile.

'Will you have a coffee, Grandma?' she asked, expecting her to decline and make some scornful comment about shop-bought ready-made coffee.

Her grandmother looked askance at the takeaway cups. 'I won't say no, but make sure it's milky and sweet.'

'Of course.' Eloise turned on her heel and went into the kitchen for the milk and sugar. Her grandmother never ceased to surprise her.

When she came back in with the coffee tray, she saw the photographer had set up the screen and was checking the lighting. 'I'll be ready in just a moment,' he said.

Her grandmother's face lit up. 'Good. I was just telling Mr Eggers about the Leica camera my father used to carry around with him. It's such a shame the camera didn't survive. He took all his photographs with it. I remember it so well, the brown leather case, the different lenses he used and the whirr and clicking sound it made whenever he took a picture. This takes me right back.' She nodded admiringly towards his camera as she lifted her coffee cup to her lips and took a sip. Eloise waited for her to make a face but instead she made an approving sound.

'I'll do my best, but I can't promise the results will be as good as your father's,' Mr Eggers said with a smile. 'May I ask you to sit on the chair over here?' He moved to help her get up, but she waved him away. 'Eloise, give me a hand, will you?' her grandmother said, turning her head to Eloise.

It took several minutes until she was comfortable. The seat

was too hard. She needed a cushion to sit on. She needed one in the small of her back. There was a draught from the window, which needed to be checked to make sure it was properly shut.

Mr Eggers quietly let her get on with it. He drank his coffee and fiddled with his camera until she declared she was ready. Eloise could see she was holding herself stiffly, and all her jolliness from earlier had vanished. He began taking photos, one after another, asking her to move her head, this way and that. And then he stopped to say brightly, 'You've done this before, haven't you? You're a natural.'

Immediately, a smile spread across the old lady's face and her eyes crinkled up in pleasure. Before she knew it, he'd taken several more photographs in quick succession. 'Excellent,' he said, then told her he wanted to change the background from light to dark.

'Whatever for? Surely you've taken enough photos?' she grumbled.

'It can make an enormous difference to the mood of a photograph. It won't take a minute,' he said, undeterred, and asked Eloise to assist him to put a black backdrop in place.

When he was ready, Eloise stood back and watched. Again, it took a few attempts to get her grandmother to smile. And when she did, her smile seemed to light up the whole room. 'Perfect,' Eloise murmured and hugged herself in delight.

She helped her grandmother back to her armchair while Mr Eggers packed everything away. He was going to meet a friend in London later, so Eloise called a taxi to take him to the station.

Before he left, he thanked them for their hospitality and said he'd be in touch with a selection of photos for her grandmother to make a choice. 'It's important that you are happy with the result. When you're satisfied, we'll get it ready for the exhibition.'

'What a fuss. And I'm not even the main subject,' her grandmother said, with a radiant smile.

Mr Eggers smiled indulgently. 'Will you be coming to the exhibition, Mrs Moses-Breslauer?'

Her expression grew serious as she drew in a breath, which seemed to catch in her throat. 'Of course I would like to, but I don't make promises to anyone – not at my age. Everything is more of an effort these days and I tire easily. If I'm well enough, I'll come. That's all I'm prepared to say.'

FIFTY-SIX

After Eloise had seen Mr Eggers out, she went back inside to spend a few minutes with her grandmother before she needed to leave for a lecture.

'Won't you stay a while longer?' her grandmother asked querulously, a worried frown appearing on her face. 'There's something I've been meaning to talk to you about. I haven't been entirely truthful with you.'

Eloise glanced quickly at her watch and calculated that she could spare half an hour. 'Of course, Grandma,' she said and sat down in her usual chair facing her.

Her grandmother cleared her throat as if she was about to make an announcement. Eloise hoped it wasn't anything serious. She'd been so cheerful with Mr Eggers, and happy to have her portrait taken – what could have caused her change of mood? Eloise felt herself tense up as she waited for her to start.

'Meeting that nice Mr Eggers today has stirred up so many memories about the past. I should never have hidden anything from you. I want you to know it's because I've wrestled so long with guilt for the way I behaved towards my parents. I simply couldn't understand what my dear papa was doing, but I see now his efforts were to keep us all safe and were nothing short of heroic.'

She paused, her mouth twitching as she struggled to regain her composure before continuing. Eloise listened with sadness as her grandmother recalled the family's flight from Leipzig to Amsterdam, where they thought they were safe, only for her father to be hunted down by Schlesinger, the Westerbork kommandant's right-hand man. It was a defining moment for the family, who ended up being forced against their will to leave their home for Westerbork. Her grandmother spared no details of their reduced circumstances inside the camp and her father's growing despair, which led him to photograph his children in order to keep the kommandant off his back.

'Papa tried so hard to keep our names off the deportation lists, but in the end it was all in vain. None of us could have foreseen the evil plan concocted by the Nazis to get rid of us. And tragically, they succeeded. On our arrival at Auschwitz, Mama, Papa, Stefan and Mischa were selected to die – they didn't deserve to. At the time, I didn't know that I would never see them again.'

A full forty-five minutes later, she was still talking, and Eloise had long forgotten about her intention to leave. Her grandmother had reached the part of her story when she found herself all alone inside Auschwitz, not knowing what fate had befallen her family.

'In a way, I'm glad I didn't know, because it gave me a slender hope to cling on to all those weeks and months during that terribly cold winter. It was horribly overcrowded inside the Auschwitz camp and we were forced to share bunks with strangers. There were no blankets. At night, I wept silently for my lost family and more than once wished I were dead. Daily, people were dying all around me, weakened by lack of food. Illness was rampant and I nearly succumbed to typhus myself after spending many long weeks trying hide my symptoms from the brutal guards. They would have shown me no mercy. I still don't know why I was spared while the rest of my family wasn't. I would willingly have changed places with any of them. It was all so, so senseless.' She gazed into the middle distance, her dark eyes misting over with unshed tears.

Eloise was about to reach out a hand when her grandmother started speaking again, returning to her arrival in Auschwitz.

'Straight after I reached the end of the platform, I was forced to go to the right and herded with a long queue of people waiting for registration. I was handed a number on a scrap of paper, which a man in prisoner's uniform tattooed in black ink on my left forearm. It must have hurt terribly but I didn't notice the pain because I was completely numb.

'After all those years I can still read the numbers on my arm. They have always been part of me, but I kept them covered up because of my shame.'

Absently, she began rubbing her arm. Suddenly, she said, 'Eloise, I beg you to look.' She painstakingly dragged back the sleeve of her best navy cardigan until her number was visible. It broke Eloise's heart to see the smudged blue-black digits that defaced the paper-thin skin on the old lady's forearm: Eight Three Seven Nine Five. Too shocked to reply, Eloise could only nod.

'It's taken me too long time to realise that none of it was my fault. I hated this tattoo, but I see now it's the only proof that I was there.'

Eloise immediately rose from her chair and crouched down beside her grandmother so she could hold her thin slight body against her own. She knew how much effort it must have taken to speak in this way and hoped it hadn't all been too much for her.

Sitting back, and with tears flowing down her face, Eloise managed to say, 'Thank you for telling me your story, Grandma. I want you to know just how much I love you.'

FIFTY-SEVEN

'It's not possible. She was perfectly well when I saw her last Friday.' Eloise's voice shook. She quickly shut the lid of her laptop and tiptoed out of the library, a trickle of cold dread seeping through her. Pressing her mobile to her ear, she heard her father sigh.

'I'm sorry to give you this news, but you're so close to your grandma. I knew you'd want to know.'

'But how come she went downhill so quickly?'

'I asked myself the same question. I've just come off the phone to the warden, who called the doctor after finding her still in bed at ten o'clock. She'd been complaining of feeling unwell and a cough. The doctor confirmed she had pneumonia and said the safest place for her right now is in hospital.'

'Can we go and visit her?' said Eloise in a small voice. How was it possible? she kept asking herself. She'd been so alert when Eloise had left her the last time. She'd even talked about wanting to see her portrait hanging at the exhibition. Didn't that mean she had every intention of going? Eloise refused to believe that her health could have deteriorated so fast.

'I'm driving over this afternoon and can pick you up on the way. Visiting hours start at three.'

'Are you sure we're allowed to see her?'

'Yes, but she might not be awake.'

Eloise began to cry softly and found that she was trembling. 'Why are we going then?'

'Because...' For a moment, he was silent. 'Grandma's in the best place where she can be properly looked after. We shouldn't jump to any conclusions. I'll get to you by two thirty. Look out for me because there's never anywhere to park round by you.'

Eloise immediately rang James to tell him the news but his phone went straight to voicemail. She glanced at the time and guessed he was in a lecture. Sighing, she tapped out a text saying she'd be in touch after she'd been to the hospital.

The hospital car park was busy and her father had to keep driving round until a space became free. 'You would have thought they'd organise themselves better round here,' he grumbled.

'Dad... please. Not now,' said Eloise, staring out of her window. She waited in the car while he went to get a parking ticket. He came round to her side and opened her door.

'I'm sorry. I've never liked hospitals,' he mumbled and held out his arms to hug her. After a brief moment he said gruffly that they should go. She was grateful for this unusual show of affection, however brief.

One of the duty staff at the nurses' station consulted a whiteboard with a long list of names and several rubbings-out. Eloise didn't allow herself to think what that meant. 'Mrs U. Moses-Breslauer. That's her,' she said with a lump in her throat. 'She was admitted this morning.'

'Follow the corridor right to the end to the last room on the left,' said the nurse, and immediately turned away because another member of staff was demanding her attention.

'Come on, Dad,' said Eloise, already hating this noisy place, with its constant hum and beep of machines and the staff who all looked so harried as they rushed about their business.

Their shoes squeaked as they walked along the long corridor that smelt of disinfectant. They came to the last room and went inside. All the beds were occupied and had curtains pulled round them. Eloise didn't want to appear nosy by poking her head round each one, and was saved from doing so when a youngish woman appeared from one of the cubicles. She gave Eloise a sympathetic smile and said, 'You all right, there?'

'We're looking for my grandmother,' Eloise said.

'That'll be the old lady by the window,' the woman said.

'Thank you,' said Eloise and exchanged a look with her dad, relieved they'd come to the right place.

'You go first,' said her father, standing aside to let her past. Eloise peered through the gap in the curtains and saw the shape of her grandmother propped up amongst a stack of pillows with her eyes closed.

'Grandma?' she whispered and moved inside the cubicle, but her grandmother didn't stir. 'It's me, Eloise,' she said in a louder voice, but still she got no reaction. She turned back to her father, who was standing looking out of the window.

'Dad, she's asleep. What should we do?'

'Why don't you stay with her and I'll go and find someone to ask about her condition.' He pursed his lips into a thin smile as he gently squeezed her shoulder. Eloise knew he was finding this difficult too as she watched him walk away. Suddenly, she felt very alone amongst the murmur of voices from the other cubicles and constant movement of visitors in and out of the room.

Sighing, she turned to sit beside her grandmother, watching her face in repose for any sign that she was about to wake up.

Ten minutes later, her father came back looking exhausted. He shook his head. 'The nurse at the front said someone will be along soon, but she couldn't say when. Typical NHS,' he mumbled.

'Dad. You can see how overstretched they are. It's not their fault.'

'I didn't say it was.' He looked as if he was about to say something further, but she silenced him with a look. She checked again on her grandmother, who still showed no response.

She stood up. 'Let's go. I can come back tomorrow and hopefully she'll be awake then. Sorry it's been a wasted journey for you.'

Every afternoon, Eloise took the bus to the hospital. The next time she was there, she was surprised to find her grandmother sitting in the chair beside the bed. Her face was drawn and her hair unbrushed, but at least she was awake. Eloise's heart soared with hope that she was turning a corner.

'How lovely to see you,' said the old lady, her dark eyes twinkling. She held out a bony hand for Eloise to hold. But she didn't give any other indication that she knew it was Eloise.

'Are you quite comfortable, Grandma?'

'Oh yes. The nurses are very nice here, but they wake me up far too early, when it's still dark. I can't see the point, because all I do is lie in bed all day. They may as well let me sleep.'

'What about the food? Are you eating enough?'

'Food? I don't think I've seen any. Would you pass me my drink?'

Eloise picked up the beaker, not unlike a toddler's drinking cup, from the bedstand and handed it to her, but she didn't attempt to drink. Eloise lifted it to her lips and she took a small sip of the thick liquid; she made a disgusted face, so Eloise put it aside, thinking she should bring up the subject of mealtimes with the nurse on duty. Already so small and frail, her grandmother seemed a shadow of her former self. Eloise hardly recognised her.

Late one afternoon, Eloise received an email from Liesbeth with a selection of photographs attached. They were all excellent, but there was one with the dark background that was most striking as it brought out her grandmother's radiant smile. Eloise gazed at it, remembering their long conversations with fondness. This would cheer her up, she thought, feeling buoyed up herself for the first time in days. Secretly, she hoped it would give her grandmother the boost she needed to help her recover. But the next time she visited, her grandmother was back in bed with her eyes closed. Eloise tried to persuade her to open her eyes and look at the image on her phone, but she got no response whatsoever. It was at that point that Eloise realised that her grandmother would never recover.

Five days after her grandmother had been admitted to hospital, Eloise was jerked awake late at night by the shrill ring of her mobile. She fumbled on her bedside table and saw the time was one fifteen; her father's name came up on the screen.

'The hospital's just rung me and asked me to come straight away.' His voice was tight, as if he might cry. 'I'm afraid Grandma hasn't got long.'

Eloise, still coming to after being woken from a deep sleep, couldn't understand what he was saying. 'Why is the hospital calling now?' she said groggily.

'It's what they always do. I'm driving straight over. I expect you'll want to be there.' Her father rang off.

. . .

Just the one nurse was on duty. She looked up from her computer screen and knew straight away who they had come to see.

'Is she in any pain?' asked Eloise's father, coming straight to the point.

'No, she's being kept comfortable,' the nurse said gently. 'You can go and sit with her. I'll page the doctor to come and speak to you.'

Eloise felt her chest tighten. She could hardly breathe. She let her father hold her hand and they walked down the empty corridor, the squeak of their shoes the only sound apart from the insistent beep of some machine or other. Without speaking, they arrived at her grandmother's bedside. Eloise was shocked to see she was attached to a ventilator. Her chest was gently moving up and down. Other than that she lay perfectly still, with her eyes closed. They sat on either side of her bed, listening to the rhythmic exhalations of the machine.

The doctor arrived, a man in his thirties with a careworn face. Eloise wondered how long his shift had already been. But he smiled for them and offered to speak privately in a nearby room that wasn't being used.

Eloise had so many questions she wanted to ask, but in the end didn't ask any of them. The doctor spoke in kind tones as he explained that Mrs Moses-Breslauer would not recover from her illness. It was impossible to say how long she had, but, as she was unable to breathe unassisted, how did they feel about switching off the machine?

Eloise was horrified that such a decision was being asked of them. 'I don't want her to experience any distress, not of our making.'

'It won't be like that,' said the doctor patiently. 'Once the machine is switched off, she'll go very quietly.'

Eloise could barely focus on him, her eyes were so full of tears. She felt her dad reach for her hand and squeeze it. When she turned her head to him, she saw he was nodding.

The doctor left them alone, saying they should take as long as they needed. At first they were silent, then gradually they began to talk haltingly and fondly about grandma, about everything except the decision they'd both come to.

When the time came, the doctor was called back and he waited until Eloise's father gestured to switch the machine off. The doctor then quietly moved away and left them in peace.

Eloise leaned over and kissed her grandmother on her cooling forehead one last time, whispering how much she loved her. She then moved aside to give her father space.

Suddenly, her grandmother let out a long sighing breath, and it was over.

A crowd had gathered outside the entrance to the museum, far bigger than Eloise had been expecting.

'Did you have any idea that so many people would come?' she asked James.

'Wait and see,' he said enigmatically as they took their place at the back of the group and waited for the doors to open. It was obvious many of the people knew each other from the way they were laughing and talking in animated voices. She heard Dutch spoken, which wasn't a surprise, but she also heard American English, and there was another language, which she didn't recognise.

She glanced down at her phone and clicked her tongue. 'Dad's just texted. Their plane's been delayed and he's not sure they'll make it in time for the start.'

James gave her a sympathetic look. There was a ripple of voices as the doors to the museum opened and the crowd began edging forward. Eloise grew anxious that her parents would miss the preview altogether. With her grandma gone, she needed their support. As they moved forward a few steps, she wondered what her grandmother would have said about all this.

No doubt she would have been her usual no-nonsense self on seeing all these people flocking to see her father's exhibition. Eloise imagined her saying, 'What a load of fuss.' But she knew there would be immense pride too in her father's achievements behind the camera after doubting him for most of her life. The thought made Eloise calmer as she passed through the doors into the foyer with James at her side.

A smartly dressed woman in a dark trouser suit and crisp white blouse stood greeting each of the guests and ticking their names off a list on a clipboard. When it was Eloise and James's turn to give their names, her face lit up. 'What a pleasure to meet you,' she said, and directed them to the exhibition hall, where Liesbeth would meet them.

'Preferential treatment,' murmured James, as they walked away, which made Eloise grin. He slipped his hand in hers and it felt warm and reassuring.

The walls of the corridor were lined with enlarged photographs of Westerbork. Some Eloise recognised, but there were several others she didn't. By the entrance hung an enormous black-and-white image of Rudolf Breslauer wearing his characteristic tortoiseshell-framed glasses, which gave him an all-knowing look. She stopped for a moment and gazed at it, her throat constricting a little.

'There it is,' said James, nudging her arm. 'Look... your grandmother.'

Right inside the entrance hung the oversized portrait of the photograph she'd chosen for the exhibition. It was the one taken against the black background that her grandmother had almost refused to have taken. Joy emanated from that lived-in face, from every small line and crease to the mischievous twinkle in her eye and radiant smile that seemed to light up the room. It hung from the ceiling next to a similar-sized photo of Ursula as a smiling eight-year-old wearing a garland of daisies in her hair.

'They're beautiful,' Eloise said, swallowing hard. 'Don't they look just perfect together?'

James shook his head in wonderment as he stared from one portrait to the other. 'Wow... the similarity between the two photos is amazing.'

Liesbeth and Stefan Eggers arrived. 'Eloise, James – I'm so pleased you were able to come.' Liesbeth held out her arms. It felt both strange and natural that she should embrace them. 'Stefan, you know Eloise. And this is her boyfriend, James.'

The photographer shook them both warmly by the hand. 'It's so good to meet you again, Eloise. And to meet you, James.'

'I think my grandmother would have loved to see what you've done,' said Eloise. 'You've done her proud and the portrait is stunning. Was it your idea to display the two pictures together?'

He looked pleased. 'When I asked her to pose for me, I hadn't seen the one of her as a child until Liesbeth showed me it. It was only when I put the two side by side that I saw how closely they mirrored each other. Liesbeth, have I time to show Eloise a couple of exhibits before we start?'

Smiling, Liesbeth glanced at her watch and nodded. 'I know you've been longing to.'

'Come with me,' Stefan said and led Eloise into the exhibition space, which consisted of two rooms. In the first room a large selection of black-and-photos were displayed, with descriptions underneath. In the one beyond a black-and-white film was being projected onto a white wall.

He stopped beside two display cases, illuminated by spotlights in the ceiling. He pointed to the first one that contained a vintage camera mounted on wooden plinths. 'We found this Leica camera packed away in a box at the back of a cupboard in the archives. I couldn't be sure when I first saw it, but it has Rudolf Breslauer's initials engraved on the bottom. I'm afraid I can't let you examine it – at least not for now.'

So this was the camera her grandmother had talked about so often. Eloise peered at it, marvelling at what good condition it was in. 'I can't believe it. Grandma would've been over the moon that you've found it. Do you remember her saying what a shame it was his camera hadn't survived?'

He nodded and smiled. 'It was a very special moment when we opened the boxes and realised what we were looking at. I'm sure this was the same Leica camera Rudolf Breslauer used to take all these pictures.' He moved to the other display case; its contents brought a smile to Eloise's face. Her grandmother's photo album lay open at the page showing the three young Breslauer children beside a piano, their mouths open in song.

'It's perfect,' she said, gazing fondly at the photo that was so familiar to her. She thought how fitting it was that this photograph of Rudolf Breslauer's three children had been given pride of place.

Liesbeth called over that the rest of the guests were about to arrive and asked Eloise to come and stand beside her. Feeling apprehensive, she caught James's eye, and he gave her a wink of encouragement. She smiled in gratitude for his contribution to making this evening happen. It had been his idea to make contact with all these people and invite them to attend. Eloise had agreed that it would be such a wonderful surprise for her grandmother to see everyone gathered together to honour her father, but now she felt bereft that Ursula wasn't here in person to meet them. As she gazed out at the assembled guests she realised she didn't know a single person, and was beginning to think this whole thing had been a mistake. A waiter dressed in a black suit came past with a tray of sparkling wine. Eloise gratefully accepted a glass and took a long sip to steady her nerves.

'I'll say a few words about the exhibition and then introduce you,' said Liesbeth. 'Are you all right with that?'

'Of course,' said Eloise, taking another gulp of her wine and quickly swallowing it down.

When everyone was inside the room, Liesbeth tapped the side of her glass with a manicured fingernail. An immediate hush descended on the assembled group.

'Good evening, everyone,' she said in her confident English. 'It is my great pleasure to welcome you to the opening of this very special exhibition, which has been two years in the making. We are honoured to present original photographs and footage taken by Rudolf Breslauer during his time as the official photographer of Westerbork transit camp. It was a role that was forced upon him by the Germans, but I am sure you will agree that he approached it with dedication and professionalism. More importantly for us is the extraordinarily frank and moving record he made inside the camp. We should never forget that in documenting the truth he would have faced enormous danger of being found out, but it didn't deter him from carrying on.

'Towards the end of his time at Westerbork, he also began filming for the Germans. He knew his time was running out and this made him all the more determined to leave behind evidence of the truth behind German lies. I would urge you to take time to view the footage he took secretly of the prisoners gathering on the platform waiting to find out if they would be boarding the trains to Auschwitz, Bergen-Belsen and Theresienstadt concentration camps. It is the only video footage taken inside the camps during World War Two that exists, making Rudolf Breslauer's record of these events unique in the history of the Holocaust.

'But more about the origin of the material that you see here today. Most of the photographs have come from our extensive archives and from donations, but I'm sure you will have noticed one notable exception.' She looked up at the portrait of Eloise's grandmother, then back at the room. 'This photograph of Rudolf's daughter, Ursula, was taken six months ago in Oxford, where she lived in retirement.'

She turned to smile at Eloise. 'It is thanks to her granddaughter, Eloise, a student at Oxford University, who came to visit us with copies of photos that Ursula had managed to keep hidden in a secret album during many long months in Auschwitz concentration camp. We are pleased to feature these photographs here today along with an album of family photographs that came to Westerbork after the war.

'Eloise persuaded her grandmother to have her portrait taken for the exhibition and we all hoped she would be well enough to attend. As many of you will know, Ursula sadly passed away at the beginning of this year, but this portrait is a fitting tribute to her, the only member of her family to survive the concentration camps.

'This exhibition is unique as it pays homage to Rudolf Breslauer's courage and unwavering belief in recording the awful reality and truth of what went on inside Westerbork camp.

'It just leaves me to say thank you to all of you for coming tonight, especially to all the members of Ursula Moses-Breslauer's family.' She glanced down at the sheet of paper she was holding. 'I am very pleased to welcome all twelve of Ursula's grandchildren, who are with us here tonight.'

A small ripple of applause grew in strength as one by one everyone joined in. Eloise looked out over the smiling faces, her eyes darting from one person to the next as she tried to guess which of these people were her family. Then, at the back, she glimpsed her parents, who must only just have arrived. Her father's face was turned to a man of similar age who looked just like him – his cousin, maybe? Her mother waved and lifted her hands to applaud her daughter.

Someone tapped Eloise on the shoulder. 'Hello, I'm Ari,' said a young man with an American accent. 'And this is my sister Ruth. We're so pleased to meet our English cousin at last.' They beamed big American smiles at her.

Eloise opened her mouth to speak as a smartly dressed man

of about thirty sauntered over and said, 'I'm Danny.' He held out his hand.

'I know you,' exclaimed Eloise excitedly. 'Grandma told me you live in Zurich and work for a medical company. She was so proud of you.'

Danny looked pleased. 'Oma was always good at keeping in touch and never forgot to send me Christmas and birthday cards. You're lucky you lived so close to her.'

'Yes, I was. I learned so much from her about the family,' said Eloise, glancing up at the photo of her grandmother, who seemed to beam down with approval. 'Did you know she had two brothers?' She looked from Danny to Ari and Ruth, and they all shook their heads. 'Come with me,' she said and led them to the other room to show them the photo album and explain why little Mischa was missing from the family photographs.

Soon they were surrounded by more people who wanted to meet Eloise, all her cousins, their partners and their parents. She had to keep reminding herself that most of these strangers were related to her, and she laughed as she tried but failed to remember all their names.

James quietly moved to her side and squeezed her gently round the waist. 'I don't think I've ever seen you this happy,' he said softly.

'It's thanks to you I've met all these wonderful people. I can't believe they're my relatives,' she said, her heart brimming with love. She lifted a hand to touch the side of his face and held it there. 'None of this would have been possible without you,' she said, but he shook his head and took her hand and kissed it.

'It wasn't me. All of this was down to your efforts to unravel the truth for your grandmother,' he said.

They both gazed up at the portrait of Ursula Breslauer

watching over her precious family with her beautiful infectious smile.

Thank you so much for choosing *Only I Can Save Them*, and I hope you enjoyed reading my book. If you would like to keep up with all my releases, please sign up at the following link. Your email address will never be shared and you can unsubscribe at any time.

www.bookouture.com/imogen-matthews

If you are familiar with my novels, you will know how much I enjoy uncovering little-known stories about real people and events during the Second World War and bringing them to new audiences through fiction. My special interest is Holland, because that is where my Dutch mother grew up and lived through five long years of German occupation in the Second World War. Her extraordinary stories continue to inspire every one of my books set in wartime Holland.

When it came to researching this latest book, my interest was aroused by a newspaper article about the German Jewish photographer Rudolf Breslauer. He fled his home in Leipzig with his wife and children after the Nazi attacks of Kristallnacht. Believing his family would be safe in the Netherlands, he was unaware that the Nazis were already planning to eliminate its entire Jewish population. His salvation, or so he was led to believe, came in the form of a job offer to move with his wife and children to Westerbork, a Nazi-run transit camp in the Netherlands near the border of Germany. He was given no choice but to comply. Breslauer's job was to photograph the thousands of new arrivals. Then, he was ordered by the kommandant to document life in the camp for Nazi propaganda purposes. He was also provided with a video camera, which he used to take secret footage of prisoners leaving the camp on cattle trains bound for the concentration camps and almost certain death.

Time was running out for the Breslauer family as he rushed to document the reality of what he was witnessing, but eventually they were put on a train to Auschwitz.

Decades later, Breslauer's photographs and film footage of Westerbork camp were discovered, and it emerged that he photographed his daughter Ursula and son Stefan as part of the work he did for the Nazis. It was never established why he risked his children in this way, although there has been much speculation about the pressure he would have been under to comply with Nazi orders to show Westerbork as a happy place for propaganda purposes.

There are many questions about how Breslauer was able to photograph and film in secret and how he managed to hide the evidence from the Nazis. This provided me with a rich tapestry of different scenarios in the context of which to write my own.

One coincidence particularly intrigued me. From historical records, I read that Rudolf Breslauer happened to be at Westerbork at around the same time as a well-known Dutch journalist called Philip Mechanicus. In Nina Siegal's *The Diary Keepers*, I read extensive extracts of the diaries Mechanicus made while interred at Westerbork. Did the two men actually meet? I have seen no concrete evidence that they did, but I imagined it would greatly enrich my story if they did. I hope that you, the reader, will agree.

I have also taken a few liberties with the birthdates of the Breslauer children in order to fit the timeline of my story, particularly when bringing Ursula into the present day. In my opinion, these are minor changes, which hopefully will not detract from readers' enjoyment of the book.

In November 2024, I was fortunate enough to visit Westerbork and see the exhibition of Breslauer's work for myself. To see the original photographs and film and the cameras Breslauer used to take them was astonishing. I also walked through the site of the original camp and was chilled by the sight of the kommandant's villa, which still stands today and is encased in glass to preserve it. I found my visit to be an extraordinarily humbling experience, which helped me greatly in my research and the writing of my book.

Rudolf Breslauer's film footage of the transports leaving Westerbork can be viewed on YouTube. It is unique as it is the only film taken inside any of the Nazi-run concentration camps.

I would love to know if you enjoyed reading *Only I Can Save Them* and would be so grateful if you could write me a review. It makes a real difference in helping new readers to discover my books for the first time.

I love hearing from my readers and you can get in touch on my Facebook page, through Twitter/X, Instagram or my website.

Thanks again for reading.

Warm wishes,

Imogen

www.imogenmatthewsbooks.com

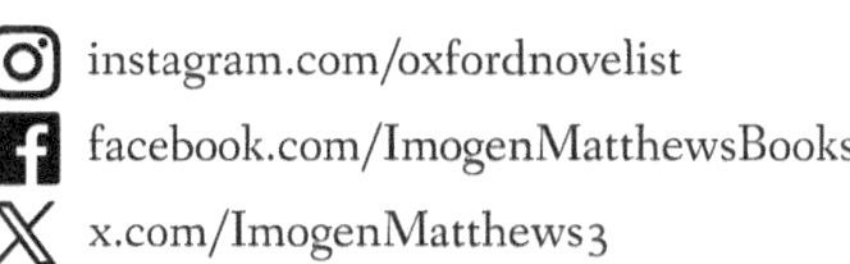

instagram.com/oxfordnovelist

facebook.com/ImogenMatthewsBooks

x.com/ImogenMatthews3

ACKNOWLEDGEMENTS

This book is a team effort and I'm grateful to everyone at Bookouture who has made it happen. First and foremost I'd like to thank my Dutch editor Nina Winters for her encouragement, meticulous attention to detail, suggestions and ideas on how to strengthen my story and make it as authentic as possible. Her support throughout many months has been invaluable.

I could not have completed this project without the encouragement and professionalism of the incredible editorial, marketing, digital, publicity, rights and sales teams at Bookouture who made it all happen. All their names are listed overleaf.

Only I Can Save Them is my eighth published book and I want to give heartfelt thanks to Matthew, my husband, for putting up with me working long and odd hours over many months to get it finished. He's also helped in many other ways, not least by suggesting that we should visit Westerbork memorial centre in November 2024. I can't think of anyone I know who would be as enthusiastic as I was to visit a former Nazi-run prison camp! And while I spent many hours at the exhibition, he was in the bookshop picking out books in Dutch and English that he thought would be interesting for my research – not only for this book, but my next one.

PUBLISHING TEAM

Turning a manuscript into a book requires the efforts of many people. The publishing team at Bookouture would like to acknowledge everyone who contributed to this publication.

Commercial
Lauren Morrissette
Hannah Richmond
Imogen Allport

Cover design
Eileen Carey

Data and analysis
Mark Alder
Mohamed Bussuri

Editorial
Nina Winters
Hannah Wilson

Copyeditor
Jacqui Lewis

Proofreader
Liz Hatherell

Marketing

Alex Crow
Melanie Price
Occy Carr
Cíara Rosney
Martyna Młynarska

Operations and distribution

Marina Valles
Stephanie Straub
Joe Morris

Production

Hannah Snetsinger
Mandy Kullar
Nadia Michael
Charlotte Hegley

Publicity

Kim Nash
Noelle Holten
Jess Readett
Sarah Hardy

Rights and contracts

Peta Nightingale
Richard King
Saidah Graham

Dear Reader,

We'd love your attention for one more page to tell you about the crisis in children's reading, and what we can all do.

Studies have shown that reading for fun is the **single biggest predictor of a child's future life chances** – more than family circumstance, parents' educational background or income. It improves academic results, mental health, wealth, communication skills, ambition and happiness.

The number of children reading for fun is in rapid decline. Young people have a lot of competition for their time, and a worryingly high number do not have a single book at home.

Hachette works extensively with schools, libraries and literacy charities, but here are some ways we can all raise more readers:

- Reading to children for just 10 minutes a day makes a difference
- Don't give up if children aren't regular readers – there will be books for them!

- Visit bookshops and libraries to get recommendations
- Encourage them to listen to audiobooks
- Support school libraries
- Give books as gifts

There's a lot more information about how to encourage children to read on our websites: **www.RaisingReaders.co.uk** and **www.JoinRaisingReaders.com**.

Thank you for reading.